MAN IN THE SADDLE

MAN IN THE SADDLE

BY
ERNEST HAYCOX

TRIANGLE BOOKS
NEW YORK

TRIANGLE BOOKS EDITION PUBLISHED FEBRUARY 1941
REPRINTED FEBRUARY 1941
REPRINTED MAY 1941

TRIANGLE BOOKS, 14 West Forty-ninth Street,
New York, N. Y.

CONTENTS

MAN IN THE SADDLE

I

OWEN MERRITT

BOURKE PRINE went into the Palace, looked around the crowd a moment, and saw the door of the back room standing ajar. He turned into that room and paused with his shoulder rested against the door's edge. Sound rolled in from the front part of the saloon, the sound of men's voices cheerfully arguing, the scrape of boots and spurs and chair legs, the dry clatter of poker chips, the sudden rush of horses coming off the Piute Desert at the dead run. A little current of air pulled smoke through the doorway and somebody's question broke above the steady racket. "When's this weddin'?"

Bourke spoke to the man sitting so alone at the table: "Thought I'd find you here."

He tried another match to the limp cigarette between his lips and a half-severe, half-amused glance slid over the edge of his cupped hands. This back room was small and scarred and bare, holding only a table and two chairs. There wasn't anything on the pine-board walls except a pen-and-ink drawing of two horse-men trying to hold a grizzly with their ropes. Every time Bourke came here he said the same thing, and he said it now. "That fellow don't know how to draw horses." But his attention returned to Owen Merritt, who sat so loose-muscled before a table which supported one bottle, one glass and a coal-oil lamp.

The lamplight threw its yellow shine directly against Merritt's face. He said in the softest voice: "Shut that damned door."

Prine closed it with his heel and came over and settled down in the opposite chair. The saloon's noise dropped away to a steady rumble beyond the partition. The smell of tobacco smoke and stale whisky and resin from the pine boards strengthened. Prine took the only glass on the table and helped himself to a drink, and pushed the glass back to Owen Merritt, meanwhile bracing himself to the shock of the whisky by pushing his shoulders forward. He was tall and heavy-chested and the muscles of his upper body stirred the gray fabric of his shirt. Solidness was the key to Bourke Prine; solidness and a dark skepticism lying deep in his eyes.

He said: "The Methodist missionary bishop just staged in from Winnemucca, so it will be a proper wedding. The hotel is lighted up like a burnin' haystack and the women have started cryin' already. What makes women cry at weddings, kid? Skull's riders are all out there belly flat to the bar, plastered with bear grease and bad intentions. You drunk yet, Owen?"

"The bottle," said Owen Merritt, by way of refuting the charge, "is still half-full." He decanted himself a drink but let it lie a moment, speculatively watching the amber shine of the liquor. His long feet were slid under the table and he lay thoroughly slack on the chair, no muscle of his body holding perceptible tension, which was a sufficient reason for Bourke Prine to study his partner with a fresher interest. Owen Merritt's hair was as yellow as the lamplight, lying well down along his forehead. Skin made a tight fit across high cheekbones, turned a ruddy bronze by sun and wind, and this freshness of complexion made his blue eyes a shade darker than they really were. At the moment his expression was wholly unreadable. It was a way Owen Merritt had of dropping a curtain in front of his feelings. He was still and he was loose, but two small signals gave him away to Bourke — the upward strike of his lip corners, as though a smile lay somewhere near, and the manner by which, after suddenly downing the drink, he laid the glass on the table and worried it with the blunt ends of his fingers. This was the signal of rashness crowding him hard.

Prine said: "I don't know where they hide but there's a lot of pretty girls in town. Helen Tague's here. Well sure, she's Sally Bidwell's bridesmaid. And Nan Melotte, and Swanee Vail's daughter and Irene Spaugh, and some homesteaders' women. Takes a weddin' to bring 'em out. Maybe it's hope."

Owen Merritt shifted on the chair. Gently, restlessly — prodded by Bourke Prine's deliberate talk. "I remember," he said, "one time when my old man was alive. We rode to the rim of the Bunchgrass Hills. It was fall. Heat smoke lay across the desert. Out Christmas Creek way we could see dust rolling up from a band of Piutes crossing down to the antelope country. Wonder what makes a man think of things that mean nothing?"

Bourke Prine's talk once more pushed against Owen Merritt. "Fay Dutcher is at the front door of this joint, keepin' tally on the Skull riders. Wearin' his pearl-handled gun for the ceremony. Maybe it's a Texas habit." His voice swung away to a lighter, quicker note. "Hugh Clagg's in town," he said, his glance touching Merritt and going away. "I saw Sheriff Medary hangin' around the hotel to kiss the bride. An easy way to keep his politics in good shape. Well, it takes a weddin' to bring 'em out."

"Antelope are running heavy over in Fremont Basin," said Owen Merritt, in a voice gently controlled. "I guess it's time I had another look at that country."

Bourke Prine took his turn on the glass and bottle. He split the contents of the bottle, drank his share, and pushed the glass back toward Merritt. He said: "That's your trouble. Always goin' off to take another look at a piece of country. Fiddle-footed. Always smellin' the wind for scent. And so you lose out." He swung his broad torso around and gave Owen Merritt a stiff, hard survey. "When I came by the hotel I saw Sally Bidwell lookin' down from a room window. She saw me and waved. She wasn't smilin' at all. Why shouldn't a prospective bride smile, kid?"

This was the way he fed it to Owen Merritt, stubbornly, slyly, with an irony drying out his words. He kept observing how Owen Merritt worried the glass around the table with his finger tips. There was a wild temper in that long man with the whalebone frame, a temper as unpredictable as dynamite.

Merritt had the last drink. "Dam' bottle's empty again. Maybe we should take a walk."

"What for?" grunted Bourke Prine. "You're always takin' a walk. Why?"

"Maybe because I'm sick of listenin' to your speeches."

They turned out of the back room, into a full and heavy racket. Everybody on the Piute Desert, it seemed certain, had come to The Wells this Saturday night to celebrate the wedding. Tom Croker's saloon could hold fifty men if the poker tables and the faro rig were pushed against the wall, but there were more than that many in here now, everybody turning and colliding, and pleased to have it that way after a long summer's work and isolation. Lamplight splintered against a long back bar mirror and smoke lay low and thick and the front swing door kept squalling on its hinges and sweat ran down the points of Tom Croker's mustache as he stood behind the bar and tried to serve this crowd. The whole Skull outfit was here. So were Mike Tague's riders from Wagon Rim way; and all the smaller ranches nestling along the base of the Bunchgrass Hills were represented. Drifters from the Broken Buttes made a show and four cavalrymen had ridden in from distant Camp

McDermitt. Juke Slover, six feet from Owen, yelled to make himself heard: "Hello, pilgrim!" Skull's foreman, Fay Dutcher, worked his way slowly through the jam, using his shoulders, using his elbows. There was a quietness to this Dutcher almost like insolence — a kind of overbearing assurance in the way he pushed others aside. It was a quality, Prine thought idly, that Fay Dutcher had imparted to his men. All Skull's riders were like that. Dutcher was short and broad, with a weather-blackened skin and a heavy cropped mustache half-hiding his upper lip and a pair of eyes that showed a slanted, short-tempered shining. He only nodded at Bourke Prine. But he took in Merritt with a full glance, a careful and far more aroused glance, and said, "Hello, Merritt," and moved aside. Other men turned to watch this scene, and then Will Isham came into the saloon and made his way forward.

Bourke Prine knew that it was a purely accidental meeting, yet Isham used the accident to a good purpose, as he always did. He stopped in front of Merritt. "Owen," he said, "I'm glad to see you. Because I want a word with you."

This room had no privacy in it, and yet men pressed away a little and gave Isham a space. Bourke Prine considered that with his sharp mind. Will Isham could have elbow room any time he wanted; for he was owner of Skull, and Skull was a quarter-million acres lying along the southern base of the Bunchgrass Hills, one of the great ranches in the state. Nevertheless, it was some other prompting which moved the crowd away. Here was Isham marrying Sally Bidwell, not Owen Merritt who had gone with her so long a time. One man was winning and one man was losing, nobody on the Piute knowing the reason, and now they were face to face. This was why the crowd withdrew and let them alone.

"Owen," said Will Isham, "I want to know how you take this. If there is to be trouble between us, I'd like to know it now."

So coolly, so softly — and yet with so much willfulness lying behind that easy speech, with so direct and unwavering a determination to have his answer. In a country of physically big riders, Will Isham was small, almost slight; in a land of carelessness and laughter, he remained grave, he held himself under stiff control. He was, Bourke Prine remembered, close to forty — at least ten years older than Owen Merritt and still older than Sally Bidwell whom he was shortly to marry.

It occurred to Bourke Prine suddenly to look over to Owen Merritt, whereupon he noticed the blond man's wide lips placed in a faint half-smile. That was all. Nothing else got through the consistently smooth expression. Merritt said: "I congratulate you, Will."

Isham's tone was thoroughly courteous, but it held the same insistence that had been there before. "You're sure?"

It seemed then to Bourke that a break hovered over these two. They were both calm, they were both softly and deceivingly gentle with their words. Prine felt the weight of Isham's will; definitely he could feel it. And he knew enough about his partner to guess at the wildness lying behind Merritt's half-smile. Owen said, in his summer-soft tone: —

"What are you worried about, Will?"

Fay Dutcher, on the edge of this scene, hauled his shoulders about and placed his agate-black eyes against Merritt. Isham kept still a moment, but Bourke Prine witnessed the minute break in the gravity of Skull's owner and identified the faint heat of a touched pride. Isham said: "I want no war of words, Owen. We'll be living in this country a long while, you and me. I should like to continue to regard you as a friend. If that is not to be, I want it made clear."

Bourke Prine, who disliked Will Isham and Skull and all that Skull stood for, had his moment of admiration for the man. Here Isham stood, asking for his showdown, side-stepping nothing, doggedly insisting on a clear answer. He wore a black broadcloth suit and a white shirt. An elktooth charm swayed in the sag of his watch chain and a diamond showed a flicker of light on his right index finger. He was sparing in his gestures and mild in his talk — and somehow very formidable to Bourke Prine at the moment. A quality set him apart from every other man in the room.

"The luck," said Owen Merritt, "is yours. I will not complain."

"Owen," counseled Will Isham, "it isn't like you to dodge. I want the truth — and I want everybody in this room to hear it. I will not have rumors going around."

"I have said I wish you luck," stated Owen Merritt. "Better let it go like that."

Isham hesitated at the answer, and Bourke Prine saw the man's steady glance search Merritt's face as though to find a direct and visible hostility. He was balancing the issue in his mind. Behind Owen's answer lay so much that was unsaid, as Isham knew, and as all the crowd knew. But in the end some caution or sense of propriety made an answer for Isham. He said, "Let's drink on that," and led the way to the bar, adding a word for the crowd. "Gentlemen, this is on Skull." Afterwards, when the drinks had been put before them, he took up his glass. "To the future Mrs. Isham."

Bourke Prine felt a chill ride down his back. Isham had turned; his eyes suddenly struck Owen Merritt. There was an expression on his face more personal than before, touched with a triumph and yet showing the bright thin edge of bitterness. The man wasn't sure. Merritt said, "Her health and yours, Will," and drank down.

Isham placed his untouched glass on the bar, and gave his apology. "I would not care to appear before the bishop with a drink on me. Croker, I'm buyin' the house for the rest of the night." He turned then and went down the alley at once made for him, a small, grave and thoroughly cool man.

Men began to talk again. Juke Slover came over to stand with Prine and Merritt — these three making an accustomed familiar group. Lee Repp, an obscure rider of the Broken Buttes, came out of the night, using his hands to clear a trail. He was drunk and his lips moved loosely across a white skin. He stared at Merritt. "I guess the Broken Buttes crowd ought to feel pretty happy, huh? Sally's old man is out there braggin' about his son-in-law already."

Owen Merritt looked at him without interest. Lee Repp described a circle in the air with his hands. "Yeah, so. Sally's old man sure has got a pretty easy thing now. Maybe — "

Merritt said: "Shut up, Repp."

Fay Dutcher plowed over from another corner of the house. "Repp," he said, "get out of here." But Repp was watching Owen Merritt and his mouth closed slowly, without further sound. Merritt's shoulders lifted. The smooth surface of the man was beginning to wear thin. Small, sudden flashes of wildness got through his eyes, the ruddiness of his cheeks glistened with an overlay of sweat, as though from strain, and the cut of his jaws showed a straight, solid line. He looked at the glass in his hand, caught in some odd debate, and put it down, and nodded at Bourke. "Let's have a look at the joyous night, Bourke." Somewhere on the street a gun banged twice, but nobody in the Palace considered the sound of any import.

Pay Lankershim shoved his way through the crowd. He tapped Owen's shoulder with a hand blackened and bony and crippled from seventy years of hard living. But his eyes, cool and bright, were still young. He stood above most men in the saloon, being Merritt's exact height. He said: "Owen — I want to see you sometime tonight."

Merritt said, "All right," and moved toward the door.

Following Merritt closely, Bourke Prine cast a quick glance across the room and discovered Hugh Clagg shouldered against a far wall. Owen, Bourke knew, hadn't noticed Clagg so far, which was a pretty good lead on Owen's frame of mind.

Out in the faint cool of the street Prine said: "Will Isham had a reason for buyin' you that drink in front of the crowd."

"Peace and good will," said Owen Merritt in a short tone.

"Don't talk like a sucker."

Love Bidwell stood by the saloon's door, talking to Mark Medary, who was the county's sheriff. Love was a thin one with a gray goatee and a windy, irritating voice. His accent was altogether Southern and he always wore a Confederate campaign hat, which now lay far back on his head. Both thumbs were well hooked into his suspenders. "I lose a daughter," he said to Medary. "Sho', I lose a daughter. I reckon that time comes to us all, Medary. But I'll be travelin' that way to see her a lot. We was always close, Sally and me.

Whut's eighty miles of distance? If my saddle horse
gives out I guess I got a son-in-law to supply me fresh,
ain't I?"

Medary listened casually, his eyes traveling elsewhere. He put out a hand to Owen Merritt. "Wish you'd
stop by sometime and talk with me, Owen. Hello,
Bourke." Love Bidwell at once checked his voice and
looked at Owen Merritt. He pushed his lips together,
as though afraid of committing himself to error in his
new situation as Will Isham's father-in-law. People
were gently moving up in the direction of the hotel.
Owen Merritt paced over the street and stopped in the
dark arch of Sam Nankervell's blacksmith shop. He
turned, leaning against the wall. There was glow enough
from all the lights shining across the dust for Bourke
Prine to see how stiff the edges of Merritt's lips had
become. The smiling ease had gone out of the big
man.

He said: "Don't seem only ten years since the Piutes
killed Bill Grandgent right where the hotel stands now.
Country's beginning to grow up."

The Wells consisted of two rows of pine boarded
buildings separated by a wide street whose dust reflected a pale silver shining where the store lights
touched it. The Palace threw off a brilliant glow; the
hotel's windows all showed yellow radiance. Elsewhere
lay the stores and sheds of a cattle town. Saddle horses
and single buggies and wagons lay banked against the
street racks, and people moved up and down the walks,

doing a week-end shopping, and children raced in and out of between-buildings alleys, and at those points where the lights of town failed to reach, in velvet-thick shadows, soft-speaking men stood, their cigarettes making firefly glints.

Wind rolled softly and coldly in from the deep distances of the Piutes, with the smell of sage and Indian summer's baked earth in it, and with the faint smell of wildness in it. This dark desert lay all around The Wells; it held the town to its flat breast, it had weathered the town to its own uniform powder-gray and bronze-brown. North and south and east there was no horizon at all, but eastward seven miles the Bunchgrass Hills lifted a long black shadow. This was 1878, and the town was only nine years old. This was cattle land, fenceless and vast, and lonely; and tied to a far away outer world only by dim, dusty trails half-lost in the ever-growing sage.

"You were a fool to take Isham's drink," said Bourke Prine. "It ties your hands." Darkness lay wholly around Nankervell's, but he saw Owen Merritt's head turn and lift, which meant his partner would be watching that bright second-story window where Sally Bidwell waited for her wedding. The bitter-pungent smell of singed hooves and heated metal and of grease and forge-fire ashes drifted from Nankervell's.

Bourke's voice had pushed insistently against Owen Merritt all evening. It did so now. "Listen. Go up the side stairs of the hotel. It takes you straight to her door. You've got time. I'll get a rig and drive around back — and wait there for you both."

"A little late, Bourke," said Owen Merritt. "A little late."

"When I saw her she wasn't smilin'," repeated Bourke. "Her heart ain't in this weddin', or she would be smilin'. God knows why you let Isham make a fool out of you."

"Maybe not her heart, Bourke. But her mind's made up to it. The damage is done."

"You sure? Something mighty odd happened between you two to make it like this. Listen, Owen, this business will eat on both of you for a hell of a lot of years. So you better be sure it can't be changed."

"I guess," murmured Merritt, "I've done my share of talkin'." He threw his cigarette far into the street and drew a long breath. He said: "I'll meet you in the saloon — five minutes. Another drink and we'll leave this damned town behind."

He cut straight across the street, going into the alley near Shannon's store to avoid the crowd gathering up by the hotel porch, and came through the back lots of town to the hotel's side stairway. This was a boarded-in affair marching up the outside wall of the building. Letting himself through the bottom door, he closed it and rose through solid darkness until he came to the top. He pushed that door partially open.

Rooms opened upon a hall running the length of the second floor, and little streaks of light crept beneath an occasional sill, breaking the blackness. At the hall's far end a stairway led to the lobby, from which came the run and murmur of a good many people's voices. Suddenly the door of a near-by room opened and he saw Helen Tague come quickly out and turn toward the lower lobby.

He came into the hall. "Helen," he said.

She wheeled with a half-startled lift of her shoulders, this tall and calm daughter of Mike Tague. She came up to him, very serious and very pretty in her half-excitement — the full light of the near-by room showing all this to him — and a sense of risk made her push him back into the stair landing, into the shadows. She pulled the door half-shut.

"Helen," he said, "tell Sally I'm here."

The shadows obscured her expression but it seemed both sad and disapproving to him. She spoke in her pleasant voice: "You're sure you want me to, Owen?"

"Tell her I'm here, Helen. I'd like to see her for a moment — if she'll come."

"She'll come. But are you sure you want her to?"

"Why not?" he said. "Why not?"

Her answer was soft and faintly regretful. "Oh, Owen." She went back into the room, not quite closing its door; and he heard her speaking to Sally, the words low and quick and insistent.

He stood on the stair landing, thoroughly motionless, his blond head tipped down. Such light as reached the landing broke vaguely against the blue surfaces of his eyes and made strong shadows beneath his jaw corners and in the exposed hollow at the base of his neck. He was quite a long man, flat and wide at the shoulders, whipped in at the flanks from all the riding he had done. Even now, in this remote corner, he kept his feelings away from his face. His breathing lifted and settled the cotton shirt gently. And so he stood as Sally Bidwell's room door fully opened and she came toward him.

II

GOOD-BYE TO A WOMAN

SHE said, "Owen," and came into the landing, near enough to see him clearly, near enough to touch him. "Owen."

Certain things were in this girl, as he had learned them through long courtship. Pride and a strong will above all. Even in this dismal corner she showed these qualities to him, her head thrown back and her deep copper hair showing its luster. And because they had been very close to each other for so long a time, he understood that she was near the weakness of tears. It was a feeling that came from her, to him.

He said, no break in his voice, no lift and no urgence: "You're sure it's got to be this way, Sally?"

"Is that all you came to say?"

"It's enough to say, isn't it? We'll live a long time. I can do a lot of remembering in the next thirty years and so can you. I can remember I didn't play my hand right. Or I can remember I came up these stairs at the last minute and tried to get it straight."

"Owen," she said, "your voice is so hard. You've condemned me already."

He shook his head. He let the silence ride a moment, staring at her. "No," he answered at last. "No, I'm just keeping back a lot of things that I can't say — or won't.

I won't beg, Sally. You're the one that made the choice, not me. All I want to know is if you're sure."

"Yes," she said. "I'm sure." Then she finished it out with a phrase that was quick and vehement and odd. "I've got to be sure, haven't I?"

She wore a russet gown that showed her arms and shoulders. She was, he decided, almost as tall as Isham, and that thought gave him an odd feeling, as though it were improper. She had a firm chin and a straight swinging body and he remembered that her smile always changed the color of her eyes, placing a frank, invitational smoothness on her lips — for him. She wasn't smiling now. She touched him with her hand, and drew back with a startled swiftness; and immediately the memory of a good many things lay between them, hot and disturbing and compelling. She murmured: "Do you really understand, Owen?"

"I wish you luck," he said. "And so-long."

"Wait. You're coming in to the wedding?"

"Why? I'd be the ghost at the banquet."

"It isn't like you to run away. From anything. From anything on earth."

"No," he said, flat and final. "I won't be there."

She said: "Then I want you to do one thing for me. When I leave the hotel to ride home I want you to be there. Wish me luck. Please. So that everybody sees you do it."

"To make the record complete," he said, dryness rustling his talk.

"Don't try to hurt me any more, Owen. It isn't that at all. I don't want anybody on the Piute to think you ran away from this. Not you."

"Thanks," he said. "Thanks for the interest."

She came a little nearer him, her lips remaining even and composed while she watched his face. When she spoke again her words were not as unerringly direct, not as certain. "Is it — is it so hard to believe — that I take an interest in you? That I'd still fight for you? Oh, Owen, you don't understand it yet."

"I guess we've talked that all out. Which was one of our troubles. We always talked too much. And did too little. You're an ambitious girl, Sally. You set your mind on certain things long ago. I couldn't break up that."

She said in almost a whisper, "Is that all? Do you really think that's all?"

"I lay no blame on you. None. You reasoned it out — the bargain and what it called for. You're getting something from Isham and from Skull. But you're an honest girl, Sally, and you'll give him more than he'll give you. And you'll stick with it, even if it gets bad."

She said, in a lower and lower tone, "Why should it ever be bad, Owen?"

"There's one thing you never found out. You're a stubborn girl and you always figured you could make your mind pull your heart along. Well, your heart ain't in this. You figure you can make it go with him. But you won't. You never will. That's why it will get bad."

She was somber and strained and still, listening to the run of his voice, listening to its repressed feelings and to all those others he could not quite keep back. She said at last, quick and broken: "Owen, why — "

He cut in with a voice on the ragged edge of anger. "We always talked too much. Nothing's any good but this." He looked at her, dismal hunger shining out of his blue eyes, the rashness of his temper having its way at last; and he seized the points of her bare shoulders and drew her against him. Her breath rushed out from the strength of his arms and a faint cry escaped her lips, and was shut off when he kissed her. She didn't breathe and she made no more protest. Helen Tague's voice came from the hall. "Sally — you've got to hurry."

Sally Bidwell drew away, with an emotion in her worse than sadness. It was like despair; it pulled her lips together until they were no longer pretty and it took the pride out of her slim, self-confident body. It was a reflex of all that which made her push at him, and sway back; afterwards it was her own desire that sent her forward again. She dropped her head against his chest, struggling against a quiet, terrible crying.

Owen Merritt stood still, holding her loosely with his arms and stirred by the fragrance rising from her copper hair; and his mind did cruel things to him then, reminding him of the sweetness and laughter and womanly softness she had once held for him. These

were things gone by. He had suddenly a sense of loss
that pumped him empty.

Helen Tague said again: "Sally."

Sally drew back. Her chin lifted, and he had this last
look into her eyes, this one unguarded moment before
she remembered where her loyalties lay. She said,
brokenly, "Why — why didn't you — " and, leaving it
unfinished, ran back to her room. Someone came up the
stairs from the lobby at a heavy tread and Helen Tague
closed the door on the outer stairway, leaving Owen
Merritt in the solid black.

He went down the stairs and let himself into the
alley. He paused here, his breath springing the bottom of his chest. So standing in the gloom, he heard
a man stumbling around from the hotel's back side;
this man went by him at a distance of two yards, walking fast, and reached the street. A light from Shannon's
store touched the area and by its glow Owen Merritt
identified Hugh Clagg.

He waited until Clagg had turned the corner of
Shannon's before following. People were still coming
into The Wells and the faint breeze had turned colder
and in the sky all the stars of the universe made a
cloudy glitter, deepening the thorough blackness lying
over this world. Troubled as he was, Owen Merritt
paused by Shannon's to have his look at that sky. High-
built and rangy, he tipped up his head and thus stood —
absorbed in the sight and smell and sound of the night.

This was the way Nan Melotte saw him. Coming out of Shannon's, she passed within a yard of him, and threw him a quick, lively glance of curiosity. He wasn't, she saw, aware of her, or of anyone on the street; and after she had gotten by him, she turned to watch him, and remained that way until he moved on, toward the Palace.

People were moving toward the hotel for the wedding. Love Bidwell came by Owen Merritt, nursing a long cheroot between his lips. He slanted a quick glance toward Merritt and his hand rose and touched his goatee, as though to hide the forming expression on his cheeks. Sally Bidwell's brother, Starr, followed indolently behind, taciturnly amused by all this and yet watching the town with the close and wary manner of one on risky ground. His eyes lifted on Owen Merritt and were at once reserved.

Owen Merritt rolled into the Palace, finding Bourke and Juke Slover established over a bottle of pale Kentucky moonshine at the bar. Bourke nodded to Owen. Liquor had stirred him up; he showed the room a small, rash grin. "Help yourself to a smile."

"Sure," murmured Owen. "Well, it's a historic occasion, Bourke. May you live to tell it to your grandsons."

Bourke said, idly: "Seems too long."

The four cavalrymen from Camp McDermitt stood along a far wall, their uniforms making a splash of color in the scene. But they were lonely in the crowd, for this was cattle land which had no particular liking for the military. All the poker tables were in full blast; the faro rig was surrounded. Owen Merritt hung over the glass of moonshine, both his elbows on the bar. He was turned away from the room and seemed to see nothing; yet the whole room was pictured before him in the long back bar mirror and certain things began to break through the heavy indifference of his mind. Hugh Clagg stood alone in a corner, which was a signal to catch Owen Merritt's rising attention. Clagg had his slender frame to the wall. His long arms hung motionless and the smoke of a brown-paper cigarette made a vague shadow in front of his narrow-shaped face. He was a roan-headed man, deliberately withdrawn from others. Quickness was written into him, still-placed as he was, and the world he saw was a world colored and changed by the smiling malice of his eyes. He had a wide, resolute mouth. A scar gouged a white dimple out of the left cheek, and his fists were very broad and very heavy for one so otherwise lean-shaped. At this moment he seemed to be thoroughly idle and thoroughly off guard.

This was the thing that held Owen Merritt — this idleness. He knew his man too well to be fooled by it.

Bourke Prine spoke out his growing dissatisfaction. "You were a sucker to take Isham's drink."

Pay Lankershim came out of the crowd. He put his thin-old shape against Merritt, speaking into Merritt's ear.

"Son, you going to let Isham do it?"

"What?"

Pay stepped back. He turned to Bourke. "What's a fellow to think? Ain't you talked to him, Bourke?"

Bourke said "No use," and turned to the bottle.

Pay lifted a finger, catching Merritt's attention. He drew the finger sharply across his throat. "That's what it is — tonight. Dammit, Owen!" He pushed back through the crowd.

Owen Merritt considered the room more carefully, which was a thing he had so far failed to do. It was a little odd to see Hugh Clagg inside four walls with a Skull outfit. The politics of it wasn't right. Searching the crowd, via the back bar's mirror, he saw four others who had come out of the Broken Buttes country with Hugh Clagg this night. Ray Neale stood by the faro rig, not playing. Pete Mariels, the half-breed, remained nearest the shadows of the back end, as he always liked to do; and Tempe Killeen and Lee Repp were at one end of the bar. Will Isham had bought the house, and here Hugh Clagg's riders were drinking Skull whisky. It was a little odd.

"Unless," he said, "there's been a change."

"What?" said Bourke Prine instantly. Juke Slover looked up from his glass.

"The charity of Skull extends all the way to the Broken Buttes tonight."

"So finally you're awake," grumbled Bourke Prine.

Pay Dutcher came into the Palace and called out: "All right, boys." Skull's men immediately milled toward the door, bound for the wedding. Mike Tague, who owned most of the Wagon Rim country outright, rose from one of the poker tables, his Irish cheeks a flame red. He came by Owen. He called, "Large night — large night," and followed the crowd outward. There remained a few homesteaders and a few riders who had no direct interest in the wedding. And Hugh Clagg and his four riding companions. Owen Merritt poured another drink into the glass and laid full weight on his elbows, looking into the oily shine of the liquor. For a little while he forgot Hugh Clagg and remembered other things. There was a growing silence in The Wells. Everybody would be up at the hotel, listening to the Methodist missionary bishop.

Bourke said: "You goin' or you stayin'?"

Lee Repp made a turn away from his partner, Tempe Killeen. He had to support himself on the bar. Tempe Killeen called, "Come back here, Lee." But Repp moved up to Owen Merritt. His long lips squashed a smile into crookedness. Killeen said again, "Repp." Something as definite as the stir of wind crossed the saloon and Bourke Prine, always alert to trouble, made a half-turn away from the bar, watching Hugh Clagg. Juke Slover, quick to follow the gesture, wheeled to keep an eye on Pete Mariels.

Repp looked up at the tall Merritt. He was unsteady on his feet; unsteady and full of some kind of secret amusement that had to come out. He said: "Listen. I guess Sally's brother won't have anything to worry about now, will he? I guess Starr's going to feel a lot safer now, ain't he? Well, it's one way. It sure is one way."

Tempe Killeen stepped forward, but it was too late to help Repp then. Owen Merritt raised one arm and hit Repp fully in the soft flesh below his ear. Repp wheeled gently around and fell with his mouth wide open. The sound of it made a racket in the still saloon; and afterwards Repp lay on his belly and kicked his legs against the floor.

"If I hear it again from you," Merritt said, "I'll rub you out."

The saloonman, Tom Croker, spoke half in apology and half as a protest. "Well, he was drunk, Owen."

"It is something I didn't care to hear," said Owen Merritt. "Even from a drunk. But maybe there's a sober man in the place that wants to repeat it."

Tempe Killeen came on up and looked down at Repp, not showing any concern. "Repp," he said, "get off the floor."

Repp rolled over, pushing himself to his knees, his head lobbing down. A round red blotch showed where Merritt had hit him. He called weakly: "Give me a hand Tempe. Give me — "

But Tempe wasn't watching him now, and nobody else in the saloon paid any attention. The people in the saloon were riders who knew the Piute and the ancient grudges of the Piute thoroughly. Lee Repp's foolish talk, meaning nothing in itself, had led into something else. Repp was one of Hugh Clagg's men and the play was up to Clagg. So the crowd watched Hugh Clagg and Owen Merritt, knowing the old, old enmity between those two.

Repp got to his feet at last and put a hand on Tempe Killeen's shoulder for support. He said to Owen Merritt uncertainly, "What the hell? I didn't — "

"Go on," said Merritt. "Go on."

Repp hesitated and at that moment Hugh Clagg broke his long silence. He called across the room, even-voiced: "Get out of town, Repp."

The wedding was over, for men's returning boots drummed on the outside walk. Repp reached the Palace doorway, turned a moment to look behind him, at Killeen and at Merritt, and at Hugh Clagg for a longer length of time — and left the saloon.

Hugh Clagg said, not changing the tone of his voice, "I'll let that ride, Merritt. He had it comin' for the remark." He was a high shape against the far wall, holding himself aloof, careful to keep his talk level in the quiet of the place.

Merritt said, "Sure," and turned to nod at Bourke Prine and Juke Slover. The three of them left the Palace just as the returning crowd reached its door. Standing aside from that thirsty current, Owen Merritt said: "I guess I've had enough of this."

Bourke said: "Repp wasn't drunk. No drunk man's

eyes pull down small like his did when he walked at you. So, one of that crowd forgot somethin'."

Owen said, irritably, "How'd you get spooked up?"

"I know enough to pay for my own whisky, son."

Part of Skull's riders were up in the saddle and waiting. Will Isham came out of the hotel and went over toward Nankervell's shop for his buggy, whereupon Owen Merritt remembered something. He said: "Wait for me," and walked toward the hotel. Short of the hotel's porch, in the shadows of Shannon's store, he stopped and waited a moment for Isham to wheel the buggy around to the porch. He laid his hand on the store wall, thus supporting his long shape; and in this concealing darkness his expression let go for a moment and an impulse almost sent him back to the saloon. Sally came out of the hotel door and stepped into the rig. People were standing all about the porch and she was smiling in answer to their laughter; but her glance came around, as though she were looking for him. Seeing that, he went on to the porch.

The people nearest the buggy gave way for him. She had stopped smiling; and Isham, now in the buggy, turned with a swift motion of his shoulders, his smooth manners unable to hold back his quick displeasure. But Merritt had removed his hat and he had bent a little toward her. Before all these eyes he was a cheerful man with no care at all on his face, with no regret on it. He said: —

"Well, I wish you all the luck."

She was trying to smile. Her hand touched his hand and he felt its momentary pressure. She said, just above a murmur: "Owen — "

Isham bent nearer, speaking only for the two of them. "I think that's enough." Anger unsteadied those soft words. "I wouldn't overdo it." The next moment the rig was in motion, with a dozen Skull riders trotting behind. Rice flailed the air.

Mrs. Nankervell turned against Merritt, crying openly — as she cried on any and all occasions requiring sentiment. He turned away and had gotten to the edge of the porch when Helen Tague said, "Owen," and stopped him.

He removed his hat for this tall calm daughter of Mike Tague's. Usually she was a cheerful girl, frank and blunt as a man; and since she practically lived on a horse she usually wore a man's overalls and shirt. Tonight she had been Sally Isham's bridesmaid and the reflection of that excitement was in her eyes, softening them, making them gently shine. He couldn't recall when she had looked prettier, and told her so. "Don't know when I saw you last in a dress. Ought to try wearin' 'em regularly."

"For whom, Owen?"

"Country's full of young men."

"Full of gophers and rabbits, too. I'm choosy."

"Any preferences?"

"Sure," she said and looked at him soberly, sweetly. "What am I offered?" Then she said, lowering her voice, "Don't make a fool out of yourself, Owen."

He laid out a cigarette between his fingers and quickly rolled it. When his glance lifted again she saw something that made her say swiftly: "Oh, Owen! Don't. It's over. I like you both, but there isn't any woman in the world worth your tearing yourself apart. I know you, you big bruiser. And you did a dangerous thing tonight. You and Sally. I don't think it was quite square."

"What's square, Helen?"

"Yes," she said, "I know. I guess I can understand."

Wagons were moving out of town, and horsemen cantered into the farther darkness, bound across the long darkness of the Piute. A small slow wind turned the night cold. Alice Langdell stopped by and said, on the verge of resentment, "I wish you'd ask Juke to come out of the saloon for a minute. He was supposed to meet me here. Seems to be one of those bottle babies that never got weaned."

"Sure," said Merritt and went on down the street. He met Slover and Bourke by the side of the Palace. "Juke," he said, "you got a call up the street."

"Yeah — well."

Fay Dutcher strolled from the hotel to join the remnant of Skull in front of the saloon. Love Bidwell came across the street, meeting him. Love was drunk enough to walk with a precise straightness and the glow of his cigar showed the red thin tip of his nose. His flat and annoying voice bore against Skull's foreman.

"Dutcher," he said, "I'll be over to see my daughter in a few days. Ain't got a very good saddle horse any more and the travelin' will take it down. I want you should pick me a good one from Skull's remuda."

Fay Dutcher answered in a cool, colorless way: "Mr. Isham say anything about that?"

"The man's my son-in-law," retorted Love Bidwell, taking quick offense. "Of co'se it'll be all right. Dammit, Dutcher, I'm tellin' you what to do."

"I hear," drawled Dutcher.

"Well, then," growled Bidwell, and marched into the saloon. When he spoke to the saloonman his voice carried back to the street. "Tom, there was a time when you called my credit into question. I reckon it ought to be all right now, ain't it?"

Tom Croker's answer was civil, nothing more. "Sure, it's all right."

"Dam' right," replied Love Bidwell. "You know who's back of me now. I'll take rye. The same kind of rye you drink, Croker. The bottle below the bar."

Merritt remained on the edge of the shadows and watched Skull's foreman with a considering interest. There was a time when Fay Dutcher would have answered Love Bidwell with a harsh brevity; but now he had to mind his manners toward Skull's new father-in-law. His black head dropped a little; his lips rolled together, displaying surliness. But this lasted for only a moment. He whipped up his chin and caught Owen Merritt's stare, and at once pulled all expression off his cheeks. He turned back toward the hotel.

"Juke," murmured Bourke, "I see Alice up there — "

"Yeah," said Juke Slover. "Yeah, well, so-long," and went away slowly.

Bourke and Owen Merritt turned on to the face of the stable without additional talk, stepped into the leather, and wheeled out of town at a pitching canter. Wagons, bound homeward toward the Kitchen Meadows, raised a high dust on the street and lighted lanterns jiggled fitfully at reach-ends, and here and there along the land's farther flatness ran the drowsy "Good night" of neighbors and the diminishing run of horsemen and the faint, irritable wail of some child kept too long awake. Gradually these lights and this sound faded away into the vastness of the desert, sinking into it without trace, until nothing was left but the everlasting shine of the remote stars and the cold slow wind roiling up the smell of sage and summer-cured grasses. It was as though all these people, saying a last farewell, had ridden at once into oblivion. The darkness was that solid, the illusion of a huge and empty world was that strong.

So Owen Merritt left The Wells behind him, too deeply engaged in his own thoughts to look back. Therefore he did not notice the particular attention of two people. The first of these, Nan Melotte, stood near Nankervell's, about to step up to the saddle of her own pony. She stood still, one hand holding to a stirrup, and followed Merritt with her glance until his shape sank into the Piute's darkness; breathing stirred and re-formed the round swell of her breasts and her eyes were dark and controlled by a dreaming, distant specula-tion.

Meanwhile, Fay Dutcher paused in the black mouth of the alley near Shannon's store watching Merritt and Bourke Prine with a strict attention. As soon as the partners left town he returned to the saloon, halting in the doorway and calling out to the rest of Skull's crew: "All right — all right. Time to ride." Hugh Clagg stood idle in a corner. Clagg looked over the room at Skull's foreman, and looked away. Dutcher backed into the street, waiting for his men. When they came out, turned surly and unwilling by their drinking, he watched them go on their waiting ponies, his mere presence subduing their grumbling protest. The last settlers from Kitchen Meadows were leaving The Wells. The hotel lights winked out one by one and some of the stores were closing up. Hugh Clagg strolled from the saloon and stood on the walk to try a fresh match to his cigarette. He was within arm's reach of Fay Dutcher and for this minute nobody else was near. Fay Dutcher said in a low, dissatisfied rumble: "What's the matter, Hugh? What's the matter?" Then he wheeled to his own horse, calling up the stragglers in the crew. "Come on — come on!" In a moment he led Skull out of The Wells at a ripping gallop, throwing the dust high behind.

Ray Neale and Mariels came from the Palace, joining Clagg. Afterwards Tempe Killeen came out. These four stood together, not speaking until Clagg broke the silence. "What was wrong with you, Ray?"

Ray Neale was waiting for it and his answer, irritably pitched, jumped back at Clagg. "Slover was watchin' me. And Prine stood there, cocked like a gun. They smelled somethin'. What'd you want me to do? No — not then. Where's Merritt now?"

"Started across the Piute."

They stood still. Mark Medary came from Shannon's and advanced on the saloon. He threw them a quick glance and passed into the saloon without speaking. A few of the town's citizens straggled over the street for a ceremonial nightcap. Afterwards Clagg said, "All right." He threw away his cigarette. His words had a sudden lift, as though he had made up his mind. The four of them went to their horses down by the stable, and left town, following Merritt and Prine.

Quiet came to The Wells. The four cavalrymen departed for McDermitt, sixty miles away. The lights continued to die and presently there was nothing left but a lone glow from the saloon where Medary and Croker and a few others kept up a last watch at one of the poker tables. The street showed no life and in the overwhelming darkness of the desert the square fronts of the buildings made a ragged outline. The street's dust cast a faded, phosphorescent glow against the dark.

III

A MAN IS SOON DEAD

AFTER that first quick run out of The Wells, Merritt and Prine settled into the customary mode of travel across the Piute — walk awhile, gallop awhile, and walk again. They aimed into the black, not speaking at all during the first few minutes. Above them lay the glittering wash of stars; on the left, which was east, the low summits of the Bunchgrass Hills made a perceptible outline. There was no sound except the hoof scuffs of their ponies and saddle leather's soft squealing, and the occasional jingling of bridle chains. Wind traveled steadily in from the west, with a sharper edge to it; for though it was Indian summer and cloudless by day, the Piute lay around five thousand feet elevation and at sundown warmth soon left the earth. In this wind, too, was the aromatic blend of sage and bunchgrass cured on the stem, and the impalpable smell of water from little marsh lakes scattered here and there along the desert; and the vague scent of an enduring wildness, which was less an actual scent than some powerful influence rising from a fresh earth to stir a man's senses.

Bourke Prine was first to break the long riding silence, at once revealing his irritation. "It was a hell of a thing to happen — and you let it happen, Owen. It is none of my business, but I'd like to know why."

Owen Merritt let the silence drag until Prine thought his partner meant to refuse an answer. But then Merritt said, quite slowly, as if the words were hard in coming, "I went to her at the hotel. I asked her if she was sure she had figured it out right. She said she had. So that was all."

"No," answered Bourke Prine. "No, that wasn't all. You put a question to a woman just like you were pointin' a gun at her head. What the hell were you doin' — just standin' there? What sort of an answer you think a woman would make, asked that way? I never saw you back up before. You just quit."

"Woman's heart is one thing," said Owen Merritt. "Her mind is another. I told you this before. Sally had made up her mind. Suppose I argued her out of it? We'd both remember she once figured the other way. We'd remember it a long time."

Bourke grumbled, "I don't get it at all."

"All right," said Owen Merritt, "I'll make it plain, and then we'll say no more."

His words came slower and dryer and with no emphasis at all. Bourke felt the big man was pushing his words up through bitterness. "She's an ambitious girl, Bourke. She made up her mind long ago to be something better than her people. Look at them. Love Bidwell's a shiftless Southerner. Poor white trash. Her brother Starr ain't worth a damn. She saw her mother work like a horse to keep the family alive and decent.

She saw her mother die — out of shame, mostly, for what the menfolks were. You know the kind of a shack they live in, and the hardscrabble outfit they've got. Sally had that burned into her. It left a mark. She made up her mind she wouldn't let any man pull her down like they had pulled her mother down. She's got a will and a lot of pride. You want to know what's back of all this? Well, here it is. She figured to do everything her dad didn't do. So here's Isham and here's Skull, and now she's got her place — the wife of the Piute's richest man, and part boss of the biggest outfit in the state. That's it."

Bourke kept still, and they rode a mile or better through the black until he had digested it. Then he said, disbelief in his voice: "A woman doesn't do a thing like that. If it was a matter of bein' poor white trash or Isham's wife, maybe yes. But it wasn't. She had another chance to get away from Broken Buttes and hardscrabble, which was you. You ain't rich but you've got a good ranch. And unless I'm a dam' poor guesser, she was in love with you. You ain't tellin' all the story, kid."

"No," said Owen Merritt, in the same dust-dry monotone. "No, I ain't. The rest of it's me. Love Bidwell is a drifter and a fellow always squattin' in the sunshine. She's put up with that all her life. It burned too deep. I'm a fellow that likes to ride over the hill, too. I like to squat in the sunshine. Maybe go see where the antelope are runnin'. Maybe follow a trail into the hills just for the fun of it. She wouldn't take the chance on what I might be when I was old as Love."

Bourke rolled his weight around the saddle. "No woman would trade off a man that way, like an old shirt for a new one. She wouldn't be much of a woman if she did. It's still out of joint, my boy. I'm not so wise, but I can smell old cheese."

"I've told you the straight of it."

But Bourke went on as if he hadn't heard that answer. "Maybe," he grumbled, "Lee Repp wasn't so wrong."

"What's that?"

"Well, her brother Starr is no good. He's been stealin'. I know that. So maybe Isham used a little pressure on her — "

Owen Merritt hauled in, which also halted Bourke. "Bourke," said Merritt — so softly, so deceivingly gentle — "I'll hear no more of that."

"All right — all right," said Bourke, full of irritation. "But Isham took your girl, which has made a sucker out of you before the country. It will get you in trouble soon or late. Mighty damned funny he should make it a point to drink with you in that saloon. It don't make sense — but Will Isham is no hand to do foolish things, so it means somethin'. And it is pretty queer Hugh Clagg should be in the same room with a bunch of Skull men."

He quit. The two men held their horses still, listening to the muffled run of a group of riders in the foreground. After the sound faded Bourke said: "Where'd Repp go?"

"Ahead of us somewhere."

"You goin' home?"

"I guess so."

"So-long then." Bourke pulled away. But he halted and called back, not sure of his partner, "Want me to ride on to the ranch with you?"

"No. Good night."

"Sure," murmured Bourke, and struck westward toward his own ranch at the base of the Bunchgrass Hills.

Owen Merritt traveled on through the solid dark, giving his horse its own head. A falling star made its faint, spectacular scratch across the low heavens; and the wind threw an increasing chill against him. Far, far away the bark of a coyote lifted up — that saddest and loneliest call of the desert. Released now from the necessity of keeping a straight face to the world, Owen Merritt let his innermost feelings carry him downward until even the little light of the stars seemed to die away. This was the way it went with him, with the thought of Sally riding toward Skull burning through him and leaving its fatal scars. There had been a moment in the Palace when, confronted by Isham, he had held himself narrowly aside from an open quarrel; when the effort to keep down the actual impulse to kill had drawn sweat into his palms. Isham, he knew, had seen the shadow of that in his eyes; and this was why Isham had proposed the drink. He could have destroyed the man at the moment and Isham had been smart enough to realize it.

Sweeping over the long miles, all this kicked its violent course through him until there was nothing left, until he was physically tired. There was a growing shadow straight ahead, which would be the Broken Buttes guarding the southern margin of the Piute Desert. His own road turned left at that point and went another four miles eastward to where Stage Coach Pass separated the Broken Buttes from the Bunchgrass Hills. A single light glimmered through a window of Nan Melotte's frame cabin by the side of the isolated Christmas Creek school.

The scene in the upper hallway remained distinct. Sally, so sad with her talk and so full of a woman's gifts, had waited for him to reveal what was in his mind. He could have taken her out of that hall and cheated Isham in the end. He knew he had that power with the girl's heart and would always have it, as she had the same power over him. Yet in that moment when he knew what he could do, he kept remembering how willfully she had set her mind the other way. And so he had let his chance go by. Distantly and dimly he could admire her for the strong will which rode over her heart's desire; he could admire what she had done, and still want her as he wanted no other woman. But in him too was a thought that would not change: He could not take half a woman.

One more thought came to him, harder than the others: Coolly and calmly as she had made her bargain, she didn't yet know to what ends she had fully committed herself. Isham was a quiet man and a slight-figured one; but behind his composed features lay a will greater than her will. She didn't know that yet.

He said to himself, half aloud and deliberately trying to break the emptiness he felt: "I guess I better ride over to Fremont Basin and see where the antelope are running."

He had been watching the light of Nan Melotte's cabin ahead, watching it and seeing nothing. Now at once his normal senses revived and he pulled the pony in. Somewhere before him two or three shapes cut across the beam of light and the beat of fast-traveling horses ran back, and presently a voice, muffled and quick and ridden by fear, said: "Hey — hey!" It was immediately drowned by the quick beat of gunfire.

Two or three guns — all going at once and quitting at once. He heard no more signaling from that voice as he laid his spurs along the pony's flank and ran dead into trouble. The yonder riders streamed across the light and a horse careened vaguely forward, causing him to veer aside. When it passed by he saw the empty saddle. In the near foreground he heard a man call, "Merritt!" And before he could stop he was in the center of a suddenly renewed firing. Gun reports flattened into the enormous dark. Exploded powder pushed little fingers of sulky light through the shadows. His horse bunched up and came off its front feet and those riders were beating toward him as he laid his own answering shots at them.

Nan Melotte's lamplight died. There was a voice calling insistently to him as he pulled his pony aside from this converging lead. "Merritt — Merritt!" Lying low in the saddle he tried another shot, ran on, and halted to listen.

They had likewise stopped, but he heard the heaving of their horses not far away, to his left; and afterwards they seemed to grow uneasy and to drift along the desert, the rustle of that travel softly coming to him. He lifted his gun, aiming it at the general sound; and gathered the pony beneath him. When he opened fire he let the pony go, driving it straight for them. Muzzle light bloomed before him. He heard a man yell, long and broken-winded. Wind breathed on his face and the smell of his own shots was in his nostrils. His horse shied from something on the ground, the farther firing quit, and he pulled in once more and heard them racing toward the Broken Buttes.

He said, to himself, "That was Clagg." Not in anger, for he was past anger or any kind of emotion. Dismounted, he waited for the sound of their retreat to sink away, at once knowing that this affair was a consequence and a continuation of the wedding. He reached for a match, walking back a few yards and squatting near a loose shadow on the ground. He scratched the light on his boot, held it cupped a brief moment over the face of Lee Repp dead on the ground, and whipped it out. There was no more echo from Broken Buttes.

Nan Melotte's lamplight reappeared in her window. He returned to his horse, thinking, "They thought I was riding ahead of Repp. They thought it was me." Nan Melotte's door came open, releasing a square-shaped glow. She was silhouetted in the doorway, one hand thrown out to touch the door's frame. He rode that way.

"Owen?"

"Yeah," he said, and got down. He saw the whiteness of her cheeks in the light; he saw the black shine of her hair. It was the strong, slow and concerned tone of her voice that dragged him out of his own tangled thoughts. "Yeah," he said.

She said, "Come in. Come out of the light."

When he passed through the door she closed it quickly. He turned to find her resting against it, her small, square shoulders dropped at the corners. He had the feeling that her glance ran over him, top to bottom, with a strange anxiety. Her lips softened and she murmured: "I'm glad." But her eyes were very dark and they watched him with a continuing interest. He had known her three or four years, he had occasionally ridden the desert with her, he had now and then danced with her. But there was a difference here at this moment. He felt it and could not reach it with a definition. His legs were heavy and all the whisky he had taken in during the evening began to have its way, grabbing at his stomach and threading his nerves. He removed his hat.

She said: "Do you need a drink?"

"No," he said.

She started to speak again and didn't, her expressive shoulders shrugging away the impulse. At the moment she saw him pretty clearly for what he was: A long, loose man with a yellow head of hair above smooth and angular features. He was, in a way, a good-looking rider who had a ready smile and seemed to take the course of his life with a complete indifference. Lazy until roused; with deep, darkly blue eyes wise in the reading of the desert's face or the shadows under the far pines. Laconic and hard to fathom. But she saw him now off guard, at a moment when he showed what he had been through, and she thought to herself: "I have been mistaken." A sun-darkened skin lay tightly across his cheekbones; his flat muscles stirred beneath the cotton shirt when he turned his shoulders.

He said: "How'd you get home so soon?"

"I left town right after you did — and rode the short trail."

"Pass anybody?"

"No. But I heard those riders come around the house and stop out there."

"Repp's still there," he said. "Dead."

He was mildly interested in knowing how she would take the news; and saw no change. There was a resoluteness in the lines of this girl, a self-reliance. And still her lips were soft and a quality in her stirred his attention.

She said: "I guess they made a mistake."

He asked: "Now how would you know that?"

"I know. Do you want me to make you some coffee?"

"No, I'll ride along."

She moved away from the door, and watched him put on his hat. He opened the door and his expression changed while he listened to the yonder night, it was keener and more alert, as though this were a game he knew very well. He looked back and gave her a faint smile. "Thanks."

"Better watch the road."

"Sure," he said. They stood this way a little while, considering each other, at once strongly aware of each other. Color showed on her cheeks. She held herself still and steady, as if waiting for him to have his look, as if willing he should consider her and draw his own conclusions. He said, "Good night," and watched her lips form the words "Good night," quite conscious of the little rhythm in her voice, somehow affected by its rise and fall. Afterwards he went to the horse and swung away, bound for his ranch on Christmas Creek, four miles east.

Nan Melotte moved over to close the door; and stood

against it, listening to his horse strike the hard foot-slope of the Buttes. Her expression relaxed. It was pleasant and warm, touched with the heat of an inner dreaming. She said, so softly: "I have been mistaken." Afterwards that warmth and softness faded, to leave her still-cheeked. For she was thinking then of Sally Isham who had once owned this man. "And still does," she thought. "I wonder if he realizes that?"

IV

"I'LL KEEP MY BARGAIN"

FIFTEEN miles east of The Wells the flat desert gave way before a hundred-foot rim which boxed in Skull River and its valley. A road cut down this rocky face, crossed a wooden bridge and went along a double row of young poplars as far as a long, deep-porched house. All in the surrounding darkness lay the out-quarters, the barns and corrals and sheds of a really great ranch. Water in the near-by diversion ditches made a liquid rustle. Haystacks showed their square patterns along the adjacent meadows. Above the ranch, rising steadily away from the Skull's other border, lay the darkling peaks of the Bunchgrass Hills.

It was midnight when Sally Isham stepped inside her new home. The lamps were bright in the place and through the open door of the mess hall she saw the long tables set for the wedding supper. Isham carried her luggage up the stairs, following her into the bedroom. They could hear Skull's crew and all the following crowd coming cheerfully across the bridge; but they had a moment alone and it was Isham who used it.

He looked at her steadily, not quite smiling. "No doubt it's been a long day for you and I think you're tired. But it is a little difficult not to take care of these folks. I hope you can manage to be cheerful."

"Will," she said immediately, "we're starting off wrong, if that's the way you feel."

He showed surprise. "I did not wish — "

"No, wait." She was cool and calm, she was almost blunt. "You don't need to treat me carefully. You want me to entertain them. Certainly I will. I'll make them feel pleased to be here. Or anyone else you bring to Skull. That's one of the reasons you married me, isn't it?"

He said, quietly, "Yes. Did we speak of that?"

"No, but I knew it at any rate."

He said, "You know, Sally, you're a smart woman."

"I want to do the right thing. I don't want to cheat you."

He shook his head. He was puzzled and he was alert. "Is it altogether a bargain, Sally?"

The visitors were in the yard, loud and cheerful. They were in the front room below, calling for Will Isham, for Sally. She said: "Yes. But we can talk about that when they're gone."

"I'd like to," he said, dryness definitely in his voice, and went out. She waited a little while, altogether still in the middle of the room, listening to the robust racket below and yet paying no attention to it. Afterwards she tidied herself and walked to a window and opened it to the wind rolling off the high hills. She stood with her hands on the sill, thinking — because she could not help it — of Owen Merritt and the way he had talked to her in the dark stairway at the hotel, the way he had held himself back, the way he had failed to hide himself completely from her. She was a cool-minded girl and an honest one with herself as with others, and she knew there had been a moment this night when Owen Merritt, had he wished, could have changed her mind by the least pressure of his hand. She had almost wanted it; and had been glad when he left her. It was that way with her. Hurt and worried by the memory, she went down to join the crowd.

They were all here, Mike Tague and Helen, and Swanee Vail and his daughter from the lower Skull, and the Nankervells, and Mark Medary, and the Spaughs who ran cattle near the Fremont, and half the families of the Piute. She knew why they came. Not so much for her sake, as for Will who was a power in the land. She came down the stairs, tall and sorrel-headed, and smiling in a way to accent the serene confidence so much a part of her character. There was one man here — Pay Lankershim — whom she was quite surprised to see. Pay was a neighbor who had a small place on the northern end of the hills, adjoining Skull. He was a thin and smart and stubborn old man, who bore Skull no love, but he came to her and took her hand, the weather wrinkles around his gray eyes deep-cut for a moment. She didn't know if he was smiling or not. She couldn't tell. But he said, quietly, "You're a good girl, Sally, a good girl," and went away.

Her father was drunk and had followed from The Wells, though she had asked him to stay behind. He had cornered Will and was speaking with a good deal of hand-waving. She watched this for a moment, observing the noncommittal expression on Will's face. Then she went over and said, "I want to see you, Dad," and drew him out to the porch. He was just sober enough to be angry at her. He said: "Ain't I good enough?"

"Get on your horse and go home."

He started to speak, but she cut in without regard for him: "It's a little bit early to start panhandling Will Isham. Get out of here and stay out till I tell you to come back."

He said, mumbling oddly, "Daughter, I — "

"No," she said, "go on. I'll never let you starve, but I don't want you here. Haven't you made people laugh at our name enough? Where's Starr?"

"Don't know."

"Tell him," she said, "to quit riding with Hugh Clagg. Tell him to quit stealing."

She waited until he had gone from the porch, and drew a long breath, smoothing her face with an effort, and turned in. She saw Sheriff Medary and went over to him, gay for his benefit. He said, deeply flattered, "Lord, Will's lucky," and then she saw Will in a corner of the room. He was watching the way she handled herself, and her slow smile went over to him, making him smile back. Presently the crowd flowed into the mess hall. She sat at the foot of the table, with the sheriff to one side and old Mike Tague, whose cheeks were vermilion-bright, on the other. Outside, the crew had opened a steady gunfire. Clay Spaugh rose and proposed a toast. This was the way it went for an hour or more, the room growing warmer and the talk livelier and livelier, with Isham all the while looking on with a kind of reserve that nothing could thaw.

Afterwards, in the living room again, she joined the women, careful in the way she treated them. Will stood in another corner with Tague and Spaugh and Swanee Vail and Lankershim. Now and then her glance went his way. He was a smaller man than the rest, but it was odd to note how they listened to him and nodded when he spoke and were, all the while, faintly ill at ease with him.

Isham said, to Spaugh: "You heard about the new brand law?"

Spaugh nodded but Pay Lankershim said, "What law?"

Isham said: "We got it through the Legislature this time. It's an offense for a rider to carry a running iron unless he's directly in the hire of some ranch. Too many stray riders in this country. They pack a straight iron and come in on the edges of our outfits. It's no trick to catch a cow and doctor a brand."

Pay Lankershim gave him a strong glance. "If I was a free rider and wanted to pack a runnin' iron I'd do it and to hell with you, Will."

Isham said in good nature: "All right, Pay, all right. But you don't suffer from stealing like I do. That is just one way of making it harder to rustle. A big outfit is always fair game for the little fellow."

Pay said, "Yeah? I always thought it was the other way around," and walked into the crowd. Isham looked at the man's high back, a remote show of irritation in his glance.

Sheriff Medary came up. He faced Isham, meanwhile bracing himself genially between Mike Tague and Clay Spaugh. He was well fed and content and said so. "But I got a couple of questions, Will. Been a couple of complaints about your fence riders. You throwin' lead at trespassers?"

Isham said, "Never heard anything about it, Mark. I'll find out from Dutcher. We try to keep riders off our range. You know. We've been having a lot of trouble like that. Maybe some of the boys wasted a few shots at the sky. Just for warning."

"Sure, sure," agreed Medary. Tague and Spaugh and Vail listened with a poker-cheeked disinterest. Isham's voice was soft, almost apologetic, and Mark Medary permitted no trace of skepticism to show on his face. "Sure. But just have Dutcher keep an eye on your riders. We don't want any shootings. Well, I'll be saying good night."

He walked over to pay his respects to Sally. Mike Tague's great body stirred with a suppressed laughter. He said to Isham: "And I thought only Irishmen spread the blarney!" Spaugh and Vail said nothing.

Isham added at once, and with a degree of sharpness,

"I've got to protect myself. And so have you, fellows. It's all right to be fair. But this country won't respect anything but strong medicine. I won't tolerate stealin'. It is getting worse. I — " He stopped on that, for Pay Lankershim had come up again.

Pay said: "I guess I know when plenty is enough. I'll make the deal."

Isham said, calmly, "All right, Pay." He put out his hand. But Pay didn't take it. The old man wasn't friendly. Isham said, to the others, "So Skull goes north another five miles."

Mike Tague shook his head. "You grow too fast, Will."

Will Isham said: "Life's pretty short and a man has to hurry. Pay, what made you change your mind?"

Pay looked at him through a sustained and unfriendly interval. "I never thought you was so tough, Will. But I made up my mind tonight that you can't be beat. If a man like Merritt won't fight for what belongs to him, I guess I'm too old to try."

Isham stared at Lankershim, and the touched temper showed. "What belonged to him, Pay?"

Pay looked at him with an old man's tight-mouthed secrecy. But everybody there knew what he meant. Tague and Spaugh and Vail remained still, vaguely embarrassed. Isham's cheeks colored.

"Pay," he said, "you're my guest and I will say nothing tonight. When you ride off Skull tonight, be sure you don't come back on my land."

Pay said: "I may and I may not. You been pressin' me a long time to sell out. You ain't very careful and you ain't very particular how you persuade a man. I ain't a fellow to forget, Isham, and I'm plumb too old to be charitable. There's a lot of people in this country who'd like to see you humble. It may come." This he considered sufficient, and stalked from the house.

The crowd had meanwhile started to break up and Sally had moved to the door. Isham joined her there, accepting congratulations, and shaking hands. Mrs. Nankervell fell on Sally's shoulders, wept a little, and strode into the night with her husband. There was a good deal of calling and hallooing through the night. The river bridge boomed from its traffic; then quiet returned to Skull, and the trickle of the irrigation ditches began to make a little melody in the overwhelming dark.

Sally left the door, crossing the long room. Will Isham's voice came over, turning her around.

"You have a way with people. You can handle them, make them feel good. I was very pleased."

She said: "That's what you want, isn't it?"

"Yes," he said, "yes, it is. The ranch is pretty big. It has plenty of enemies. Size always brings parasites. I can make friends, but a man's wife can do a good deal — as you did with Medary. It has been a rather lonely house. I'd like people to drop in — and feel welcome. That's what you can do. The bigger the place gets the more I'd like people to come in."

"Is it going to be a bigger place, Will?"

"Much bigger," he said. "It grew ten thousand acres tonight. Pay Lankershim sold out to me. I've been after the man a long while."

The distance of the room lay between them and the odd constraint lay between them, hard to fathom and yet quite definite. He crossed over until he stood before her, not altogether as composed as he seemed to be. She was a shapely, beautiful girl, she had a dignity that placed her apart from all the women he knew. It was a quality he had noticed long before; it was the thing that had drawn him so strongly to her. Standing against the room's side-lamps her shoulders showed him a lifted silhouette. Her hair was deeply and richly auburn and her features — so smooth and gently colored — were very grave. He was thinking that a man and a woman at a time like this should be compelled to warmer words; that an intimacy and a gladness ought to be touching them now. But he could not seem to break through that strange, quiet distance.

He said, as near impulsiveness as was possible to him: "I watched you tonight. You belong here, Sally. You belong in the best of surroundings. You've got a manner. You can handle anybody. I think I'm pretty lucky. I want you to know that."

"You're very ambitious, aren't you?"

"Why yes," he said, really surprised. "I didn't think you knew me that well."

She drew a long breath. She turned, more squarely

facing him. "Maybe you don't know me very well, Will.
I'm ambitious, too. Perhaps that's why I see it in you."

He considered it, and spoke with a dry restraint.
"What is it you want?"

She answered quickly, as though he had misunder-
stood. "Nothing more than I'm getting now. We've got
to be honest, Will. You know my family. You know
what my father and brother are. That's what I come
from and that's what I'm getting away from. I'm grateful to you. I really am. I won't let down on my part of
the bargain, not ever. Remember that — I'll play the
part you want me to play."

A small tone of regret lay in his words. "Is it nothing
more than a bargain with you, Sally? Nothing else?"

Silence came. She continued grave and serene; she
was a slim, erect shape against the light and as he
watched her, hoping for an answer he knew he wouldn't
get, he recalled the scene at the buggy and the way she
had turned and placed her hand on Owen Merritt. The
memory dug into him, it threw him out of his calm, and
the narrows of his eyes showed her a flicker of distrust
and anger. She saw that, but she said evenly:

"It is a bargain, Will. Did I ever give you another impression?"

"No," he told her, short and hard. "No, you never did.
I'll give you credit."

"Sometimes," she went on, gentler than before, "am-
bition can be bad for people. It can hurt them so much.

Sometimes it makes them pretty hard." Then she thought of something else. "My father won't trouble you again very soon."

He shrugged his shoulders. "I'll put up with him. That's part of the bargain too, isn't it?" He brought a cigar from his coat and held it in an open palm, looking at it a long time, meanwhile trying to find the words he wanted. Presently he looked up to her and she saw him then as few people ever saw him — openly disturbed and embarrassed by the things he felt. "Sally, I had hoped for more. I'll still hope for it, as time goes on."

She gave him a small smile and turned to the stairs. But afterwards she swung around, waiting for him to come to her if he wished it that way. He recognized the gesture and said: "Good night," and didn't move.

She went on up to the room and crossed to the window again. The thin quiet of the desert lay about Skull and the stars were all aglitter in a thorough-black sky. This was the end of the wedding and weariness was real in her, made heavier by an uncertainty like fear. Will Isham was steel-strong in so many things and she knew he expected much of her. It would be hard, sometimes, to know what he wanted; and it would be hard to change her ways to meet his will, though she would do it. In one thing lay danger. The memory of Owen Merritt unsettled him, and would always bring that quick distrust into his eyes. She had to watch for that. These were the things of which she thought now; these and so many others. And always, as a picture that would never leave, the shape of Owen Merritt was before her, his turned-down face hungry and hurt and reckless.

Isham poured himself a drink and settled before the empty fireplace, nursing his cigar with a keen relish. He was like this when Fay Dutcher came in from the yard, deep-eyed from want of sleep and a steely stubble blackening his square face. Isham said: "Thought you'd be in the blankets."

"Night's gone — it's three-thirty. I'm on my way up to Corral Flats. The boys will be starting out for Winnemucca in another hour."

"Help yourself to the whisky."

Dutcher found himself a glass and poured a good drink into it. He jiggled the glass at Isham and said, "How," and downed the whisky at a swallow, afterwards standing before Isham with his lips well drawn back, braced against the liquor's jolt.

Isham said, "We'll talk this over, Fay," and considered his foreman more carefully than before. This man was huge and surly and had his weaknesses, all on the side of violence. But whatever his faults, he was loyal. Skull was Fay Dutcher's passion. He was jealous of it before the country, he would stand no abuse of it, and he had taught all Skull's hands to be the same way.

Dutcher said, "About this Love Bidwell. He came to me and said he wanted a horse. What do I say to that fellow?" He didn't like Bidwell and took no pains to conceal it, which made Isham smile slightly.

"Give him the horse."

"If you do he'll be around here moochin' all the time."

"That's all right, Fay."

"Dam' bum."

Isham slid a hand through the air, which was a signal Dutcher knew. It meant the subject was closed. "Fay," said Isham, "Pay Lankershim's sold out. So our north side extends to the head of Christmas Creek now."

Dutcher nodded. "Pressure got a little strong for him, I guess. He was a stubborn son-of-a-gun." He watched Isham carefully, and Isham looked at him with that characteristic quietness which meant so much. The short silence which followed contained its own understanding, for these two knew each other very well. Isham was not a man to change his ideas. Once fixed they stayed fixed, and the foreman never was at loss to know what his own duties were.

Isham said: "Mark Medary made a complaint tonight about our shootin' at trespassers. Who's been on our land lately?"

"Couple of homesteaders."

"Use your judgment, Fay."

The foreman considered this. "We didn't hit 'em — just scared 'em. But you want I should ease off on them fellows?"

"No. You keep right on being rough. I want everybody to know it's a damned dangerous business coming across Skull's fences. People always figure a big outfit is fair game. They figure that what Skull loses it won't miss. So we got to throw the fear of God into these easy riders. Skull keeps what it owns, and never mind how the little outfits or the homesteaders yell. Only, use your head. Be sure you've got a good reason for everything you do. I can handle Medary, so long as you furnish me with a decent reason every time you rough up a trespasser."

"I'll rough 'em up," stated Dutcher, and showed a surly pleasure in his eyes. He moved around the room, turned back. "Well, that puts our line up against Owen Merritt."

"Yes," said Isham; and silence came again, very thoughtful, until Dutcher murmured: —

"Maybe we put the pressure against him now, huh?"

"There's a horse of another kind, Fay."

Dutcher pulled himself together, touched by Isham's caution. "Listen, I never saw the man I couldn't handle."

"Be careful."

"You tellin' me to go ahead with him, or to leave him alone?"

"I only said," repeated Isham evenly, "to be careful."

Dutcher put down the glass. "I never thought much of Owen Merritt and never will."

"Why?"

Dutcher shook his shoulders together. There was weight to them, a latent crushing power. His broad hands moved idly before him. He spoke with a remembering darkness: "The man's a little too brash. Well, I'll be going."

He went into the yard, changed his saddle to a fresh horse and swung aboard. But instead of immediately lining out for the hills, he came back to the front of the big house and stopped there, and laid his hands on the horn, watching Isham through a window. He saw Isham march up and down the room, and turn and settle into a chair. Thereafter Dutcher raised his glance to the house's second floor, to the window of Sally Isham's room. He hated this woman with a sultry, secret thoroughness; he hated her for her intrusion, for the extra problem she created. Loyal to Skull, he felt she was a trespasser, and he knew at once, from the one brief glance she had given him during the night, that she distrusted him. But there was more to his resentment than that; there was a reason deeper and more personal for his instant antagonism. She was on Skull now; she was one of Skull's owners and its inheritor if Isham died. He thought of that quite carefully, his heavy mind weighing the fact against his own inner ambitions. Isham, he told himself, was a fool in this regard.

The light in Sally's room died, whereupon Dutcher wheeled away from the yard and turned to the hills.

Isham meanwhile listened to the delayed run of Dutcher's horse. He lighted his cigar and settled into a chair. There was no sound in the house. Chill came into it and daylight, long after, grayly stained the windows and his cigar burned out. But he continued to sit before the fireplace, small and half-rigid; and he kept thinking of Owen Merritt because his mind would not leave the big man alone.

V

ON TRAIL

CLIMBING steadily out of the valley of Skull into the heights of the Bunchgrass Hills, Fay Dutcher reached Corral Flats at five o'clock and found an empty camp. He pushed ahead energetically through an open pine country, across the bright flash of an occasional creek, over little meadows marked with elk and antelope sign. All the sky was bright with first sunlight but the shadows in the timber were quite cold and the expelled breath of his pony made steamy impressions on the air. Half an hour from the flats he overtook the Winnemucca-bound trail herd of five hundred steers and the accompanying four riders. Skull's riding-boss, Theodore Bale, was in charge. Dutcher went at him in a rough voice: "You got away late. By now you ought to be clear beyond the head of Christmas Creek. Damn a man that waits for daylight to get up."

"Sure," said Bale, ignoring the hard words. "Wasted some time tryin' to find a feller. Was a couple of shots over west about four o'clock. Couldn't find anything."

"I'll take a look when I go back. Be sure you make the King River crossin' by tonight. Another thing. Keep out of fights in Winnemucca. Be back here the sixth day. If you get in the cooler you can rot there."

"Sure," said Theodore Bale, whose small, tight-skinned face showed the ancient bruise of many a barroom fight. "Never started a quarrel in my life."

"Never won one, either," grumbled Dutcher. The trail herd made a scattered file ahead, tramping up the dust. A Skull man rode point, far ahead; two swing riders were off on either side of the beef. Dutcher and Bale held the drag position. Dutcher said, "I'll go as far as Christmas Creek — "

Some flash of light, or some bit of motion in the timber at the right, caused him to pull up instantly; and searching the scattered timber he saw, perhaps three hundred yards away, the rump of a horse slide from sight. He turned immediately, calling to Bale "Come up, Theodore," and rushed on. Yonder, a rider came into view, emerging from a thick stand of pine, and saw Dutcher approach. Immediately the rider swung about and stopped. It was, Dutcher saw, Juke Slover, and Juke had a quarter of antelope lashed behind his saddle. Theodore Bale, galloping behind, said: "Well, that's where them two shots came from."

Dutcher pulled in, confronting Slover. He said, short and darkly tempered: "You know the rule, don't you?"

Slover was a young man with a gawky diffidence about him, with a broad and rather pleasant face. "Where's the fire?" he complained.

"Maybe we'll find out," said Dutcher. "Get down. Throw off the game. And stand fast."

"Hell with you," said Slover. He saw trouble storming up but he kept his seat. "Wasn't hunting in your territory. I chased this thing over from Pay Lankershim's land."

Dutcher snapped up his gun. "Get down," he repeated.

Slover left the saddle reluctantly and, with equal reluctance, loosened the quarter of antelope and let it fall. He said bitterly: "You people are entirely too proud. One of these days you'll get gentled."

"Pull out your gun and let it fall," ordered Dutcher.

"What for?" demanded Juke Slover. "Not on your tintype."

"Lift it and drop it," said Dutcher. "I'm going to tie you to a tree and beat hell out of you. Maybe it will be a lesson to the country."

It was dark in this timber, dark and cold. Dutcher had dismounted. He was a huge, blunt shape before Juke Slover. The surly will showed in his eyes, and a slow brutality rolled with his lips, pretty clear to Juke Slover. Theodore Bale came up and stood a little way from Dutcher. Bale was grinning. Juke Slover straightened, he pulled up his chin. Breathing quickened in him and then he was pale and fear pinched his features together. He knew these men too well, and all the black reports of the country came back to him. But he said, knowing it could be no other way: "Not me, Dutcher." There was no change in Dutcher's expression, but Bale's grin got wider and whiter and more wicked.

Early this same morning Owen Merritt stood in his yard and had a look at the brightening land. Christmas

Creek came out of the high timber and dropped over a twenty-foot fall at this point, flowed evenly across the narrow bench and, dropping again along the slope of the hills, toward the Piute. On this bench sat the ranch house, backed by timber and facing the desert which, a thousand feet lower, ran on under morning's transparent light to the distant shape of the homestead windmills on Kitchen Meadows far away. Four miles distant lay Nan Melotte's cabin, and the adjoining school which she taught. This was the southern edge of the desert, at which point the Broken Buttes rose and heaved away, fold on fold, poor of graze and timber but slashed by a hundred criss-cross ravines and canyons. Between the prow of the Bunchgrass Hills — which was where he stood now — and the beginning of the Broken Buttes lay the low pass used by the stage road.

Cultus Charley, who was Merritt's full-blood Piute cook, came out of the house. "You back when?"

"Thursday sometime — maybe."

"Maybe," repeated Cultus Charley, who knew his boss pretty well. Merritt grinned and turned the gelding up through the timber. Two miles away he came upon George Vird, who held a hundred of Christmas Creek's knotty steers for the drive. There wasn't any delay. The trail to Winnemucca lay plainly down the side of the hill and ran its yellow way out across East Desert toward Nevada; the cattle were fresh, well watered and well fed, and already on the walk. George Vird took point, leaving the dust for Owen Merritt, who rode out to cover either flank as the occasion demanded.

After he had reached the desert floor he sighted Skull's long crooked column dropping off the east flank of the hills, behind him. He had not known that Skull was driving at the same time, and didn't care much, though it was a satisfaction to be in front. Later he caught sight of a lone rider dropping down from the Broken Buttes, advancing toward him. Presently he recognized Nan Melotte.

She came up briskly, riding with the swing of one accustomed to the saddle. She wore a riding skirt and a gray jacket and a hat pulled low over her very dark hair. She said, with a low and lazy voice: "Need a hand, mister?"

He was pleased and showed it. "You're hired if you can cook."

"Well, I can make mince pie, if you brought your mince meat."

A steer moved off the column, to the right. Nan Melotte put her horse around by a turn of her hips and cut the steer back into the column. She returned and fell beside Merritt. Color deepened the smooth surface of her cheeks and fresh sunlight showed its flash against her hazel eyes. There were ways about her Owen Merritt had never observed in another woman. A kind of indifference that covered her, a kind of bluntness, a kind of reserve. She was a girl of average height, supple and shapely, with long and full and expressive lips.

He said: "What happened?"

She knew what he meant. "Hugh Clagg came out of the buttes this morning before daylight and took Lee Repp away."

He had not thought of it before, but now it seemed odd to think of her living alone at the base of the buttes. Odd and risky. It impelled him to say: "Clagg bother you?"

She didn't immediately answer. Instead her eyes came around and watched him a little while, as though he had aroused some kind of speculation in her. "No. What made you think of that?"

"Just occurred to me."

"Well," she said, smooth and grave, "it was a nice thought. But I can tell you one thing. It's been a comfort, on more than one occasion, to look across the desert and see your light shining on the hill."

He spoke quickly. "That bad?"

She had a way of turning certain things aside with a lift of her shoulders and did so now, as though things past didn't matter any more. Her voice held a lazy, indifferent note. When she talked it was as though she didn't expect him to answer, and didn't care. "I'd like to be in Winnemucca now. I'd sit on the edge of the loading pens and watch the train go by. It would be something different."

"Thought I hired you for cook?"

She looked at him again with the same slanting, speculating interest. Her lips showed the faintest of change. "Isn't it a shame, but I forgot to bring the rolling pin."

"Anything I can get for you?"

She smiled and produced a sample of cloth from her jacket and reached over and slipped it into his pocket. "I need five yards of that, if you can match it. If not, use your judgment. The pattern doesn't matter much but the color does. Stay away from brown."

"Sure. Anything else?"

She stopped, and caused him to stop. Turned and ready to hit the back trail, she showed him the smallest, sweetest and briefest of smiles — as though she were afraid to offer more. "Why yes, Owen. Stay away from trouble, too. It comes easy to you — and it will come still easier, because you're in a frame of mind to have some."

She went away at a dead run, turning in a short while to lift a hand and call, "Good luck."

He reversed his neckpiece and pulled it above his nose to cut the trail dust, and settled down to the long day's grind. The coolness of night had gone completely from the desert, and sunlight began to bite his skin. Skull's outfit, being larger and therefore slower, had dropped farther behind. Slack in the saddle he watched the day march on, now and then leaving his position to round in a straying beef, now and then rolling up a smoke. At noon they threw off for an hour, eating cold bacon and bread by the wet seep of Lizard Spring. When they pushed forward again Merritt went up to point and George Vird took the drag. All this was done without talk, for Vird wasn't a hand to waste words and

Merritt had his mind full of many things. Heat crowded around them and the alkali soil glittered between its patches of rock and dried bunchgrass. To the left East Desert ran toward the smoky rim of Idaho. To the right the near-by buttes grew more barren and more rugged. Before them, in an empty land, the packed cattle-trail ran up and down across gentle sea-swell undulations. Twice or so, riders appeared in the far distance, stirring up vague spirals of dust. In the middle of the afternoon a band of antelope scudded down a barren draw and crossed the trail with the speed of gusty wind, racing into the desert. Four piled cattle skulls marked the Nevada line and at dusk of that long day they came to the crossing of King River, which, at this point no wider than an irrigation ditch, lay half-hidden in the rank-growing tules.

They watered the herd and turned it off the trail to graze. Over the campfire they boiled coffee and made a quick supper of bacon and canned tomatoes and bread and settled back to smoke away the last of day's light.

Long afterward the column of Skull beef broke through the violet dark, whereupon George Vird speech-lessly rose and pulled his Winchester from its saddle boot and squatted beyond the fire's light. But Skull swung aside and made camp down the river two or three miles. Suddenly the stars were shining out of a sky blacker than any black could be and the night wind turned quite cold and Owen Merritt saddled his night horse and went out to the herd.

Singing gently at the cattle, he rode his continuous circle. The land's wildness ran with the wind and the coyotes were calling out of the near hills, and at a time like this a man's thoughts ran freely, and odd, and a little sad. In the still and massive earth, pressed by the black and pressed by the weight of all the overwhelming sky, was a feeling. In the wind was a feeling. It touched his skin and his nerves and got in his bones. He couldn't name the feeling, but it made him listen to the long, weird calling of the coyote with understanding; it made him lift his eyes to the high blackness and grow larger, brushed by sudden mystery. Riding like this, a man's mind got closer and closer to something like an answer to all his mortal questions — so near that a sensation ran up and down his spine; and then the answer faded away, and left him riding, and wondering. Then he was thinking, because everything led back to her, of Sally Bidwell.

At twelve o'clock when he returned to the fire he found George Vird hunkered before it, cross-legged like an Indian. The light showed the long, half-bitter lines of the man's face, the thin pressure around the lips. Vird was near forty, small and tough and wiry, and showing the knocks of a pretty hard life. He was a deceptive man, and though he had been with the Christmas Creek ranch five years he had never spoken of his past other than to say that once he had been in the Seventh Cavalry. All Merritt knew was that this man, so taciturn and melancholy and secretive, had the instincts of an Indian. He slept light, he rode always with an odd vigilance, scanning the country and the ground around him and seeming to listen after dark for the little sounds of night. He never went without his revolver and never put himself far away from the carbine lashed to the horse, and at those times when strangers came to the ranch he invariably disappeared from view. He had ash-white hair and the steadiest blue eyes Merritt had ever noticed in a man and his language was better than average, and though all these habits pointed to some kind of past, Merritt trusted him without reservation. He was a good hand in time of trouble.

Merritt said: "Night-owlin' again?"

Vird looked up at him oddly. "Can't sleep," he murmured, and rose to saddle his spare horse. Merritt had rolled up in his blankets when Vird came back, in the saddle; and Vird remained there a little while, looking down with a plain impulse to speak. But his habitual silence controlled him and presently he turned out of the herd. Looking up at the cloudy glitter of the stars Owen Merritt thought: "Maybe I did wrong. I could have taken her away from that wedding. Which is the worst regret? Not to have a woman, or to have half a woman?" And then, with the cold, wild-scented wind blowing against him, he fell into a healthy man's instant sleep.

He awoke to find himself standing on his feet and his gun lifted against the night. A quick burst of firing

rolled over the dark and a voice howled in the near
shadows and ponies' feet made a solid, arriving rumble.
Racing for his saddled night horse he called, "George,"
and caught George Vird's answering halloo through a
fresh volley of gunfire. Up in the saddle, he turned and
rammed the pony straight toward the herd. The shadows
there were stirring along the earth; all this racket had
spooked the steers and they were on the edge of running.

George Vird plunged toward him. "We better keep together! Those fellows are comin' dead off the hills!"

Pale shafts of light stabbed the night and died, and
bloomed again. He swung beside Vird. They rushed on,
cutting around the edges of the herd. Lead laced around
them and the attacking party wheeled in the foreground
and began to turn the far edge of the beef, pressing it
toward Merritt and Vird. Merritt heard a man's easy,
unexcited call, "Here, here," and thought it was the
voice of Hugh Clagg. He went ahead with Vird beside
him and laid a sight on a vague yonder shape and let go.
Vird began firing with him and that group over there
wheeled again and came back around the side of the
herd, straight on. Steers pitched past Merritt and his
pony bucked against this pressure. The campfire was
scuffed out. Clagg's voice was more definite: "Here!"
Merritt saw shapes clearly above the general line of
the herd. He fired and kept going, and smelled powder
smoke's rank back-drift. There were, he thought, four

of them, and suddenly they wheeled and ran back and were absorbed in the black, and a man's voice, Clagg's again, let out a long whoop. That was all.

The cattle were not yet on the dead run, but they kept drifting along the margin of the river. Merritt yelled: "Take the right!" and turned out to the left. He got clear of the melee, ahead of the steers, and he began to sing, in a soft way, "Easy, easy, easy," and bucked the pony against them, moving along the line, back and forth. George Vird was singing: "Way down south in the land of cotton, go to sleep you knotty horns." Alkali dust rose thick as smoke and in the distance he saw the still-shining point of the Skull campfire. The sound of the retreating party died completely in the direction of the hills and the pressure went out of the herd. Owen Merritt turned the edge and started them into a circular milling. Presently George Vird slid from the black and said, "Guess that's all. It was Hugh Clagg. And I heard a yell that sounded like Starr Bidwell."

"Maybe."

"We can remember it," murmured Vird, and moved away, singing gently again. Merritt rode the edge a little while longer, afterwards returning to locate his blanket and roll up. When the dust had settled he was asleep.

In the middle of the afternoon, two days following, Merritt and Vird drove the beef down a gentle hill-slope, crossed the Humboldt and threw the beef into a loading pen adjoining the Central Pacific. Winnemucca town, raw and dusty and bare, lay adjacent, its single street paralleling the track. Lee Benneckdorf, who did a cattle-shipping business here, came pegging down the gravel and tallied the beef and gave Merritt a receipt, whereupon Merritt and Vird took their horses to the stable and idled into the saloon to wash away the dust of the drive.

Merritt had his drink. He said, to Vird, "We'll stay over till morning. I'm going to get a little sleep."

Vird was nursing his thirst with a kind of jumpy, taciturn humor, and so Merritt left him like that and went to the hotel. The room was on the second floor, facing the depot and eating house. Stretching on the hard bed, he felt the trapped heat soak into him and loosen up sweat. Heat had likewise warped apart the rough partition boards; and in the next room a man and a woman were violently quarreling. The woman said: "Not in this Godforsaken country. I'm taking the next train out!" Merritt fell asleep with this in his ears. When he awoke, dusk had turned the room blue and he lay thoroughly soaked in his own sweat — and Bourke Prine stood at the foot of the bed, calling his name.

VI

IN THE BARROOM

I᷈ brought Merritt immediately upright.

"What're you doing here, Bourke?"

"Just the ride," murmured Bourke. But he had something on his cheeks that gave him away. Merritt pulled off his shirt and sloshed around a basin of lukewarm water; the heat wouldn't leave the room. He said irritably, "Let's get out of here." They went down to the street and stood in a faint breeze drifting off the hills. The lamps in the yellow depot restaurant came on, across the street; a train sounded its whistle out on the far reaches of the Humboldt. Sleep had made Merritt groggy. He said, "What's up?"

George Vird sauntered from the saloon, walking with a stiffness that showed he was drunk. He looked hard at Bourke Prine but said nothing. His eyes turned to Merritt, round and strained, and somewhat wicked.

"Owen," said Bourke, "we found Juke Slover dead last Monday morning, up on Skull's land, just beyond Pay Lankershim's line. He had two bullets in him and had drawn his own gun. There was a quarter of antelope on his chest, which they laid over him deliberate. They shot his horse."

The train hallooed again in the nearing distance, the flare of its headlight beginning to show. George Vird wiped his mouth with the back of his hand, watching Bourke Prine.

Merritt said, "How did you know it?"

"He came by Pay's house pretty early and told Pay he was going in to hunt. He didn't come back. Pay went to look." Bourke cleared his throat. "Pay said he thought he heard the shots. About the time Skull's trail herd passed out of the timber into East Desert."

"Same time I left," mused Merritt.

Vird broke his long silence: "Skull just got into the loadin' pens."

The train came ringing into Winnemucca and stopped with a huge blast of brakes. All the coach windows threw out squares of yellow light; people stared through the glass. The conductor called, loud enough for train and town alike to hear: "Twenty minutes for supper!"

The three partners moved over the dust, into the railroad dining-room, and sat up at a long table set ranch-style, with all the food before them. Easterners came in from the train and took places around them, making a great racket. A woman, alone and stylishly dressed, sat at the end of the table and watched Owen Merritt with a full, frank interest — until his glance came up to her. She held his eyes a moment, and lowered her own with a warm color showing on her cheeks. A man across the table murmured sibilantly, "Cowboys," but Merritt and Bourke Prine and George Vird ate rapidly, with a glum indifference. When they were finished they rose to go. George Vird lagged back, and at the door Owen turned to see the cause and found Vird paused in the middle of the dining-room with an odd half-grin on his mouth, with a sort of deviltry showing; and suddenly Vird lifted his revolver and fired twice at the ceiling and let out a long wolf-howl. A woman screamed, and faces turned toward Vird, very pale in the lamplight, and one man knocked over his chair and rushed toward the track door. Vird wheeled from the room, stopping in the street's dust until Prine and Merritt came up.

"George," grunted Merritt, displeased, "that's the first time I ever saw you make a sucker out of yourself."

Vird wasn't smiling now. He said: "Just wanted to please the pilgrims. They expected it." His face was solemn, it was gray. A long-legged man came over the dust, pointing his hand at Vird. He was in his shirt sleeves and a star glittered high up on his chest. "Friend," he said evenly, "do your shootin' after the train's gone. You got no call to scare hell out of travelers."

"Yeah," murmured Vird, and watched the marshal go away. Rashness stirred again in his odd eyes. He was, Merritt saw, on thin edge. Twilight came down from the roundabout hills; it swept up the Humboldt flats and laid its softness over the unlovely edges of this desert town. Dust was in the air and the smell of scorched boards was in the air, but the heat of day was fading before a slow wind out of the east. Lights laid yellow bars across Winnemucca's single street and riders drifted into town from ranches deep and lonely in these hills, and a row of Indians sat on the edge of the walk, all humped over. Looking toward the saloon Owen Merritt saw Skull's trail crew — Theodore Bale and three others — standing by its door. He said, "Come on," to Prine and Vird and led them back to the hotel.

The room was still hot. Light crept through the interstices in the board partition and he heard the woman in the next room crying with a stifled, heavy labor. The train's bell began to ring and in a little while it pulled away from Winnemucca. Vird stood by the window, watching the street with a surly expression. Merritt spread out on the bed. Bourke Prine, standing with his back to the door, said, almost sharply: "You got nothing to say, Owen?"

Merritt shaded his eyes. "It's a funny thing — what a man will think. I've been remembering that girl Juke was going with. Alice Langdell. She rode him pretty hard sometimes. I wonder if a woman ever thinks of things like that when it's too late. Well, Juke was a skookum man. We had some good times. Now he'll ride no more. Bourke, the country's changing pretty fast."

Vird, still watching the street, said in a low tone: "They're goin' in to eat — Skull."

Bourke continued to watch Merritt. His glance was sharp, it was impatient. "You keep dodging."

"I keep thinking," murmured Owen Merritt. "It must have happened pretty near where Theodore Bale was camped with the trail herd. Corral Flats. Was it Bale? I don't know if he'd cool a man off — unless Fay Dutcher was along to start the play."

Bourke said: "You're still dodgin'. Dutcher stands behind Bale. Sure. But somebody stands behind Dutcher. That's what you keep dodgin'."

"Why should I dodge?" said Merritt. But before Bourke Prine answered, he added, "We'll keep off one subject, Bourke. I told you that before."

Bourke said: "Two things I never argue over with a man. Whisky and women. But maybe you don't know something else. Pay Lankershim sold out his hill range to Skull. Isham wanted that and got it. You're up against Skull's fence now, my boy. If Isham wants your graze he'll get that too. I figure he wants it."

"Why?"

"Growin' big is like playin' poker. It gets into a man's blood." He came over to the edge of the bed. He had a temper, this Bourke Prine, and sometimes it got away from him, as now. He reached out and pushed aside the hand which shaded Merritt's eyes. He stared down at Merritt. "Listen, you dam' fool, wake up. You lost a girl and you go around moonin' over that while other things are happenin' to you. I said Isham had made a sucker out of you when he married Sally. You lost a lot of standin' when you let him do that. Now he'll scare you off the hills, because it's the way he plays. Likewise, maybe you don't remember Lee Repp was one of Hugh Clagg's men. What you figure Clagg's going to do?"

Vird said, "Come over here, Bourke." Bourke walked to the window, looking out. He turned back, a change on his cheeks. "Fay Dutcher."

Merritt said: "Here?"

Vird crossed the little room and opened the door. "I'll be on the street," he said, and went out.

Merritt sat up on the bed and rolled and lighted a cigarette, and lay back again. Smoke swirled around his face until Bourke, tramping back and forth in the drab room, couldn't see his partner's eyes at all. Bourke paused at the window again, watching the street. His big shoulders bent down and rose, and he shook them, as though irritated by what he saw and felt. "What's the man here for?" he grumbled. "Well, for something. What you going to do, Owen?"

Owen Merritt let the question hang in the heated air. The woman in the adjoining room quit crying. A man plugged up the stairs and went into her room, his voice pretty plain to the partners. "I thought you figured to take that train?"

The woman said, in a sadder voice than Owen had ever heard, "I guess I've got to stay with you, Claude. Pillar to post. Always broke and always in trouble. Is it always going to be like this?"

The man said: "I know. I'm leadin' you a hell of a life. Caroline, I'll try — I'll try to make it up!"

Owen Merritt rose; he went to the window. Store lights brightened the street's deep dust. Night lay black and star-brilliant across the great arch of the sky and riders drifted like vague shadows in from the surrounding desert. He turned to observe Bourke Prine's face.

"What did you come here for?"

Bourke shrugged his shoulders. "You're a fool to go battin' around the country without help. It's too risky."

"Bourke," said Owen, "you keep pushin' at me. You keep telling me something I don't seem to get."

"All right. You're a gone coon, but you don't know it. Your mind's cluttered up from thinkin' of a woman, and you don't realize that Will Isham is after your hide — and will get it, because he never lost a play yet. I know why you don't say anything. You figure you won't fight Skull because Sally is there now. I know Isham better than you do. The man can't bear anything to stand in his way. You do. Not just your ranch, kid. But you had Sally before he did and he won't forget. He's an Indian. I'm telling you."

Merritt shook his head. "After all, Isham can't afford — " He stopped, a new thought cutting across his mind. He came away from the window, jerking open the door. "Come on, Bourke. I just remembered about George Vird." He took the stairs two at a time, and came to the street, Bourke close behind. Vird wasn't on the street. "Saloon, naturally," Merritt grumbled, and turned that way, at once noting Fay Dutcher's big sorrel mare standing at an adjoining rack. Men came out of the saloon, and turned and made a little group by the door, a dozen of them or more. When Prine and Merritt came up, one man said, in clear caution: "A little warm in there, mister."

There were two windows to the place, both painted over, and a single swinging door that was closed. Another man came out, opening it long enough for Merritt to see Vird standing in the middle of the room, alone and motionless, with his face pointed to one corner. Merritt couldn't see into that corner.

Bourke called, "Wait — " and touched Merritt's shoulder. Merritt shook free, kicked the door open again and stepped into the smoky, ill-lighted room.

The place was square, with a few poker tables on one side, a bar at the far end, and a hallway leading off one corner of the bar to rear rooms. This much he caught at a glance, meanwhile watching Vird's head turn, watching Vird's shoulders loosen in real relief at sight of him. A barkeeper stood behind the counter, not moving. Near the hallway corner the bar turned at right angles, and here, half protected by it, three of the Skull riders stood in apparent idleness, side by side. Vird had his back to these men, more interested apparently in Theodore Bale, who had maneuvered himself over to the bar's other end. And then, looking to the near-by poker tables, Merritt found Fay Dutcher's big shape planted in a chair.

The quietness of this place was a thorough thing. No man stepping into it could mistake its meaning or the intent of all those quiet shapes in the dismal light. Dutcher sat in a manner to command whoever might come in the front way. It was, Merritt considered, a deliberate situation; and now Dutcher's long and surly face came together at all its angles. He stood up, kicking the chair back of him. He said: "Hello, Owen, what's news?" It wasn't a question. It wasn't anything except so much sound flattening into the silence, calm and unhurried and very deliberate. The saloonman took half a dozen steps deeper into the room, the squeaking of his boots very loud.

George Vird was sober, as Owen Merritt saw. But the rash and crazy temper which had ridden him all evening still held. He looked around the room; he made a complete circle on his heels and showed Merritt the pale surface of his eyes. He was smiling his insolence at them, eager for what was so surely on its way. "Owen," he said, "these boys are a little tough. Go back outside a minute and let me oblige 'em."

Merritt turned to Dutcher: "What's the matter here, Fay?"

Dutcher said: "You can see, can't you?"

"George," called Merritt, "shut up and come on out of here. You're drunk again."

"No," broke in Dutcher, "he ain't drunk."

"Wait a minute," broke in Merritt, actually curious. "You're all standin' around here braced for a fight. Now just which one was going to handle George — or was it the whole four?"

"You can find out," said Dutcher. He was affected by the talk. His bold face turned complexion and the surly temper came up into his eyes more powerfully.

"Skull style," murmured Merritt. Then he said, "You're a fine bunch of dogs."

"You want some?" said Dutcher.

"I'll just cut in," agreed Merritt coolly. "And I'll call my ball, to boot. You and me, Fay."

George Vird said in his high, taunting voice: "A little fun, Owen. But I don't think they like the odds."

"Why you damn fool," said Theodore Bale in the far corner, "you're dead when the fun starts."

"Me and Juke Slover, hah?" said George Vird.

Silence came down then. On Dutcher, Merritt kept a steady eye, waiting for the break. There wasn't any fear in Skull's foreman, and no doubt at all. The man hated everything that stood against Skull and he had a contempt that was very real for everything in Skull's way. He remained dark-faced and taciturnly composed; physical power flowed out of him. But there was something else that Owen Merritt clearly caught, something that told him more than he had hitherto known about Skull. Fay Dutcher wanted this fight. He was playing for it.

Theodore Bale called to Dutcher in a quick, disturbed voice: "What's it goin' to be, Dutcher?"

Owen Merritt let his arms hang. Coolness came to him. He said, "Let's find out, Dutcher." A man's life was full of trouble and full of question — and so it was like relief to stand up to certainty, to know that he was in front of reality. He would survive or he wouldn't, and at once he realized that for him there was no fear of going out. He lived this long, long interval with a sureness, with a strength; and then he was thinking of Juke Slover and mercy went out of him.

This was the moment when Bourke Prine, having circled the outside of the saloon, came down the little hallway back of the bar and laid his risen gun against the three Skull men in that corner of the room. He said: "You fellows scratch for it."

It knocked them out of the play; it evened up the fight instantly, and some reflection of this showed on Fay Dutcher's face. His eyes grew round, grew blacker as he stared at Bourke Prine. His words flattened into the silence. "Better stay out of this, Bourke. You ain't so big." Theodore Bale was obviously disturbed. He scraped his feet on the floor and threw Dutcher a silent appeal, and afterwards, for a reason Owen Merritt never understood, Dutcher left his corner of the room and walked deliberately over to Bale. He turned there, pushing Bale away. Bale came half down the room, clearly puzzled and not knowing what Dutcher wanted. At this instant, the saloonman rose from behind the bar and shot out the saloon's three lamps.

Darkness crashed down upon the room and Owen Merritt cat-stepped aside, hearing the rip of cloth and Theodore Bale's long loud cry fade into a full roar of aroused gunfire. Everybody opened up at once. Owen Merritt kept side-stepping toward the wall to clear George Vird in the middle of the room. He spotted the flash of Dutcher's gun, and laid his shot on that. He saw muzzle light leap from Vird's piece, flashing and fading and flashing again. Something seemed to come apart in the corner where Bourke was. Merritt heard the smash of bodies against the wall and the fall of table and chairs. Sound battered the saloon room, it shook the walls and rang painfully against Merritt's ears. He kept moving, he kept shifting his feet like a dancer, he kept throwing his bullets at the corner. Everybody in this place stirred around, as the powder flashes showed. Somebody went down, striking with a dead solid weight. A bullet hit the bar's back mirror, dropping a shower of glass to the floor. The saloonman shouted. A rolling body clipped Owen Merritt behind the legs and threw him flat on his chest. One man went out of the saloon doorway low and fast, falling on the yonder walk, and greatly swearing. Rising, surrounded by blackness and oppressed by the stink of close-held powder, Merritt heard the heavy run of a man's feet in the back hall. The firing had quit and somebody's breathing sawed up and down. He stood there a long while, sweat crawling down his cheeks. He said: "George," and stepped aside quickly. But it was Bourke who answered, from the far corner: "All right." Bourke's voice had a flat sound, a faraway sound. This was what the racket had done to Merritt's ears. The saloonkeeper said: "Wait a minute, boys," and a little later a light went on by the bar.

Vird was still in the center of the room, impossibly surviving the crisscross of fire. He said, "Put out that damned light."

Merritt spotted Bourke immediately. Then he saw a man lying near Bourke, one of the three who had been in that corner. Theodore Bale huddled, face down, near the opposite wall. Vird repeated, "Put out that light." His cheeks were pale and his ash hair was disheveled. He was a good-looking man, a little tired around the mouth and no longer showing the trace of wickedness in his eyes. His expression was almost serene.

The saloonman whipped his hand across the globe and the room fell into darkness again. A single shot smacked through the saloon's flimsy wall and boots scuffed the walk. Merritt jumped to the door. Bourke and George Vird were rushing over and both were warning him, but he charged through the doorway and faced a street fast emptying. Men were vanishing into alleys and into the smooth velvet shadows surrounding the depot. He put himself flat against the saloon wall, looking to his left where Skull's horses were. Fay Dutcher was an obscure shape yonder, backing unhurriedly away; the two other Skull riders had paused by the horses, but now they moved farther into the street. George and Bourke ran out of the saloon. Merritt turned from the wall and walked toward Dutcher. He fired when his left foot hit the walk, and moved on, and fired again in rhythm with his pacing. Dutcher gave ground slowly, saving his lead. Bourke and George Vird were out in the middle of the street; they pounded away at the two Skull men, who whipped their bullets up from the shadows.

Dutcher halted and raised his gun, taking careful aim.

The steady racket of all this fled away into the high night sky and instantly faded in that vastness. One of the other Skull men cried, "Dutcher!" and dropped in the dust. Dutcher took his aim and pulled the trigger, but the hammer fell on an empty. He wheeled and rushed for his horse and the other surviving Skull hand raced back. In a moment they were mounted and rushing away.

Merritt stopped. Bourke Prine sent a useless shot after those two and George Vird walked toward the dropped Skull man. Quietness came back to Winnemucca. Light flowed freshly through the saloon windows, and people of the town began to drift from the shadows. The sound of horses diminished in the black distance beyond town. Bourke and Vird came back to Merritt and for a while the three of them stood together. George Vird's face maintained its gentle expression. "I can sleep a little better now. It kind of takes care of Juke Slover."

VII

DANGEROUS INTERVIEW

WHEN Dutcher returned from Winnemucca with the other survivor of the Winnemucca fight, Isham was in the home meadow watching a crew work on an irrigation ditch. He came straight up to Dutcher. The first thing he said was: —

"Where've you been?"

Dutcher's solid face was covered with a steel-black beard. His eyes were red from dust and from the need of sleep, and the man's surly temper made it hard for him to be civil. "Winnemucca."

"I didn't tell you to go there," said Isham. Part of the home crew had come up. Isham said to them, "Go on, boys," and waited until they were out of earshot. His own hard temper was rising, but he was cool enough to spare his foreman embarrassment in front of the men. He said: "Where's Theodore Bale? Where's the others?"

Fay Dutcher stood with his legs apart, with the powdered dust of the trip clinging to him. He had lost a fight. This was the thing that burned in him. He said, "In the graveyard by now" — and then this man, who was afraid of almost nothing on earth, dropped his glance. It was the bright heat of Will Isham's eyes that made Dutcher look down.

Isham said: "Come in the house," and led the way. He walked over to close the dining room door; he looked at the stairs. Sally stood on the upper landing. She called, "Is there something wrong, Will?"

When Isham was really stirred, his manner always turned quiet and smooth and very soft. It was now. He said, "Nothing, Sally," and waited till she went back along the hall. He listened to the tap of her footsteps. Dutcher was a huge, waiting shape in the center of the room. Isham said: "You went down there and started a fight, and took a licking. What did you go for?"

Dutcher murmured: "Merritt started down with some beef the same mornng. I got to thinkin' . . ."

Isham made a sliding gesture with his hand, instantly cutting off the explanation. For Dutcher didn't need to explain what he had thought. The hint of it was in the corners of his eyes, it lay arrogantly in the thick-fleshed line of his lips. Isham said: "I told you to be careful."

Dutcher burst out: "Before God, I'll make up for that!" A raging sense of defeat unsettled him. "I'll take care of Merritt. I'll — "

Isham's hand once more checked Dutcher. Against the bulk of his foreman, Isham was a small, almost ineffectual shape, thin in all his features and possessing little hint of physical power. But his coolness grew and his talk, so soft and so smooth, was nevertheless like acid on the dismally listening foreman.

"I warned you about him. Merritt's different from other men. We can scare most riders out of the country.

We can break most of them by fear. But it won't work with him."

Dutcher said, sullenly: "The hell it won't. I'll find out about that."

"Be quiet while I talk," said Isham with a lecturing insistence. "In some things, Dutcher, you can't be beat. In some things you are a fool. I give you credit for being loyal to the ranch. But you have caused me a lot of trouble. I'll have to share the blame for telling you to be tough. The thing is done and we've got to stand it somehow. But why didn't you use your head?" He stared at Dutcher. "I'm not talking about Merritt now. I'm talking about Juke Slover."

Dutcher gave his grumbling, heated answer. "We caught him cold. He had a quarter of venison on him. I told him I figured to beat hell out of him, for warnin'. That's the way you got to treat these people unless you want 'em all swarmin' over our fence. The man wasn't smart. He decided he'd try a fight. What else could I do?"

"You could have put him out of sight," said Isham. "Instead you leave him for Pay Lankershim to stumble over."

Dutcher said earnestly: "Well, what's the matter with that? It'll teach the country a lesson. Dead men ought to be seen."

Isham weighed his foreman unfavorably, at last saying: "After this you let me know when you figure to do something."

Dutcher immediately hoisted his great shoulders. "Listen, Mister Isham. I have done my best for Skull. If I don't suit you any more just say so and I'll pack my bed."

"If I wanted to fire you," said Isham dryly, "I wouldn't waste this much talk on it. You're all right, Dutcher, but just leave the thinking to me. And let Merritt alone until I say something to you."

Mention of Merritt's name increased the somber glow in the foreman's eyes. It hardened the muscles of his face. His defeat cut deep in him. He couldn't forget it — and wouldn't rest until the injury had been wiped out. Isham saw this much and warned Dutcher more definitely. "Do you hear what I say?"

Dutcher said, "Yeah," and scowled, and turned to the door. But protest swung him around. His own philosophy was too positive to let him alone. "It won't work at all. The man's got to pay for what he did. If we don't do something about it everybody in the country will be shootin' at us. You got to keep 'em afraid, Mr. Isham. Maybe I ain't so smart, but I know this country. You can't crowd a fellow and expect him to grin. You been crowdin' this country. Well, those folks will crowd back if they can. That's my job — to keep 'em humble. You can feed 'em at your table all you like, and you can set up the drinks in the Palace all you like, but you ain't goin' to make any friends that way. Skull is too big to have any friends, and it has been too tough. I don't think you got that straight, Mr. Isham. You can have things your way — if you're prepared to fight. Well, you've got things your way, and it is too late now to think of soapin' people to make 'em forget. You got a lot of enemies and there's only one way to keep on top, which is by beatin' hell out of 'em. If you ain't prepared to do it that way then you never should of started to crowd other folks in the first place. People don't forget. Think that over."

Isham opened his mouth, and closed it again. He studied his foreman carefully and in the end only nodded, whereupon Dutcher left the room. Isham took a fresh cigar from his pocket and lighted it. He stood by the fireplace, hands locked behind him, considering Dutcher's talk. Considering it and vaguely feeling its truth. Slover's death would be a scandal and Medary would be questioning him about it. He'd have to smooth things down somehow. It left a bad impression on the Piute, it made the rest of his plans that much harder to accomplish. He thought of all this as he smoked, his little shape motionless and drawn together. Of this and of many other things.

Sally came out of an upper hall and down the stairs. She said: "Are you going to town with me, Will?"

He said, "Yes," and studied her face, wondering how much of all this she had heard. He couldn't tell. Her expression was smooth, almost willfully so, and she had nothing in her eyes that gave him a clue. She was, he thought, a poker-faced girl when she chose to be; and always just beyond his reach.

Immediately on returning from Winnemucca, Owen Merritt took a swim in the creek behind the house, and saddled a fresh horse and lined out for The Wells. Within a mile of town he met Mark Medary, who turned back to The Wells with him. "I was comin' to see you," said the sheriff.

"I'm on my way to Skull."

The sheriff gave him a considering glance. "We'll have a little talk first."

They were on the edge of town then. Merritt pulled up at the Palace and went in with Medary. They had a drink and walked on through to the back room. Medary took a moment to adjust the door so that it was within an inch of being shut, which gave Merritt an idea of the sheriff's state of mind.

"Owen," he said, "there's trouble enough for a lot of us. Yours, the other fellow's, and mine. We'll talk about your troubles first. Who was with you when you went home from the weddin'?"

"Bourke, for half the distance. Alone the rest of the way."

"And who was with Repp when you ran into him?"

Merritt said, gently: "I wouldn't know about that, Mark. Did I run into him?"

Medary said: "You remember what you did to Lee Repp in this saloon? And what you said you'd do to him?"

"I remember," said Merritt. "But I didn't do it. Somebody saved me the trouble."

"It may be," murmured Mark Medary. "But the remark does you no good. I hear you had trouble in Winnemucca."

"That got here in a hurry."

The sheriff gave him a sad nod. "Sure. Bad news always does. You'll find it's like a smell in the wind. And the smell sticks to a man. Then Juke Slover dies, who is a friend of yours, and now you're on the road to Skull. I believe I wouldn't go, Owen."

"I'm not after trouble, Mark."

Medary said: "Trouble just comes." He made his long appraisal of Merritt. The big man sat loose in the chair, his arms idle on the table and his face composed. But his lips made a solid roll across the tanned skin and his eyes were fathomless at the moment. It made the sheriff say: "If I was you, there's a couple of things I'd do. I'd be mighty careful of my own temper, and I'd look sharp at the other man's. Things are kind of rollin' up on you. That's what I came to say."

"About Repp," said Merritt, "what was it you meant?"

"Nothin'," said Medary. "Nothin' yet — and maybe nothin' ever. But . . ." He stopped, searching for a word. The years had made Medary pretty smart. "But if you should ever see me comin' toward your house in the next couple of weeks, Owen, I'd just say to myself: 'There comes Medary — and I wonder what for?' "

Merritt grinned. "Thanks, Mark," he said, and rose. Medary turned to the door, looking back. He answered the grin, but was soon sober again. "My boy," he said, "I'd hate to see you laid out, like I saw Juke Slover."

Merritt said: "You talk like Bourke Prine."

"Bourke," said the sheriff, "is a pretty sharp man. Use your eyes like he uses his." With this admonition he went out.

Merritt built himself a cigarette and lighted it and sat a little while in the room's heated silence. Afterwards he walked through to the street to his horse, got in the saddle and went on toward Skull's road. Passing the hotel he saw Helen Tague in the doorway. She said, "Hello, traveler," and beckoned. He went over there, smiling at the sight she made. He said, "You're the prettiest thing — " and then heard the quick run of horses around the bend of the hotel. A moment later Isham and Sally galloped in.

They rode to the hotel's porch and for a moment silence was a solid wall between these four people. Owen had removed his hat for Helen Tague. He held it in his hand, watching Sally's face change. It was this way between them, and had always been, and always would be. Nothing was any different. She had her effect on him, her eyes and her lips and the flow of her smooth body holding something for him, something he remembered and couldn't forget. There was a riding color on her cheeks, a color that remained while the moments passed, and this was what Will Isham saw with his suspecting glance — this scene between his wife and the man she hadn't married. At that moment he was ignored, and knew it. Helen Tague, so quietly in the background, saw the dangerous lines on Isham's cheeks just then, the pale composure, the stiffening of his small shoulders.

Sally's eyes dropped and Merritt turned his attention to Isham. He said, "I was riding your way."

"Glad I saved you the trip," said Isham, the rustle of emotion in his talk. He got down and gave his hand to Sally. She stepped to the porch, joining Helen Tague, and called: "I'll be here quite a while, Will." Both women went into the hotel.

Merritt left the saddle and for a moment was close to Isham, standing head and shoulders over the Skull owner. Isham, always quick to feel the affront of such comparison, moved quickly back from Merritt until the added distance made the disparity less pronounced. Ruffled pride put a change on his cheeks. He showed it, as a man shows weakness in an unguarded moment.

Sun slanted out of the west and late summer's light was golden, clouded here with the street's disturbed dust. Sam Nankervell's hammer pounded hard echoes into the drowsing day. Medary came from Shannon's store and turned toward the hotel. But he saw the two men here and wheeled around. Owen Merritt used a fresh match on his cigarette; when he cupped his hands around the match the knuckles of his hands made solid shapes underneath the tanned skin. Little things like this showed his physical toughness, the punishing power of his body, as Will Isham noted with a slow, deep jealousy.

It was hidden and no man suspected it; but the feeling always came bitterly to him when he stood by Merritt.

"Will," said Merritt, as direct as he could be, "did you send Dutcher down to Winnemucca to start a fight?"

"No."

"I'm glad to hear that."

Isham said: "Don't draw your conclusions too fast. I didn't send him. But he went on ranch business and I'll stand by him. Skull takes care of its people. Who started that fight?"

"Ask Dutcher," said Merritt, constantly watching Isham. The little man's eyes were cool and uncompromising; they were not friendly. Merritt said then: "Better make it a little clearer, Will. If you stand back of Dutcher, then you stand back of everything he does. He had his fun down there. I don't propose to be a target for Skull. If that's what it is going to be, I want to know."

Isham took it with a growing restlessness. He showed it. He said, suddenly: "It comes poorly from you to complain of that affair when you killed three of my men. I can't let that go by." They were on the border of a quarrel, but his feelings kept pushing at him, and afterwards his talk went at Merritt with a greater and greater intolerance. "You can't expect to bait Skull's riders and not get a play. Well, that's what you've been doing a long time. You're like the rest of this country, figuring Skull is fair game for anything. If Winnemucca was in Oregon I'd ask Medary to lock you up."

Merritt said: "I get this a little bit clearer. All right, if you want it that way you tell Dutcher to take care of himself."

"Hold on," challenged Isham. "I won't listen to a threat. If I told that to Dutcher the crew would be on your trail before night."

"It's been on my trail longer than that," pointed out Merritt. "Which I'm just beginnin' to realize." He grew calmer and dryer-voiced as Isham's temper slipped.

Isham realized it and made a strong effort to pull in his talk. For a moment his voice was conceding. "Wait now. The fat's in the fire and I can't answer for the men. It wouldn't make any difference what I said. They'll be remembering Theodore Bale and the other boys. There's one way out of it. There's always been a way out. I'll buy Christmas Creek from you, Merritt."

Merritt said: "You been playin' freeze-out with me a long time. So far, no luck. You can go to hell."

"Wait," demanded Isham. He stepped another pace backward and stopped and made a thin shape in the golden daylight. Something bitter and implacable came out of him, clearly reaching Owen Merritt. A state of mind that wouldn't yield, a pride that burned higher and higher. "I don't care for that, Owen."

"No?" said Owen. "You don't?" His tone was summer-soft. It was within his power to reach forward and break Will Isham with his hands, and some of the old anger ragged at him and the old sense of loss had its hard effect on him. He held it back, knowing that for once he

turned to Helen Tague and murmured: "I've got to see him, Helen."

Helen Tague said, gently saddened: "Oh, Sally. No. It isn't right."

"Nothing's right."

Helen looked at Sally carefully. "Have you found that out already?"

"Don't, Helen. I've got to have somebody I can turn to."

"Why, honey," said Helen, and put her arm out to Sally Isham's shoulder. "I'd never draw away. I'm so sorry for you. And have been since the night you married him."

"That won't do either." Sally came from the window and a moment later, unable to hold in her curiosity, went back to it, watching her husband walk toward the saloon. She made a tall, supple shape in the room. Even her worries couldn't take away that sense of vigor and self-sufficiency and readiness to do what had to be done. She was darkly composed and color made her pretty and her lips were even and sweet. "Don't be sorry for me, Helen. I'm not sorry for myself."

Helen Tague asked her a quiet, softly-insistent question. "It was a mistake, wasn't it?"

"How can anybody know when a mistake is made, Helen? There are things we know we must do. Good or bad, we do them. Because there isn't any other way."

"You're thinking of Owen now and wanting to see him. And you're not happy."

"No, I'm not happy," Sally admitted. She turned on Helen and added at once: "But I never expected that kind of happiness. Most people fool themselves. I have tried not to. I wanted something. Now I have it. I can't explain, but if you had been brought up to see and hear and feel the things I have, you'd know. I just can't tell you. But I've got to see Owen."

Helen Tague was thoroughly honest. She said again: "That's not right."

Sally looked at the girl with the firmness of her will showing through. She had a tilt to her auburn head, a kind of unresting vitality that would not die. She said, "He's in trouble, Helen," and watched the girl's eyes widen with concern. "You see," said Sally, "I know how you feel, too."

Helen drew back, alarmed and turning color. "If you ever breathe — "

"Sometimes," murmured Sally in a softer voice, "I have thought . . ." But she suppressed whatever the thought was and faintly moved her shoulders. "Now, whatever I say, back me up."

They went to the street, toward the store. Isham was returning from the saloon and met them. Sally said: —

"Irene Spaugh is coming in later. We had planned to meet her, but it's late — and I think Helen and I will stay over tonight at the hotel. You don't mind?"

He said, "No," civilly, and clapped on his hat. From the porch of the store the women watched him ride out of town on the Skull road.

Helen murmured uneasily: "I don't feel right about it."

It was then early afternoon. Much later they ate in the hotel's dining room; when night swept in Sally Isham turned her horse down Skull's road a mile or more to throw off the town's curious eyes, and turned south toward the Broken Buttes. Night lay solidly about, relieved only by the crystal wash of stars above. A small breeze brought on the desert's wild and stirring incense, and she was thinking — because Helen Tague had brought it back to her harder than she could ever admit — of a forbidden happiness: of Owen Merritt and herself.

VIII

SALLY AND NAN

MERRITT was on the porch of the Christmas Creek House, well to one side of the beam of light flowing through the doorway. George Vird, lost in gloomy silence, squatted on his heels against the wall, and Cultus Charley rattled around the kitchen, making his customary racket with the pots. The falls behind the house maintained a rustling sound that was pleasant to hear, and far off on the lower desert the light of Nan Melotte's cabin drilled a glittering point through the black. It was Vird, very sharp of ear, who heard the horse coming up the slope. He rose and put his back to the wall, murmuring to Owen: "Better kill that cigarette." Always a spooky man, he had grown more wary since the affair in Winnemucca, as Owen observed now. "You're on edge, George."

"I feel it," admitted Vird. "Close. Like a man feels a gun pointin' at him even when he can't see it." He stopped talking so that he might listen more carefully, afterwards adding in a dull, dry voice: "Not that I give a damn about dyin'. Life ain't that valuable to me, or to any man. But when I go I figure to take company along. One horse yonder and a light rider."

They saw the silhouette of horse and rider against

the shadows. For a moment Owen had a definite reaction of pleasure, believing it to be Nan. He stepped from the porch. When the rider called his name he stopped in his tracks and whirled around, throwing George Vird a warning altogether unnecessary: "You haven't seen anything, George." She came up and swung down and paused before him, and the little ease went out of the night. It had always been this way before, and was now — her presence reviving old memories, old hunger and a sense of incompleteness that would not let him alone.

He said, very slow with his words and very gentle: "Not a good place for you to be, Sally."

Her voice had a quick swing of uncertainty, a singing melody, as though nothing had changed. "Is there anyone on Christmas Creek I couldn't trust?"

Vird went into the house, closing the door and cutting off its light. A narrower glow came from the window, vaguely staining the dark; and that was all. Her presence here was strong and compelling and the fragrance of her hair, so close she stood to him, had a way with his feelings. He said, "Sit down," and watched her turn and sink to the porch steps. This silence ran on, hard to break.

"Owen," she murmured, "what are you thinking?"

He said, brusque with his answer, "Things I shouldn't. You know that."

A long sigh came out of her. "I was afraid you would," she murmured. But then, because she was too straightforward to hide her thoughts, she immediately added in a low, faintly pleased tone: "And afraid you wouldn't, too."

"You had better make up your mind, Sally. You know where your bed is now."

She said, quickly and humbly: "I know — I know."

The old sense of irritation drove him on. "What was it you came here to say?"

"Owen," she said, "Fay Dutcher means to kill you."

"Is that all?"

She stood up. She stepped close to him, placing her hand on his shoulder. "Don't try to hurt me, Owen. Not now. I know more than you think I know."

He said: "What does Isham say to that?"

She didn't immediately answer, but held her arm where it was, her fingers hanging to the cloth of his shirt. Her face was vague and white in the darkness; the fragrance of her hair drifted to him again. She said, more quietly: "I can't repeat the things my husband has said. You wouldn't want me to. But it is different with Dutcher. I have no reason for liking him. He's a dangerous man, Owen. Dangerous even for Skull, I think." She stopped and the long pause told him how difficult this was for her. Then she added: "I wish I could tell you the rest of it."

Merritt said: "The rest of it, Sally, is that Isham agrees with Dutcher. We threshed that out in front of the hotel this afternoon. I have got my walking papers from him. I can sell him the ranch or I can make out my will."

Her tone was low and weighed with concern. "Owen
— Owen!"

"What else would you expect? Skull's up against my
fence and it won't stop there. I thought, one time, that
maybe we could work it out without trouble. Since what
happened in Winnemucca, I know better."

"It isn't just a matter of land, Owen. It's Will — the
way he feels about you. He keeps remembering . . ."

He waited for the rest of it, and afterwards prompted
her: "What, Sally?"

What impelled her to finish the sentence was an utter
honesty that now, as in times past, had made her so
desirable to him. There was no evasion in this girl. "He
keeps remembering," she went on, so slowly, "that you
once were first. His pride is so terribly strong. It makes
him wonder now if I still feel about you as I did."

In a calmer moment, in a more clear-sighted moment
he would never have asked the question he did now.
Her presence caused him to say: "Do you, Sally?"

She was very near to him, so near that he saw the
change on her pale-shining face. She was not a girl to
cry or give way; she was stronger than that. Yet she
was a thorough woman, with a woman's dreams and
desires making riot in her; they showed through, on
her lips. This was what he saw, and this was what made
him reach out and seize her and draw her in to him. He
had his kiss, and felt her arms push him away. He
stepped back, hearing the uneven rush of her breathing.

"Owen," she cried, "don't! You make me feel dirty, you make me feel so ashamed."

"Maybe," he said dismally, "you'll remember what I told you the night you were married."

She flung her protest at him. "You could have had your way that night. If you'd wanted me — if you'd only said it — I would have gone down those side stairs with you. You knew it, too! But you spoke as though you hated me. Why, Owen?"

"Because," he said, "you made up your mind the other way. Half a woman ain't enough, Sally."

Her voice fell down to a tired, throaty whisper. "I wish you had known how tired I was of making up my own mind." This was her moment of weakness. Afterwards her will came back. It pulled her together. "Listen, Owen, you have never really known why I married Will. I never said I loved him. He knows that. But there's my father, a shiftless liar and a panhandler. There's my brother, a thief. Will knows it, for Dutcher caught Starr a few months ago. Do you know how hard pride can be? I grew up hating my family, and I made up my mind I'd make myself into something, no matter what it cost. I told Will this. He knew what he was getting, and what he wasn't getting. I'll keep my bargain. But, Owen, I wish you'd sell out to him and leave. Dutcher is too dangerous."

"Dutcher?" he said.

"All right, it is Will I mean. There are many fine things about him, but Skull is his whole life. And even if he wished, I don't think he could keep Dutcher from hunting you. Why don't you sell, and go over to East Desert?"

He said, "No, Sally."

Her breath drew in and went out as a long, long sigh. Her shoulders dropped and she murmured, "All right," and moved past him to her horse. He came up to her. They stood without talk, both looking into the yonder desert. Wind ran brisker and colder from the high timber behind them, and coyotes were lifting their mourning voices along the bench. The darkness held a kind of silver fog. She said: "You've made up your mind to do something."

"Yes."

"I can hear it in your words. You see, I know you better than anybody else knows you. But, remember, Will controls the country." Suddenly she changed the topic. "Is that Nan Melotte's light down there?"

"Yes."

She watched it a moment and presently turned, coming nearer him and looking into his face. Her voice changed. "I hadn't realized you were that near as neighbors. Do you visit?"

"Sometimes."

She spoke with a controlled indifference. "She's rather pretty. I never knew her very well. In fact I have thought, from the few times we've met, that she didn't like me. I have often wondered how she puts up with so lonely a place."

"Seems to find her own pleasures," commented Owen.

"Perhaps," said Sally and stepped to the saddle. But she kept looking at him through the darkness and all at once a surprising resentment came out of her. "Owen, you aren't very wise about women. Don't be a fool."

"What have I said?"

"It is what you haven't said that gives you away," she reported, and spurred down the slope.

Darkness covered her. She reached the bottom of the slope fifteen minutes later, skirted the black mouth of the Christmas Creek Gulch, and turned north toward town with the light of Nan Melotte's house shining insistently over the flat. Now and then, riding at a fast clip, she looked back at the light and each time something like fear went through her, although she didn't recognize it.

She had made the trip without trouble, and thought that the night protected her. In this she was mistaken, for in passing the mouth of the gulch she had been very close to Hugh Clagg, who stood slightly back in the gulch's shelter. All he definitely saw was the shape she made in the saddle. But there were few women in this country, and of the two who might possibly have reason to visit Merritt, one was in her cabin a few miles away, as the light showed. So this, he decided, was Sally Isham. He brought his horse from the gulch and cut back up the Bunchgrass Hills, aiming for Corral Flats where he thought Fay Dutcher might be.

After Sally's departure George Vird rode in from the rear of the ranch. He said to Merritt, "Going back of the north fork. Can't sleep and might as well be doing something."

"Better let it go. Skull's got cattle in there, just over the fence. You might run into somebody."

"I wouldn't mind that," grunted Vird, and wheeled away.

Merritt built himself another smoke, aware of the loneliness of these hills. It was a queer thing, for this was a land he knew as a man might know the pages of an oft-read book: its covert places, its silence and sunlit spots and deep ravines, its mystery. He loved it and was at home in it. Yet tonight the stirring of Cultus Charley in the kitchen was a single sound accenting emptiness. It bothered him, it turned him restless, and when his glance came about to Nan Melotte's far-shining cabin light he made up his mind without second thought, went in to get the roll of gingham he had bought in Winnemucca, and strolled to the gelding. Half an hour later he knocked on Nan Melotte's door.

He heard her come across the room and stop a moment, and this pause made him think of the cabin's isolated position and of the risks any woman took in living alone on the mysterious Piute. A moment later the latch turned and the door was open and he saw her grave face show a fleeting expression — a lightening and a softening. It passed over her features and went away, leaving her sober again. She stepped aside, saying, "Come in," and closed the door behind him. In the middle of the room he turned about and found her with her shoulders against the door, her hands placed behind her back. She was a dark and silent girl and it was hard to know what lay behind that composure, whether it was indifference, or speculation, or some other feeling closely guarded.

He felt better for coming, he felt eased by the cabin's warmth and by her presence. He said: "My house is empty and I'm just ridin' around, making poor company for myself."

Her voice was steady and soft and pleasant to hear. "I know how that goes. But I hadn't thought you'd ever feel it."

"Why not?"

She shrugged her shoulders, and he remembered that this was her way of explaining or dismissing many things; she had the trick of using her hands and her body to fill in the meaning of her words. "You are pretty self-sufficient. And always very active. Sit down."

He said, "Is it all right?"

She said, instant and direct: "Why not, Owen?"

He remembered the package he carried and laid it on the table, and sat down, his long shape sprawling in the chair. She said: "I didn't think you'd remember to get that, after what happened in Winnemucca."

"How did that news get here?"

"It's all over the hills." She remained by the door, watching the way ease went over his muscles, relaxing them. The lamplight brightened the surface of his eyes, it built up the solid angles at the base of his ears, at the bridge of his nose; it deepened the ruddy coloring of his skin. On Nan, he always made definite impressions. Of a kind of lazy indifference covering a tremendous strength he had never used. He had long, full lips set in a faint smiling and even in repose his chest seemed very wide to her. She was thinking that he showed the world a deliberate indolence but that behind this indifference were perceptions keen and grasping, and a hungering zest for the sensations of life. She felt a lurking gaiety about him, a strong and vital sense of humor, and emotions that could powerfully lift him, and powerfully depress him.

All this while she stood against the door, her expression quite sober. Her thoughts, though she did not know it, colored her cheeks a little and changed the soft curve of her lips. She was not quite as tall as Sally Isham, nor did she have that other girl's driving, willful temper. Or if she had it, it was hidden. Supple-shaped and idly placed at the door, she waited for him to speak. Her hair was black and had a strong shine, and when she suddenly came away from the wall, prompted by something that lay in this deep quietness, he noticed the round turn of her arms and the graceful way her hands stirred and were still. She was a woman thoroughly. He had not noticed this before, and saw it with a slow surprise; there was more to her than a man might see unless he had a careful look.

The silence had run away with both of them; she said rather quickly, "Wait," and went into the adjoining kitchen.

He put his head against the chair's back and closed his eyes, listening to the tap of her shoes along the floor. Comfort loosened him; a sense of pleasure ran through him. Listening, he heard no sound in the outer night, and at once his thinking carried him straight back to Will Isham. When, ten minutes later, Nan Melotte came in from the kitchen with a cup of coffee, she found him crouched forward in the chair, his long arms lying across his knees. He had rolled up a cigarette. Its smoke trailed over his face and a single crease tracked across his forehead.

She handed him the coffee and stood in front of him, putting her arms behind her. There were little things about this man she kept observing. He had wrists almost as broad as his hands, with a white scar cutting across one of them. She said: "Owen, don't ride so much alone."

He put the cup on the table, and rose. "Maybe," he said, "you know something that I haven't caught."

"I know what's ahead of you."

He watched her, he was increasingly aware of her. She was smart and she was quick-eyed. He said so. "You don't miss much, Nan."

"Listen," she said. "Skull is on one side of you and Hugh Clagg is on the other. You're going to fight. I saw that on your face just a moment ago. Is it so hard to

guess? What else can you do? You won't be left alone.
Tonight, or tomorrow — or someday — they'll come
after you. I don't . . ."

He said, after a while, "What?"

Her voice dropped. "I don't see how you'll do it." She
gave him a long, direct glance. "You could do it the easy
way, Owen. You could leave. But you won't. I know."

He said, "I guess not." He was at the door, his hand
on the knob. She said, "Wait," and went to the table.
"You're thinking mostly of Skull. But don't forget Hugh
Clagg. If . . ."

She stopped, and after a while shrugged her shoulders.
"Good night," she murmured, and blew out the lamp.

He called, in the darkness: "Nan, you sure you're all
right in this place?"

Her answer to that was rather odd. She said, more
quickly than before: "Good night, Owen."

He thought about that, and put the thought aside.
Opening the door he stepped to his horse and struck
across the flats. At the base of the hills he looked back
to see her light shining through a window.

IX

THE PIT OF NIGHT

AFTER the sound of Sally Isham's fast-traveling horse faded in the distance, Hugh Clagg turned up the slope of the Bunchgrass Hills, thinking to catch Dutcher at Corral Flats, which was where Skull's foreman could usually be found. Following the cut-bank of Christmas Creek, Clagg reached the bench near Owen Merritt's ranch. He had, at the moment, no definite idea, but curiosity caused him to drift in toward the ranch until he was scarcely more than two hundred yards from the front door. Here he stopped, observing Owen Merritt swing around the yard into the beam of light coming through the open door, speak to Cultus Charley, and presently travel down the slope. In a moment darkness absorbed him.

Clagg was a man with a deep streak of curiosity. It impelled him to keep drifting along the creek, still nearer the house until he reached a point from which he might look directly into the lighted kitchen. The kitchen was empty, but while he watched a shape momentarily blocked out the doorway's light causing Clagg to back his horse away. Cultus Charley's voice ran out through the night at him: "Who there?"

Clagg wheeled and drifted into the hillside, followed by Charley's repeated call, "Who there?" He cut into the trail and started climbing toward Corral Flats. He was amused by the Indian's nervous voice, and he chuckled to himself, murmuring: "That's turnin' the thing about — white man huntin' an Indian." But the humor didn't last long. A new thought stopped him and turned him and sent him back along the trail at a gallop. What was Merritt doing out there on the flats of the Piute?

This was Hugh Clagg, a man with quick and restless nerves and no solid bottom. Impulsive, quick to change from hot anger to laughter and back again, few things held his mind steady. His temper could swing to startling extremes in the space of a long-drawn breath, from tolerance to a streak of thorough brutality. A word could soothe him or a word could set him afire; such was the way his tremendous egotism jerked him about. If there was any dominating thing in a life as impermanent as a shadow on the earth, it was a consistent jealousy of Owen Merritt, who in almost every respect was his opposite. For Hugh Clagg was a man cursed with the ability to see his own weaknesses; and so he hated Owen Merritt who seemed to be all that he, Hugh Clagg, was not.

This was the reason he went pounding down the long slope of the hills into the Piute again. Halfway to Nan Melotte's cabin he saw light flood through her opening door. He knew then it was Merritt who had gone into the cabin. And, paused near the place, Hugh Clagg waited out a long half-hour, nursing almost ungovernable impulses. Nothing kept him from putting a shot through the window but Nan's presence. When the light died in the cabin Hugh Clagg literally ground his teeth together and started on at a dead run. But a natural slyness soon stopped him, and presently he listened to Merritt's retreating echoes. For a moment he had the strong urge to follow Merritt, to close in and make a quarrel of it. What changed his mind was the appearance of light again from Nan's cabin. He went up to the place, dropped out of the saddle, and knocked.

It was a long minute or more before she opened the door — and he saw the surprise and half-fear on her face. It was a comfort to him to know that he could make this girl show that concern; it soothed his vanity a little as he stepped through the door and shut it. He said, in a swift, grating way: —

"That's a hell of a thing for you to be doing, Nan!"

He had rust-red hair and blue eyes below sun-bleached eyebrows. His face lay rather long, sharpening chin and nose; and a constantly plainer jealousy kept changing the set of his cheeks. Nan knew how dangerous Hugh Clagg's temper could be, and was never certain of the way he looked at her, and never felt safe when he visited her. But she let none of this show, presenting him an unstirred countenance.

"Why not, Hugh?"

"My God, Nan! You're alone out here. It's a bad thing — "

She understood the way to handle him. "I trust Owen," she said, evenly. "Just as I trust you."

Change went over him swiftly. Her words had that effect on his pride. He said, "Sure," grudgingly, "sure you do. But it's a bad thing to let men in this place at night."

"You're here, Hugh."

"Yeah," he said, and drew a long, long breath. "Why not? Did I ever do anything that wasn't right?" He was fair-skinned and quick to flush up. A blood vein showed its heavy track on his forehead. There was a note in his talk, a little wild, a little overinsistent. "If I thought you gave Merritt much of a show, I'd —" He cut it off. He looked at her, the hazel light in his eyes bright and bold. "Don't give that man any rope. You hear?"

"Why are you riding around here tonight, Hugh?"

He said, at once cautious: "Just riding." But his quick-changing thoughts veered to something else and he was smiling in a gray, ironic way. "Maybe you'd like to know that Sally came down from his ranch about an hour ago. Just before he came here."

He had quick eyes, and noticed the instant shading on her face. Her lips tightened, her breathing drew deeper. "Hugh," she said, "what are you up to?"

"Never mind," he said, irritated again. "You keep him out. One woman's enough for Owen Merritt. Maybe Isham would like to know that. Merritt must figure

Isham for a fool, and that's about the biggest mistake Owen Merritt will ever make. Thinking so."

She said in soft-voiced prompting: "How, Hugh? What will Isham do?"

He gave her a slanting, bright glance. He had at once turned smart and ironic. "Maybe you're curious. I wouldn't be curious, Nan."

"It's time for you to go, Hugh."

He said: "There's a dance in town Saturday night."

She watched the way he considered her, and was afraid again. The man's assurance held something on the faint edge of danger; in the corners of his eyes — as she delayed her answer — the bright suspicion began to grow. He had a possessiveness she couldn't manage. So she said: "All right."

The faint lines loosened away from his mouth and his confidence somersaulted up into a broad grin. "Fine," he said. "Fine!" But it carried him on, so odd and so unstable were his emotions, to an intemperate outburst: "Nan, why don't you smile at a man? Here I am — and what's the matter with me? I'd tear off my arms, I'd burn The Wells down to ashes if you'd want it! My God, you don't know what I feel! Sometimes I've come out of those hills after dark and stood yonder — just watchin' your light. Sometimes I've come close to your door. Maybe it's been a good thing, those times, you had the door barred. I'm honest — I'm telling you how it is. But I'd do anything — anything! Honey, is there a chance for a man?"

She said, her calmness covering quicker fear: "Time to go, Hugh."

That outburst, so startling, so passionate, brought the ruddy color heavily to his face; it had laid a fine glitter of sweat on his forehead. Wildness lay in his eyes, clear to see; and for this moment he was suspended on the very edge of rash desire. The silence got deeper and she heard the run of his breathing and saw the tightness in his shoulder muscles, as though he meant to jump at her. It was that near. She said again, her tone like the cool strike of silver on crystal: "Good night, Hugh."

He could be swayed by the tone of anybody's voice. And this swayed him. His head, held high and stiff, dropped a little and he shrugged his shoulders and said with a dry, faintly shamed amusement: "I guess maybe I'd better."

She stood entirely motionless, afraid to make any gesture that would rouse him again, and watched him go out. After the door closed she went swiftly to it, drawing the bar, quietly so that he wouldn't hear how soon she had done it; and put her back to it, turned weak by the scene.

Merritt had been quite tired earlier in the evening, but now the chill of the night whipped him wide awake. When he reached home he found Cultus Charley squatting in the yard. All the lights of the house were out.

Merritt said: "George come home?"

"Not here. You ride by here maybe one hour back?"

"Not me."

Cultus Charley's head bobbed in the darkness. "Somebody he ride over there an' stop — and go up trail around falls. Same way George do."

Merritt had dropped from the saddle. He climbed into it again. "I'll go that way."

Cultus Charley grumbled. "Everybody always go. I always stay. Dam' place."

"Spooky, Cultus?"

Cultus Charley was an old Indian with a long memory. "Like long time ago when Chief Egan come through here with his warriors. Bad feeling. Same as now. I hear trees talk. I hear water talk. Not good."

Merritt said, "You quit drinkin' that vanilla extract, Cultus," and trotted from the yard. A short bridge carried him across the creek pool. Beyond the pool the trail ran steeply around the falls into the pines. Darkness here was like the darkness of deep water. The grade continued for a mile or so, underneath the steady rustle of wind in the pine tops. After that a meadow of yellow grasses showed a faint ghost-glow on the earth. Beyond this the forest crowded the trail again.

The meadow marked the northern edge of his land and the beginning of what had been Pay Lankershim's graze but was now Skull's. Here he stopped, listening carefully into the night for the sound of travel. Corral Flats, which was where Skull kept a chuckwagon crew the year around, was about four miles ahead — far beyond any reasonable trip for Vird. Yet he recalled Vird's words earlier in the evening and wasn't satisfied. The man had been jumpy since Winnemucca, and in bad temper, and it would be like him to go prowl for trouble.

He went on with a greater care and a greater worry. Skull patrolled its land pretty thoroughly and no doubt there'd be riders somewhere along this stretch — riders who made short work of those who trespassed. As with Juke Slover. Now and then in the perfect black he came to forks in the trail and chose his fork from memory; and kept on.

Slover, he realized, had been a laughing young man, full of hell and fun. The three of them, Slover and Bourke Prine and himself, had made many a campfire in the Bunchgrass Hills. High up in the Broken Buttes they had shaken night's frosts out of their blankets to watch sunrise break like fire across East Desert. A lot of riding and a lot of laughter . . . Now Juke was dead and Skull's line came up against Christmas Creek, and he knew in his heart his own careless life was gone. Dutcher would never let him alone, and Will Isham would never rest.

Owen Merritt hated to come to hard-and-fast decisions. This land was pleasant for a man who liked to cruise the deep, high hills — to hear the owl hoot by night, to see the red heart of the campfire deepen and die, to watch antelope scudding in fluid motion across the distant dry lake-beds. To live and let live and feel the wine of freedom sink deep into his flesh, into his bones. A little money was enough and a few cows were enough; and for the rest the trails beckoned and of a Saturday night town was not far away. He knew his weakness, which was to drift. This was what Sally Isham had told him; this was why Bourke Prine kept beating at him with hard, violent words, trying to rouse him. So now, Juke was dead and Sally was lost, and Skull pressed against his fence. The good days were gone.

In Winnemucca he had discovered that he could stand under fire, and in Winnemucca some sense of security had left him everlastingly. Leaving that saloon he had known he would fight. Yet he had not told Bourke of this, for his thoughts kept reaching far ahead and seeing things Bourke had not yet seen. If he fought it would be to stay alive, but he could not stay alive as long as Dutcher and Isham remained on Skull. So, to stay alive he had to ruin Skull. It made an outlaw out of him, it spoiled Sally's life, and maybe it put Mark Medary on his trail. So —

The gelding stopped short, its muscles bunching; it let out a trumpeting breath and cat-walked nervously on the dust. Ahead, a vague shadow appeared in the night's blackness; the vaguest of shadows, at once defined by a whinny. Merritt flattened against the gelding, reaching for his gun. He slid off the gelding. He said: "Who's that?"

The yonder horse whinnied again. Night's wind got colder and the rustling echoes up in the trees strengthened. Squatted against the earth, he caught a slanting silhouette of the horse against the pale-black sky, but observed no rider. Rising, he clucked his tongue gently, stepping nearer the adjoining trees. The horse moved toward the gelding.

There was this long, risky moment in which all the sounds of the night came in with a gathering completeness — a continuous wash and scrape and snap and murmur. Merritt said, "Steady — steady." He reached forward, catching the horse by the bridle. He moved against the horse, making a shield for himself, his palm touching a hide that held only a faint warmth, so telling the animal had been standing here quite a while. Shoving his hand back to the beast's hind quarter he traced its brand with the point of his finger.

What he discovered brought along an actual shock. He went around the horse, still holding his gun against the impenetrable night, continuing up the trail. He had not gone three yards when the toe of his boot pressed into something that yielded, softly and terribly, to his weight. He jumped back. Sweat cracked through his forehead, and his nerves began to move and the pit of his belly tightened. Dropped on his knees, he reached for a match, raked it along the barrel of the revolver and made a downward cup of his hand. The light burst into the black violently enough to have almost the quality of sound; and threw its oil-yellow glow upon the shape of George Vird on the trail. George lay on his stomach, both arms stretched forward, one of them still holding a gun; his face was tipped so that Merritt saw a final composure engraved on the waxen skin. This was all, this one moment. Merritt whipped out the light and drew back, waiting. The flare of that match had been bright enough to draw down the whole hill, or so it seemed. He kept waiting for trouble to break.

But afterwards the rustling silence ran on and then he knew that George Vird had been dead a good hour and that Skull's riders had long since ridden away.

For it would be Skull's riders. As he stood there, he knew that with as much certainty as he knew anything in life. Skull, jealous of every acre it owned, had put its patrols out on this trail and Vird had run into them. For a moment he had one clear impulse, which was to ride on to Corral Flats, where they would be camped. But he held himself still, and let the first hot fury pass away. There would be plenty of sign on the soft dirt, which he wanted to see before he moved ahead.

He put away his gun and bent down to his foreman. He had a bad quarter-hour lifting Vird onto the waiting horse. He put Vird across the saddle and shook out the rope hanging to the saddle thong, and made a few quick ties, speaking to the uneasy horse. "So, Babe, so." Stepping into his own saddle he turned back to Christmas Creek with the other horse in tow.

It was a long, long ride. When he came down by the falls into his own dark yard, he had searched his mind with a completeness that left nothing behind. It was like going through an empty house, looking into cupboards and closets and locking the windows, and at last turning a key in the door. Nothing remained. There wasn't anything to hold him. So he came into the yard, calling: "Charley — light a lamp."

He had no answer. He said, more impatiently, "Charley, where the hell are you?" and got down. He went into the house, he lighted a lamp and traveled back to the kitchen. He went from the kitchen to the side room, which was the Indian's. The blankets were gone from the bed and Charley's handful of little possessions removed from the washstand. Merritt left the house, forgetting for a moment that the lamp he carried made a fine target in pit-black shadows. The tan horse was missing from the barn. Charley's bridle and saddle had been taken.

Halfway back across the yard it occurred to him to blow out the lamp. He walked around the house and stopped at the edge of the porch. The sky showed its vague star-glitter, and wind breathed out of the south, colder and colder. Far away on the flat he saw Nan Melotte's light wink two or three times, as though somebody had passed across its beam. George Vird was dead and Cultus Charley, turned spooky, had gone from the ranch for good. He stood here thoroughly alone.

X

OWEN RIDES OUT

MERRITT drove a flat bed wagon into The Wells around one o'clock that night, with the gelding tied behind. A single point of light showed from a second-story window in the hotel; otherwise the town was asleep and darkness solidly crowded the street. He put the wagon against Luke Gilder's harness shop and walked down a narrow alley and kicked his boot against the shop's back door. Luke was, among other things, coroner and undertaker, and accustomed to midnight calls like this. He took his own good time opening up. He had put on a pair of pants and shoes and the lantern he held up showed the tangle of his gray hair, the taciturn sleepiness of his eyes.

"Come around front," said Merritt, and went back to the wagon. While he waited there, hearing Gilder kick his way through the shop, he rolled a cigarette and lighted it, and listened to the shuffle and stamp of restless horses in M'Garrick's stable at the far end of town. It was that still in The Wells. Still and cold and black. Gilder emerged from the front door of the shop. He ducked the lantern into the wagon box and saw George Vird's palely composed face above the edge of the blankets. It was a pretty familiar sight to Gilder. All he said was: "When did this happen, Owen?"

"Three hours ago. Medary in town?"

"Yeah."

Merritt's boots raked hollow echoes out of the loose boards as he walked, those echoes traveling over the street and coming back to him until it sounded as though two men tramped through the midnight. At the courthouse, which was a single-story house running back from the street like a shed, he turned to the rear jail office. The door was ajar but Merritt hit it twice with the flat of his hand, calling, "Medary." The sheriff's voice came right back to him, "All right."

When he came out a few minutes later he said: "Was that you driving a wagon into town?"

Merritt nodded and the two of them went back to the wagon. Luke Gilder hadn't done anything; he slouched against the wagon box while the sheriff looked at George Vird. Medary said: "When was this, Owen?"

"I found him up on the trail behind my house about ten o'clock."

The sheriff put both hands on the edge of the wagon box. Gilder's lantern played a yellow light on Vird's face, showing its established gravity. The sheriff said nothing for a little while, seeming to wait for Merritt to finish the explanation. When it didn't come, he asked: "That all?"

"You figure out the rest of it. What the hell are we waiting here for?" He moved around and let down the tail gate. The three of them took Vird into Gilder's shop, into a small side room, and laid him on a bench. Medary and Gilder moved back into the main part of the harness shop, but Merritt stood over the bench a long while, trying to make up his mind about that grayly definite composure on Vird's cheeks. The longer he looked the more it struck him that Vird seemed younger than before and less careworn. He reached down and smoothed the man's hair back and drew the blanket over his face and left the little room, pulling the door to behind him.

"Gilder," he said, "do me a favor. You take care of George. I won't be here the next few days."

Gilder said, almost indifferently, "Sure."

Merritt and the sheriff went out to the walk. Medary noticed the gelding tied behind the wagon. "What's that for, Owen?"

Merritt had his own question to ask: "What are you going to do about Juke Slover, Mark?"

"What can a man do? It would be a wild goose chase. I don't know who did it — and I'd have a hell of a time finding out."

"Figure to do anything about Lee Repp?"

The sheriff didn't answer that one quite so soon. Gilder had closed his door against the cold night air, but his light came through the front window and by this shining Merritt had some view of the sheriff's face. Medary said finally, and with a considerable reluctance: "Not unless I'm pushed to it, Owen."

"Who'd push you to it?"

"You're not that foolish, Owen. You know who would."

"Well, suppose he did? What would you do?"

"I'd have to think about that," answered Medary quite slowly.

Merritt dragged cigarette smoke into his mouth, watching the pressure change the cast of the sheriff's face, watching reserve come there. Medary was under strain; something made him cautious. This was what Merritt felt and he knew then he could put no trust in Medary. He said: "So that's it?"

"Which is what?" spoke up Medary, quick to catch the tone.

"Never mind." Merritt climbed to the wagon's seat and kicked off the brake.

"Owen," called the sheriff, "don't be too sure about that. But if I was you I'd raise a lot of dust between me and this country before morning. You can't beat Isham."

"Why can't I?"

Merritt drove down to M'Garrick's stable. He unhitched in the runway, stalled the horses and led the saddled gelding back to Shannon's store. Medary's light was still on. Medary would be watching him from the jail office. For his own part he had sounded out the sheriff deliberately and the sheriff's answers had helped him to make up his mind. He was pretty close to being a man on the dodge and had to know who his friends were. Medary wasn't one of them.

He kicked on Shannon's door and stood back and yelled to the second-story window. "Shannon." The echo knocked around the cold black silence. It made a great racket. The upper window squealed open and Shannon called gloomily, "Go on home you dam' drunk. Who's there?"

"Open up."

"Merritt? Wait a minute."

When he came down Merritt went in, got half a side of bacon and a package of ground coffee. He took several boxes of cartridges for the Winchester and for his .44. Shannon was an old-timer and knew the country inside out, and the ways of men. He shook his head rather sadly. "It's too bad."

Merritt was on his way out. But he stopped and turned to ask a question: "What do you think of Isham now, Shannon?"

Shannon again shook his head, caught by the same set of circumstances now controlling Medary. Shannon made his money largely from Skull, and could not afford to speak; and Medary held his office because of Skull and the other great ranches in the country. This was the way it would be with most of the people in The Wells. Skull was too powerful.

He made a roll behind the cantle to hold his supplies, swung up and left The Wells at a fast run. Once in the outer darkness, he looked behind to see a lantern swing across the street from the courthouse to Shannon's, which would be Medary coming over to find out what he had bought. Four miles along he passed the side road into Bourke Prine's place, and saw, far over, Prine's late light shining. But having already made up his mind to leave his partner out of this, he went directly to his own place.

It was then almost three o'clock. He threw the saddle on Vird's white mare, put a halter on the gelding and on one other pony and started up the hill trail with these extra mounts in tow. All this he had worked out in his mind during the ride into The Wells. The air was thin and cold and the shadows at their blackest. This was the ebb hour, when a man's inner fire was only a heatless flicker and all his thinking ran a discouraged channel, and hope got lower and lower. The meadow, when he reached it, showed almost no shine. At the spot where he had found George Vird he pulled in, but only for a moment. Somewhere during all this riding he had discarded the idea of waiting for daylight to trace the prints on the trail. There could be no doubt as to where those prints led. Later, when the slope of the hills leveled away, he turned into the timber, picketed the two extra horses and came back to the trail again. Faintest light began to dilute the night sky.

In his mind were many pictures to keep him company as he rode, some faint and turned vague by time, some so vivid and strong that they had a force for him. He thought of the way Juke Slover used to speak, soft and diffident and full of humor. He thought of George Vird, whose silence had covered so much personal bitterness and so much that was solid. He remembered the honk of geese high overhead, heard only yesterday as a reminder of winter soon coming; and this turned his mind to Sally who once, a year before, had ridden the Fremont with him to see antelope scudding out of the iron hills into the white glare of a dry lake-bed. The memories of her stayed with him, detailed and warm, for a long while, until by some obscure connection he saw Nan Melotte looking across the mellow light of her cabin to him. Not smiling but near to a smile; with her shoulders risen a little and a color on her cheeks, and an odd feeling behind the shadow of her eyes.

Then it was gray first-dawn and he was off the trail, halted on the edge of timber. Ahead of him a hundred yards stood the Corral Flats cabin where Skull's chuck-wagon crew still slept. Horses stirred in the corral just beyond.

He dropped from the saddle and drew his rifle out of its boot, softly working the lever. Its faint metallic click disturbed the huge silence of the hills; he could hear somebody in the cabin groan. There were, he recalled, five or six men stationed at the place and in another fifteen minutes they would be stirring. One end of the cabin, and its window, faced him. A bench outside the door held a bucket and a white tin basin that began to reflect the growing daylight.

He had the rifle steadied against the side of a small pine, knowing well enough what he meant to do. But for a little while he held his fire, going back over his thoughts with a greater care, trying to find another answer, and failing to find it. Bourke Prine had continually urged him to fight and he had resisted, knowing that when he opened up he provided Will Isham legitimate excuse to turn the whole weight of Skull's crew on him. It was the old game of prodding the other man into a draw. Afterwards the rule of the country made anything fair.

But Skull was against his fence and his fence couldn't hold Skull out. Sitting on the porch of his house on Christmas Creek was pretty useless business. What he did now would start a jump-and-run fight, and make the hills tough for Skull to ride. When he pulled the trigger of the Winchester he said good-by to Christmas Creek and to the flat country. It would be high trails and fast horses; beans and bacon over a quick campfire, and fade away.

A voice in the cabin grumbled: "Rise and shine!" Merritt took aim on the high corner of the window and let go.

The flat and dry crack of the shot spread through the hills. It split into fragments of sound that rolled down the clear spaces and struck the solidness of trees and bounced back. One man in the cabin yelled.

All of them struck the floor with a heavy smash. The window's shattered glass jangled down. The door swung open, slowly. Merritt turned the Winchester's muzzle. One bullet clunked through the filled water bucket; the next sailed the basin off the bench. The basin struck on edge and rolled three or four feet with a waggling motion and fell. The door slammed shut.

Somebody in there fired through the window, but it

was a high slanting shot that struck nowhere in the timber. Merritt turned to the window again and fired through it, hearing lead flatten against the inner side of the logs.

He filled the gun and waited. There was a faint sound in the cabin, like the furtive scraping of a body on the floor. Light came out of the east in higher and higher waves and dew began to glitter on the clumps of bunchgrass in the meadow. All the horses were milling around the corral, raking up a cloudy dust. He watched them a moment and shook his head; and saw the cabin door show its crack again. His shot hit the door's lower corner, knocking it partially open. A man yelled — the quick and incomplete yell of pain — and the door slammed. Merritt called: "Better not."

They were cursing him. He listened to that full-hearted rage, and began to make out the shape of the stovepipe in the middle of the room. He turned loose on that target, stilling their voices for a while. His shots went through the pipe without knocking it down, but soot made a little cloud at the top. Stepping back from the tree he faded into the timber and ran parallel with the clearing. When he came up to the meadow again, behind another tree, he commanded a slanting view of a window on the cabin's front and knocked it out with a few quick shots and aimed at the door again, at the latch. It took half a dozen bullets to break the latch. The door swung inward and was kicked shut, but he laid his fire along the sill and a man howled and moved away; and when the door swung next time nobody seemed near enough to kick it. Through the opening he spotted the stove, reloaded the Winchester, and began to crack away at it. This was cast-iron and brittle, and made a racket at each direct strike. One shot struck a leg and broke it and then the stove collapsed and the stovepipe fell.

Backing once more into the timber, he circled to his original spot and laid another shot through the side window. Full day swelled up from the east, the chill began to fade out of the air. Behind him the dark corridors in the pines slowly lost their heavy shadows, so that he could see farther into the timber, and could be seen as well. They had quit talking to him, but he heard them stir around a little and now he could look through the broken side-window to the window on the far end; by way of persuasion he put a stray shot through to it, and spoke.

"I'll be here all morning. Settle down."

It was time to go. All this racket was enough to wake the dead, and before very long other Skull riders would be patrolling up from the Wolf Creek cabin. Slipping back from his position, Merritt led his horse quietly down the trail a distance, got in the saddle and drifted away. When he was quite beyond earshot he put the pony to a quick run. The trail here dropped gently, winding with the land's contours, and so presently brought him to the place where he had picketed his extra horses. Catching them up, he slanted across the trail, aiming for the high ground on the southern prow of the hills. He had not quite cleared the trail when a dry, dry voice said: —

"Wait a minute, Owen."

Merritt's nerves this morning were quick-strung. The sound came out of the timber, at his right elbow, and his reaction was to throw himself flat against the saddle and wheel the horse around, at once drawing. He saw a shape duck back behind a pine. Afterwards Pay Lankershim called in the same rustling, amused way: "Now you were a mite careless, Owen."

He waited until Merritt said, "All right," and then stepped from shelter and came on to Merritt's stirrup. Pay was a long, wire-tough old man with hatchet features and ink-black eyes that kept sliding quick glances all about the trees. He had a week's whiskers and a big chew of tobacco prominently nested in his cheek, and it was plain that he had slept in his clothes a long while. He seemed to be enjoying himself. "What," he wanted to know, "was all that larrupin' up yonder?"

Merritt told him, observing the thin smile it brought out. Old Pay had always been an Indian for drifting, even in his prosperous days. He was the kind to light a campfire deep in the hills and sleep well away from it; he was the kind to rise without sound from some covert spot where least expected, as now. And he had a permanent hump in his back from leaning down in the saddle to study the signs on the earth. This was Pay.

He said: "What you goin' to do for a ranch? Hell, you can't go back there and make a target."

"Nothing on the ranch," said Merritt, and told him the rest of it, about Vird and Cultus Charley. Pay listened solemnly, never ceasing to place his bright-black glance here and there into the timber, like a fisherman casting a constant fly. "Well," he said, "I never thought you'd come to it, Owen. It sure puts you on the dodge and I dunno how you figure to come out. I think I better go tell Bourke Prine. Where you goin' to be?"

"Up on the knob somewhere."

"See you later," murmured Pay and faded into the timber. Presently he reappeared on an old brown horse and trotted down the trail with his bony shape jiggling at all its joints. The first flash of sunlight from the eastern rim flushed the high sky a light pink. Merritt turned south again and traveled into a rising, rougher country. An hour or so later he threw off in a brushy bowl on the heights of the hills, put the horses on picket and cooked himself breakfast over a quick fire. Later, he crawled well back from the bowl and stretched out for a short sleep.

When Hugh Clagg left Nan Melotte's cabin he started again for Corral Flats, this time by the roundabout route through Stage Coach Pass. This eventually put him out on the margin of East Desert, at the southern base of the Bunchgrass Hills; here he turned into the hills, cutting across the high corner of Owen Merritt's range. Merritt's beef grazed through the thin scatter of pines, and after an hour or more of riding of the district he knew where the bulk of that beef lay. And later, riding northward, he began to see Skull's cattle in the timber. During that time he heard three quick shots break the immense stillness of the night, higher up and quite distant. Around midnight he reached Corral Flats and paused at the edge of timber, knowing too much about Skull's crew to ride into the meadow without due warning. There was a light in the line cabin and the drowsy sound of voices. Hugh Clagg put a hand to his mouth and whistled through his knuckles.

The voices quit and the light went out. A man's feet scraped the cabin floor. Somebody in the yard called: "Who's that?"

"Dutcher there?"

The Skull man repeated his question in a shallow, suspecting tone: "Who's that?"

Hugh Clagg spoke his own name and drifted his horse over to the cabin. He saw the shape of the Skull man before him. The Skull man came up and seized the bridle of Clagg's horse, his tilted face appearing as a narrow white blur in the dark. The light in the cabin came on again. Other men stepped out.

"He ain't here," said the fellow holding the bridle.

"Been here tonight?"

"No."

They stood in front of him, carefully placed beyond the beam of light shining from the cabin — all five. They were motionless and close-mouthed and he felt their dislike rise as solidly as a stone wall. They were a tough lot, most of them having records of violence in other districts. But these were the kind of men Dutcher deliberately hired, knowing they would be loyal to the outfit which fed them. Dutcher had pounded into them his own hatred of anything that wasn't Skull, his own surly brand of vengeance.

Clagg was a tough man himself and recognized toughness in others. So he said, "I'll ride to the Wolf Creek cabin. Maybe he's there," and drifted on, and was relieved when Corral Flats was well behind him. These men remembered that he had once rustled beef from Skull and wouldn't forget it, regardless of what his present politics might be. He had to be careful when he met them in the hills.

The trail ran through the mealy blackness of the timber for another six miles and arrived at the small spring marking the headwaters of Wolf Creek. Another cabin lay here, formless under the night. He caught the faint scent of woodsmoke and paused at the edge of the pines, calling Dutcher's name.

Dutcher answered immediately, not from the cabin but from the trees near by. "Clagg?"

"Sure. What you night-hawkin' for?"

"I heard your horse comin'," said Dutcher, and moved forward. Clagg stepped down and the two came together at the edge of the meadow. "You be careful how you ride around this country," added Dutcher.

Clagg grinned in the darkness, ironically amused. He had his agreement with Skull but Dutcher, like the others, couldn't forget he had once lived on Skull beef. It clung to the foreman's mind. It was an injury he would never be quite able to forget. As well as any man, Hugh Clagg knew nothing but an uneasy and patched-up truce existed between them and one day when the need for this was ended Dutcher would go after him without mercy. The trickiness of it amused Hugh Clagg. It was a joke he enjoyed. He said: "I got something to make you feel good, Fay. Sally Isham came up to visit Merritt tonight. I saw her leave."

He was laughing, softly and audibly. Fay Dutcher's talk lunged at him. "What's so damned funny?"

"You don't like that, Fay," said Clagg. "I knew you wouldn't."

"The little flossy!" grounded out Dutcher. "She comes up the line from nothin', onto Skull. A kid out of a no 'count, nigger-poor family. And she starts cheatin'. By God, I'll fix her."

"Tell Isham? No, I guess you won't."

"Why not?" said Dutcher in his growling tone. "Why not?"

"A man don't like to have his wife talked about. He'd throw you off Skull in a hurry."

"Me?" said Dutcher. "Throw me off? What would he do without me? He can do the thinkin', but I'm the man that does the work, which he knows." He quit speaking.

Clagg knew the foreman was grasping at his thoughts and having a heavy time. It made Clagg repeat: "You won't tell Isham."

Dutcher grumbled, "No, I guess not. There's other ways." He shot his next phrase at Clagg hard and fast. "Listen, you keep your mouth shut. I won't have it known around that a woman can fool Skull. Keep your mouth shut."

"Sure," said Clagg. "Listen, Fay. Hold the boys at Corral Flats out of the timber tomorrow night. I'm going in to pick up some of Merritt's beef. It ain't so far from the Flats and I don't want to have any accidents with your boys. Keep 'em at the cabin."

"All right."

"What are you going to do about Merritt?"

"Never mind," said Dutcher, at once suspicious. "How did you know I was here?"

"Just a guess."

Dutcher said, "Your guess is too good." He stepped nearer. "Hughie, you know too damned much."

"A man," answered Clagg, a repressed laughter in him, "likes to keep track of his friends."

"No," contradicted Dutcher at once. "You're no friend of mine, and I'm none of yours. You're a little slippery for me. I gave you a piece of business once — and you didn't do it."

"About Merritt," murmured Clagg. "About Merritt in the saloon. No, it didn't work. I tried again, out on the Flats. Repp, the blamed fool, got in the road."

"Two tries and two misses," pointed out Dutcher. "No, I don't believe it. That's the trouble, Hughie. You're too flashy. A man can't lay his finger on you. Which is too bad. I could put a few things your way."

"If," said Clagg, pleased with his own audacity, "you had my head, Dutcher, you'd be farther along with the bug in your bonnet."

Dutcher flared back. "What bug?"

"Which," continued Clagg, "is why you don't like Sally Isham. She puts your nose out of joint. Makes it tougher for you to get what you want."

Dutcher said: "Go on, ride. And quit comin' around this side of the range. You might get hurt. I'm through with you."

"Sure," answered Clagg. "But I can still do you a good turn. Keep your men at the cabin tomorrow night."

He cantered away, repressing his amusement. Beef was beef. With Skull out of sight that outfit's cattle was just as good as Merritt's. All cows had four legs. It was a joke.

Dutcher returned to the cabin and lighted a lamp. He closed the door and dropped a burlap curtain over the window, distrusting Clagg too much to present him with a chance. It was far past midnight, but Dutcher, a born nighthawk, stoked up the stove, rolled a cigarette, and squatted Indian-fashion before the heat. The line of his black hair lay low on his forehead, narrowing it; his ears were small and flattened back against the scalp. Otherwise his features were quite large, heavy of bone and heavy of flesh. Small, vertical wrinkles broke the roll of his lower lip; his brows bushed out, throwing added shadow into his eyes. Lamplight glistened against the natural oil on his skin. He took up a piece of kindling and thrust it through the stove's front grate and as his solid, sulky thoughts had their way with him he slowly turned and crushed the live coals. Dutcher had his deep-lying ambitions and if he sat here in hulking silence while the night ran on, it was because he saw those ambitions blocked by Sally Isham and by Merritt.

XI

COLLISION

AT NINE o'clock in the morning Tuck Ring raced through the pines with the news of Merritt's raid and found Fay Dutcher on the way to the Home ranch. Dutcher's immediate reaction was to turn and start back. "We'll pay that gentleman a visit," he swore. But after the first shock wore off he drew in again. "No, I got to tell Isham first. Never know what he'll want to do. You keep the boys out of trouble, Tuck. If Merritt's on the warpath he may go to pot-shootin' again. So drag back from the Flats. I'll be there later." At eleven o'clock he stood in Skull's big living room, giving the story to Isham.

Isham said: "He didn't hit anybody?"

"No," answered Dutcher. And he showed his open contempt for that. "He just wasted a lot of lead. Was I out to make trouble I'd save powder till I saw somethin' to hit. I don't think Merritt's got the sand."

Isham showed his foreman an irritated impatience. "He's smarter than you are. If he'd killed one of the boys we'd have something to hang on him. I'd have Medary pick him up. But he does it the other way. Now he's telling us to clear out of the Flats."

"He can tell us nothin'," grunted Dutcher. "We'll go down and pay that fellow a visit."

"You don't seem to understand the kind of a man you're up against," retorted Isham. "He won't be there."

"Neither will his house, when we get through with it."

"Wait — wait," Isham interposed. "That won't do — yet. The Piute won't like it."

"What's that got to do with it? Is that your ranch or does it belong to the folks on the desert?"

"We've got to have a better reason," insisted Isham.

"He came on our land," pointed out Dutcher. "Reason enough."

Isham looked at his foreman, cool and calm. "We've been on his also. Ever occur to you that the people in this country can get damned good and mad?" He went past Dutcher, to the doorway, and called up a rider. He said: "Go down the valley and ask Swanee Vail to meet me in town. Circle over to Tague's — and to Spaugh's."

Dutcher's contempt for public opinion was always pretty close to the surface. "What of it? What can they do? This is your land. Let 'em shout. If they tried to come in here, a whole damned army, they wouldn't get beyond the front gate. I been tellin' you a long while about this, Mr. Isham. You can't run Skull and play possum. I'll keep folks off Skull and I'll take care of Merritt. But you got to make up your mind about it. Who's going to kick? The Wells? Hell, if it wasn't for Skull The Wells would dry up and float away. Those people ain't going to do anything. Ain't nothin' else but

homesteaders and they got to mind their own business."
He stared down at Isham's slight, pointed shape. "What
you afraid of?"

Isham flushed and Dutcher closed his heavy lips,
knowing he had made a mistake. Yet it was a sly mistake, working both ways. It offended Isham, but it
roused his pride as well. "That's enough of that,
Dutcher." Then he got to thinking, and said: "What
started this?"

Dutcher moved his vast shoulders. When he spoke
he didn't quite meet Isham's eyes. "A little trouble, I
guess. One of the boys ran into George Vird on the trail
last night. There was some smoke. Vird's dead."

Isham's face showed actual shock. He looked at
Dutcher with an expression wild and unsteady; and this
anger brought him up against Dutcher. He reached out
and seized Dutcher's shirt front, twisting the cloth until
Dutcher bent from the pressure. "Dutcher," he said in
a voice half-breathless, "if you go against me again I'll
kill you."

Dutcher brought both his arms down against Isham's
hands, knocking them clear. He stepped backward into
the center of the room. "By God," he said, "that's far
enough for you to go, Mr. Isham."

"Answer me!" yelled Isham.

"No," said Dutcher, "I had no part in that. I told
you once I couldn't hold those boys back. They had Vird
marked and they got him. And that's the way it is with
Owen Merritt. What kind of men you think work for

Skull, Mr. Isham? You ought to know. You told me to hire 'em."

Isham turned from Dutcher and walked to the corner of the room. He swung, pressing the palm of his hand across his forehead, scrubbing away the fine sweat formed there. His voice had flattened out; he had himself checked. "All right, Dutcher. Now listen to me. You find Clagg and tell him to work on Merritt's beef."

"He's doin' that tonight," said Dutcher, observing his boss with a quite close glance. Hard man as he was, he had been set back, he had been actually astonished. Isham had shown him something he hadn't seen before, which was a temper that could kill. Dutcher had seen the yellow-white flame of that emotion in the Skull owner's eyes; it was something a man couldn't mistake.

"All right," said Isham. "And leave Merritt alone until I tell you what to do next. Better stay away from the Flats for a while."

"Suppose . . ." said Dutcher, and afterwards closed his mouth as though caught in mortal confession. Sally Isham came down the stairs. She had heard a good deal of this, as both Dutcher and Isham immediately realized. Both men watched her with a reserved attention. She faced them at the bottom of the stairs, cool with her eyes and throwing their interest back at them.

She said to Isham, "Should I go, or stay to hear the rest of this?"

"I think there's very little left to hear," observed Isham, dry as dust with his answer.

She pulled up her chin, meeting his glance with the same cool gravity. "If I am not to hear your conversations, Will, then you had better warn me beforehand. Both of you have been talking rather loud."

Isham said to Dutcher: "What did you say?"

But Dutcher shook his head. "Nothing," he grumbled, and kept his eyes on Sally Isham. He had turned sullen. There was this little silence, with its very evident feeling. Isham stared at his foreman and then, quite quickly, turned to see what was on his wife's face to cause Dutcher to close up. He had sharp intuitions and he knew something was wrong, though he had no information from her contained expression. It made Isham call out in half-irritation: "What is it, Dutcher?"

Dutcher repeated, "Nothing," and left the room.

"The man hates me," remarked Sally.

Isham at once said: "Been discourteous to you in any way?"

"No. If he were I'd take care of it. I can't blame him, for he knows very well I despise him."

Isham's glance kept searching her. "Why?"

"Will," she said, "I don't think he's a good man for Skull."

"For Skull," replied Isham, very smooth, "he's the best man in the world." He said it smoothly, yet it had its challenge for her, its faint ring of insistence, as though he put his will against her will and wanted her to submit.

She stood her ground, clearly realizing how perilous this moment was for her and how swift his latent suspicions would rise at anything she might say. Yet she had a will that was, in its own quiet fashion, equal to Isham's. It compelled her to speak. Paused before him she looked across the little distance at his set, self-disciplined expression. Her eyes were level with his eyes — and then he stepped away from her, a touched pride showing at the angle of his mouth because of that equality in height. She knew it irritated him, but she could not help it. Her shoulders squared a little and her lips, long and fresh-colored and pleasant, lay in a firm line. She had a resoluteness that heightened her and steadied her body.

"Will," she said finally, "do you have to break Owen Merritt to get what you want? Is there no other way?"

"Our bargain," answered Isham, dry and distant, "didn't specify I should protect Merritt, did it?" He was watching her with a narrowing interest; he was weighing her expression and each word she spoke.

"No. But is it fair?"

"Sally," he said, "maybe you'd better quit dreaming. When I want a thing I get it. Skull is too big for sentiment, and I'm in too much of a hurry to stop to grieve about any one man. Didn't you know my disposition when you married me?"

She had her long, calm glance. "I did, Will. But I never saw in you any desire to destroy, or kill."

"Have I killed?"

"Your men have. You hire them and you support them."

His voice withdrew from her; it denied her. He had drawn himself straight. He was indomitable, he was quietly relentless. "Merritt's got himself to blame. He was in the party that killed three of my men in Winnemucca. He riddled my line cabin this morning. You think that's all right for him, Sally?"

"If you had been in his place, Will, what would you have done?"

"I'm not in his place. It seems you are."

"Oh, Will, do we have to quarrel?"

"It is interesting," he said, "to get the truth out of you. Maybe you figure you have made a mistake."

Her pride was as strong as his pride. Her cheeks flushed, her chin lifted at him; and her temper, then, could not remain humble. "Lately," she said, "you have turned to sarcasm."

"What is a man to believe?"

She drew a long breath, steadying her temper, and then was calmer than Isham. "We shouldn't fight, Will. I'm your wife — and I'll never do anything to hurt you. But if I'm to help you I've got to say something. Don't let Dutcher push you into too much trouble. There isn't any reason why you should try to break Owen. He's fighting you now because Dutcher started trouble. Buy him out if you can. Or if you can't, let him alone. Skull is big enough without Christmas Creek. And I can tell you something, though you won't like it. Merritt is popular with people on the desert. If you ruin him or if you kill him you'll make those people hate you."

He had never ceased to watch her. Malice laid its faint impression on his lips. His reserve remained unbroken, impenetrable. He said, as courteously insistent as ever: "I have wondered about something. Suppose you had known, before we were married, that I meant to go after Merritt. Would you have married me?"

"What a brutal question," she said in a breathing tone. "Do you want me to answer it?"

"I want the truth out of you, Sally. It seems I have not had it before. Either that, or you have changed."

She said directly: "I wouldn't marry a man who told me he intended to commit murder, Will. Or who hired others to commit it for him."

His eyes widened a little and a degree of paleness came back to his small cheeks — betraying the disturbance inside. And yet he showed her a small, thin smile and bowed his head, saying, "Thanks for the compliment," and went out of the room. Never moving, she heard him later pound across the bridge. It meant he would be going into The Wells.

She knew she had destroyed any chance of peace in this house, for his was the kind of pride that could not stand injury. He would never forget her words. Behind his deadly courtesy would lie an everlasting resentment. She felt like crying. Yet, looking back over that scene with a good deal of curiosity at its sudden coming, she suddenly realized that Isham had deliberately pushed her on. There was at times an intentional malice in this man which made him hard to understand. As though he took pride in hurting her.

She thought: "He wants no advice from me. I shall have to keep still. This will have to be patched up somehow. We've got to go on." Still-placed in the quiet room and thinking it over with a long, long care, she knew she could have said nothing else. She was seeing Owen Merritt now and at once a greater thought went through her like a shock. Her marriage had been a mistake, a tragic error that could never be remedied. It hit her all at once, knocking down her courage and her resolution. She was caught and could not escape. She could do nothing and say nothing. Living in this house she had to watch Isham pursue Merritt. For he would not change now. If anything, her words had hardened his will only so much the more. She had gone to Owen once. She could not go again. She was Isham's wife.

Dutcher's voice said: "I want to speak to you, Mrs. Isham."

It whirled her around. Dutcher came into the room, walking with an aggressive swing of his shoulders. He had long arms and he carried his fists closed as though always prepared to hit at something; and his knees gave a little at each stride. He looked at her in a way leaving no doubt of his dislike. Only it was more definite than it had been before. It was an open hostility that he no longer tried to conceal.

"Mrs. Isham," he said, "you don't like me and I don't like you. I don't understand how you tricked Isham but I guess a smart man's got to be a fool once. Anyhow, you got a nice livin' out of the deal, and Skull will have to pay the way for them deadhead people of yours."

"Why don't you tell that to Mr. Isham?" retorted Sally.

"Maybe you'll tell him."

"I can take care of myself, Dutcher. It's time you knew that."

His talk came out of the bottom of his throat. Everything about this huge man was black and heavy and guttural. He had his head down and looked at her with a slanting contempt. That too, she understood, was another characteristic of his — a contempt for most things and most people. He had a savage, brutelike belief in himself. From her observation she had noticed that only Isham could turn this foreman of Skull into respect. He said: —

"Sure you can take care of yourself. But some things you better not do any more, like goin' up to see Owen Merritt. You do that again and I'll find a way of breakin' you apart. Nobody's going to cheat this ranch while I'm around. From now on you ride close to this house, or else take one of the crew along. Remember that, Mrs. Isham."

He turned to the door. Before he reached it another thought pulled him around. "Maybe," he said, "you ought to get out of here. Go back to the Broken Buttes. Isham's going to go after your friend Merritt. If you like the man so much, why stay here? Go tell him we're on his trail."

He blocked the light of the doorway as he left. She went immediately up the stairs, her legs weak from a real fear.

Isham, going a roundabout way, reached town rather late in the morning. Vail and Tague and Spaugh were in Medary's office; and Isham went there at once. He said: "This morning pretty early Owen Merritt shot hell out of my line cabin on Corral Flats and ran for the timber."

"Why now," murmured Mike Tague, "he shouldn't ought to have done that."

None of these men bothered to ask Isham why it had happened. They were old hands and they knew why. Tague looked a little uncomfortable, for he liked Merritt. The others said nothing.

Medary spoke up mildly. "Maybe you ought to add, Mr. Isham, that George Vird's dead. Merritt brought him to town at midnight."

"Vird," said Isham at once, his voice quick and arbitrary, "was in on that Winnemucca shootin'. He's been lookin' for trouble and finally he found it."

"Hate to see it break like this," the sheriff murmured. "Maybe . . ."

"Never mind about that, Medary. Skull's been bothered too much by men nighthawkin' its range. Merritt had no right to come on it and start shooting. It's a bad thing to set up before the Piute. You start that in one place and it spreads to another. I'm telling all you men that it might happen to you. So I'm going after Merritt. What I say is, don't give him any help."

"He shouldn't of done that," said Tague regretfully.

"Well, I guess you got to stop it," said Clay Spaugh, and no more. Swanee Vail, being nearer Skull and therefore more under its shadow, only nodded.

"Mark, you go out and bring Merritt in," said Isham.

Medary looked at him. "What for? A trial? No, that won't work, Mr. Isham. You won't get a jury to help you. He'd be turned loose."

"You do it," insisted Isham.

But Medary had his own stubborn streak. "I ain't going on a wild goose chase. If Merritt's on the jump I'd have a hell of a time catchin' up with him. If I brought him in it wouldn't stick. Maybe you don't know something, Mr. Isham. There ain't twelve men on the Piute who like Skull well enough to stick Merritt in the jug for you."

"What's the matter with you, Medary?" asked Isham, very sharp.

Mike Tague, always a peacemaker, came into the argument. "I guess maybe that's right, Will. You better go after him yourself." He got up, waving the smoke of his cigar away with his hand, and this move brought Spaugh and Vail likewise up. Isham gave them a close, displeased glance.

"You fellows run cattle, don't you? You want to see this business get out of hand? If they can shoot at Skull they can shoot at you."

"Sure," agreed Tague. "But when they shoot at me, Will, I'll do my own huntin'. I'll never ask another man to do it for me."

"All right. But I'm telling you what it will be like. Don't give Merritt any help."

The three filed out, leaving Isham with the sheriff. Medary said: "Well, what you want?"

Isham got up. "Nothing," he answered. "I've changed my mind. I'll take care of it personally."

"Maybe best," murmured the sheriff.

Isham gave him a critical glance. "Mark," he said, "you're crawfishing. Maybe, next election, you ought to take a rest."

Isham rode directly back to Skull, arriving there around two o'clock and meeting Dutcher. He said: "Saddle me a fresh horse. We're going up to Corral Flats." He went into the kitchen and had a quick meal. Dutcher was outside waiting for him, but Isham walked to the living room and stood there a moment, hearing Sally's steps somewhere in the upper part of the house. Presently she came down and, as always, his glance went to her face and searched it for expression. But it was smooth and cool and, as before, he felt that odd barrier between them. It brought back his temper to hear her speak as she did.

She said, driving at once to the trouble between them, "Will, do you want me to leave?"

He answered that with a small malice in his words. "What would you go back to?"

He had his moment's pleasure from knowing his question hit her hard; it broke through her composure. She looked at him so oddly, repeating, "Do you want me to leave?"

"No," he said, "that's the last thing I want. You will stay here." He showed her the edge of the smile she knew so well and had begun to fear.

"Then we've got to talk this out. I can't have you looking at me like that, as though it were all a terrible joke. I can't have you go on believing the worst about me. We've got too many years ahead of us."

He said, smooth and distant and unstirred, "We'll talk about it. When I come back we'll do all the talking you want."

"Will — "

But he had turned through the doorway with a small dismissing motion of his arm. He stepped into the saddle and rode over the yard, Dutcher beside him. He said, "We're going up to Corral Flats. I have decided to visit Mister Merritt."

"He won't be there," Dutcher said.

Isham threw a quick, amused glance at his foreman. "Don't worry about that," he answered. "Don't worry

about it." Dutcher said nothing more, and so they rode
into the hills, Isham entirely silent.

After Isham had gone Medary sat before the desk
with a wry and troubled look on his face. Politics was
a game of survival, of guessing where the power lay. In
this country the power belonged to Skull and to the four
other big outfits controlling three quarters of the country's range. The little people, the two-bit ranchers and
the folks in the Broken Buttes and the homesteaders,
didn't count very much, and never would. The division
was quite clear and he had, in the course of his own
career, played with the big owners, his reward being an
undisturbed tenure in office. His course now was pretty
simple, as it had always been. Yet the more he thought
of it, the worse it got; and presently he rose and crossed
to Tom Croker's saloon. Tom was another foxy one.

"Tom," he said, over his glass of whisky, "what do
you think?"

"Merritt? No chance, Mark, no chance."

"Sure," murmured the sheriff and downed his drink.
He dawdled over the bar, tracing a pattern on the wood
with his finger. His face was screwed tight, his expression showed a distant irritation.

"Ain't a thing you can do to help him," said Croker
by way of consolation. "Like the boy, don't you? So
do I. But he'll cash in his chips. I know Isham. He's
an Injun for rememberin'. You know what he remem-
bers?"

"Yeah: Sally." Then Medary added with a quick discontent, "What'd she marry him for?"

"He's an Injun," repeated Tom Croker, "and he makes my hair stand when he's around. It takes a pretty tough fellow to do that, Medary. What you goin' to do?"

Medary had his second drink, which for him was unusual. He said, "I'm going to do the first damfool thing in a long time, Tom," and went to the door. "I'm goin' down to the Fremont to hunt antelope and I won't be back for two weeks."

He went to the stable and presently reappeared in the saddle, leading a pack horse behind; he struck straight into the Piute, aiming for the blue blur of hills in the distant southwest. He could not help Merritt, whose troubles were past repairing, but in leaving town he knew he'd anger Isham. It was, as he had said, a foolish thing for a man to do who had cut his milk teeth in the obscure politics of a cattle country. He said to himself with a philosophic resignation, "Well, the huntin' ought to be good anyhow," and faded from The Wells.

From his hideout in the hills late that afternoon Merritt saw two riders appear on a little meadow below. He walked down the slope to intercept them. Pay Lankershim grinned, as though all this were a good joke. But Bourke Prine turned his temper loose on Merritt.

"Why in thunder didn't you come over to my place and let me in on this? I rode to your house this morning. No fire in the stove and nobody around. I went down to

Nan Melotte's but she hadn't seen nothin' of you. I pick up your trail in town — and I get worried. Then Pay comes along."

They squatted in the heavy shadows of the pines, Pay Lankershim still smiling. Bourke Prine rolled himself a cigarette, now and then shooting his sharp glance at Merritt who lay idle and untalkative. "Well," challenged Bourke, "what you going to do?"

Merritt said: "You been asking that question for a month. I did something, didn't I?"

"Just a beginning. Isham will follow you to hell now. You can't go back to your ranch." Bourke moved his heavy shoulders to express his dissatisfaction. "Well, we better think of something."

"You think of something," drawled Merritt. "You're the man that wanted to make a fight."

Bourke said, "You got an idea in your bonnet when you talk like that. Let's have it."

"I'm going up to Corral Flats again tonight."

Pay Lankershim chuckled. "That's the way. We'll all go."

The three of them sat around, considering it, until Bourke got up and moved to his horse. "All right. I'm going home. Then I'll cut into the high trail and see if I can spot anything. I'll be here when it gets dark."

Pay had a new thought, and went likewise to his pony. "Think I'll drift up toward the Flats and keep an eye open. Be back same time as Bourke. Meet us here."

Bourke studied Merritt a little longer. He said, "You got something in your coco." Then the two moved out on their separate trails and Merritt returned to the high bowl from which, when the spirit moved him, he could scan the long vistas leading down through the open timber.

Bourke, he thought, was a pretty hard man to fool. And Bourke was right in believing he had something on his mind. Waiting was hard work, and as this day went on his original idea seemed less effective than at sunrise. Lying here, he felt thoroughly outside of everything and out of touch with the Piute. To raise a little hell and run for shelter was, when a man looked at it in cold blood, a defensive gesture but it wasn't fighting. Meanwhile Skull had the country to itself. His ranch house was exposed and probably by tomorrow morning would be burned to the ground. His cattle would undoubtedly be run off. This was what happened to a man on the dodge.

Flat on his back, he rolled up a cigarette, dragging in the smoke. One small white cloud drifted over the tree-tops and disappeared. There was a little wind coming over this high point and somewhere a jay made a great racket in the timber. It wasn't Bourke's affair and it wasn't Pay Lankershim's affair, but here they were doing the work while he remained idle. Nor did it seem any better when he thought of the risk Sally Isham had taken in coming to his ranch.

He rose and scanned the lower pines, and circled the

bowl. He moved his saddle around and sat on it and watched the sky deepen in color while time dragged and the shadows in the timber began to creep upslope toward him. It was a long day with nothing to do but think; and after a while it occurred to him that a man's thoughts could only go so far until they turned and followed the same trail back. He remembered the way Sally Isham had held to him the night before, he remembered the intensity of her voice and the fragrance rising from her hair; then presently, by one of those strange skips of the mind, he found that the image of Nan Melotte was before him, vivid and very real.

At sundown he rose and saddled the gelding, caught up the two extra horses, and rode downgrade toward his ranch. Not until he was well away from the high point did he realize how quietly the change had come. Running wasn't any good. A man had to stand fast and do his fighting. This was what it amounted to. So he rode on through twilight, deliberately avoiding Bourke and Pay because he didn't want them mixed up in what seemed certain to come, and arrived at the edge of his ranch yard just as full night rolled out of the sky.

The darkness and the emptiness of the house hit him hard; it was as though he saw his own ruin in advance, and this was the reaction that roused his anger, quick and personal and hot. He had come off the left fork of the hill trail, avoiding the creek. It brought him in behind the barn and here he left the horses and went on to the back of the house. At the open door he delayed a moment, listening for trouble, then went in. A little later he lighted a lamp, left it on the table, and walked through the front room, stopping on the porch. Nan Melotte's light cut its diamond sparkle through the lower blackness of the desert.

He had been here only a few minutes — and was turning to go into the house again — when he heard the scuff of horses above the steady rustle of the waterfall. Wheeling back against the wall, he made out Isham's voice. Very cool and very plain, it rose from the slope directly across the creek. "Go straight on. Merritt, is that you? I want to talk to you." Dutcher shouted and horses splashed the shallows of the creek and a gun broke the night, its slug going through the wood of the house wall with a small, rustling echo. The shape of Skull's men appeared. Little yellow and purple rosettes of muzzle light began to flash from all their guns.

Merritt stepped backwards, dropped off the end of the porch and put a shoulder against the wide wall. Half-sheltered here, he waited while they rushed on, and laid his quick fire at them. Bullets skimmed the porch boards. One bullet hit the porch post with a definite spat. A horse grunted and fell and a man yelled, "Dutcher — Dutcher!" Isham's voice came on. "Keep going!" Some of them had cut back toward the rear of the house.

He ducked along the wall and came out at the back yard and saw a man's dismounted shape streaking toward the barn, which was where he also wanted to go. He threw two bullets at that fading shape, and saw the man fall — and heard him fall. Somebody was in the house, kicking through it at a dead run. The lamplight was killed. Halfway to the barn, Merritt saw a rider gallop in from the back trail and race toward him. He swung sharply away, barely clearing the horse. He took a snap aim at the rider, but held his fire, hearing the man call anxiously, "Dutcher — Dutcher," and rush by.

Dutcher burst through the back door, howling: "Back here! Mr. Isham, stay out of this for a minute! Come back here — he's in the barn!" Merritt wheeled and whipped a shot toward the house door, but it was wild, for Dutcher's yell was like a terrific whoop of triumph and afterwards he laced the night with his answering fire. Other men were rushing up, on foot. Lead scraped around Merritt's feet and his hammer dropped on an empty. Isham called from the side of the house, calm and cool as ever: "Keep on, Dutcher. Keep on." Somebody swung in from the darkness and raced for the barn, and so he was surrounded on three sides and the barn was, for all good use, a hundred miles away. He gave ground toward the waterfall, thumbing in fresh shells as he faded back. All this was in a night turned swiftly and completely black. They were pinching in on him, but he saw only the vaguest of shadows, and would have missed them entirely except for the flare of their guns. A man had reached the barn and was shooting from there; the hard-packed yard began to give up its dust, acrid to smell.

He had his revolver loaded and had raised it to fire again when something like a huge scythe cut him off his feet at one stroke and dropped him, knees and hands, to the ground. He felt, at that moment, no pain at all. Nothing but shock and a complete lack of feeling in his left leg. Searching slugs went *thwutt* on the near-by hard-pen, making him roll over and over. His arm hit the edge of the creek and the faint slope carried him down into the water, the coldness of the water kicking pain through his left leg at once. Dutcher howled, "Watch that barn, Tuck — he's goin' that way!" Two men ran from the house, passing him within a yard, and trotted toward the barn. He knew then he was through. He pulled himself around in the shallow water and crawled toward the fall. Its spray reached out to him and after another twenty feet the whole solid fall hit him in the back of the neck, knocking him flat. He pushed through it to the little basin inside the fall, his one sound foot supported on the basin's bottom. Resting this way, up to his ears in water, one hand hooked around a rock on the bank, he heard Isham's men as from a great distance. They were in the barn and afterwards their voices came near him, and then they were in the house. He heard furniture and windows smash. He heard doors go down. These sounds grew fainter and fainter and the rock to which he hung seemed to slide beyond his fingers. His leg was solid fire, the pain growing pretty bad. There was, at last, no sound at all from the house, and after a long interval, he pulled himself beyond the rock and, with his chest flat on dry land and his feet afloat in the restless surface of the pool, he drifted into a completely black world.

XII

NAN MELOTTE

THESE hills, and the desert of the Piute, made up a vast whispering gallery wherein the acts of men, no matter how isolated and secretive, soon were known from the remote edge of the Broken Buttes all over to the northernmost side of Wagon Rim. At noon Starr Bidwell came from the buttes and paused long enough at the schoolhouse to give Nan the news.

"Merritt," he said, "went to Corral Flats this mornin' and shot up the line cabin." He looked at her with a sly interest. "I hear he was visitin' you last night. I'd be careful about that." He went on to The Wells. Returning from town late in the day he paused at her house to drop fresh information. "Isham's on his trail with a crew. Well, Merritt won't be fool enough to come back to his ranch. He ain't got anything left to come back for anyhow."

Nan said: "How do you know that?"

Starr Bidwell grinned again. "I know," he answered, and trotted up the grade, into the butte country.

He was a Clagg rider and she could draw her own conclusions from what he had said. If Owen Merritt had nothing left it could only mean that Clagg had raided Merritt's range. After her evening meal, Nan stood in front of the cabin and watched night drop layer after layer of enamel-black shadow across the land. Low in the west a new moon showed the palest and thinnest of arcs and the southern wind began to strengthen. This morning a thick crust of ice had formed on her water bucket. First snow wasn't far away.

All this while she faced the east and waited, as she had done so many times, for Owen Merritt's light to break the black. This night, she told herself, it would not show. After all that had happened Merritt would keep to the hills, avoiding certain trouble from Skull. So when the light did suddenly cut its clear small flash on the heights she was both puzzled and a little bit alarmed. He was too smart a man to walk into a trap. Thinking of this, and of what Starr Bidwell had told her, she went to the adjoining leanto barn, saddled her horse and started for his place. She had not gone far when the light faded. Well across the flat stretch she began to hear the sound of firing. It grew stronger as she approached, and kept bursting through the stillness until she reached the bottom of the long grade. At this point it petered out. Going up the grade, and halting within a few hundred feet of the house, she heard them inside the place tearing it to pieces, crashing into anything that would break. Part of the crew roamed the yard. They were calling across the dark, and once she recognized Dutcher's voice — there could be no mistake about that heavy tone — calling out: "Mr. Isham, where are you?" Another man in the barn shouted: "He ain't here, that's a bet."

A man stepped from the house, drifting toward her.

Nan remained thoroughly still until, quite a while later, he swung away. Dutcher said: "Get those horses, Tuck, and come on."

Isham's voice was quite clear, quite insistent. "Look around once more. He may be hiding out. Look every place."

This went on for a good quarter-hour longer. Somebody struck a match — and quickly killed it when Dutcher roared: "You dam' fool, don't do that! Mr. Isham, he's in the brush by now."

Isham said, "All right." The reluctance and the steel-cold way of his words was something that went through Nan Melotte and made her afraid. They were collecting, they were talking. Dutcher spoke again and the creek rustled to their passage and in a little while all sound of them died in the timber. Nan slid from the saddle and went toward the house with soft steps. Within twenty yards of the place she dropped to the ground.

This was her country. She had been raised in it. She knew its people and the way they acted; since childhood she had listened to its stories of trickery and violence and fury until they had become a part of her thinking. This was a part of her nobody knew — this attentive silence that absorbed so much, this stoicism covering ways of thought that could be so earthy and practical and without illusion. This was why she dropped and waited.

It was as she suspected — Dutcher had left a man behind; for presently he grew weary of his watch and came to life, dragging his boots across the porch. He reached his horse, murmuring at the bottom of his breath, and rode once around the yard, passing quite close to Nan. She heard him grumble, "Oh, well." In a moment he crossed the water and galloped into the hills. Risen, but paused, Nan thought: He must be hurt. If he hadn't been he wouldn't have quit firing. So he's here somewhere. But not in the house, because they've searched it. And not in the barn.

She called, "Owen," listening to the faint, oncoming sounds of the night. The crickets were chirping again and the wind, colder and colder, brushed through the near-by pines and added volume to the sound of the waterfall in back of the house. She said again, "Owen," in a stronger tone and rose and walked directly toward the barn. "Owen."

She went into the barn, passed through it to the little corral butting against the pines. He wouldn't run. He would stay near the house and fight. Why else had he come back if not for that? So he was here, somewhere — and hurt. She circled the barn, crossed the yard and stopped at the house's back doorway. She murmured, "Owen," and heard the echo sibilantly through the empty rooms. Her feeling now was tight and fearful and increasingly desperate. She walked through the house, kicking against broken chairs and capsized furniture. On the porch she called his name again, going to the edge of the creek and following it to the rear of the house. The fall's mist touched her face. She repeated: "Owen — where are you?"

She heard him as from a great distance. He said: "Over here," but his voice was so dim that it didn't help.

"Where — Owen? Where?"

"Here," he called. She knew he was hurt. His tone was thin and faded — and might be anywhere. He seemed to realize it for he said: "Behind the falls."

The rush of water dimmed the tone. She ran through the spray, circling the straight curtain of water, and got to the gravelly edge of the basin. It was like a steady heavy rain here, wetting her immediately. She bent down and touched his shoulders.

"Owen, can you walk?"

"Try," he said. "I'm a little weak. Left leg's no good. Get around on that side."

She felt him make the effort; he kept grinding his boots against the gravel. His muscles stirred and he got one leg beneath him. She steadied herself beneath his left arm. "All right, Owen. You've got to get up."

He was up, bearing harder and harder against her. He made a try on his right leg and stepped out of the water. His breathing was quick and shallow and his voice got rough. "Let me down, Nan. I can crawl better." He fell on his knees, taking her with him. His elbow struck her across the chest. She held back the cry it brought up. He said, between the in-and-out rush of his wind: "They took my horses."

She ran over the yard and brought up her pony. He had pulled himself a little farther away from the water. He was on his knees and his arms reached out for her. "Left side," he called and, braced by her shoulder, he rose again. She turned the pony around so that he could grasp the horn; and helped him lift his left leg into the stirrup. He said, quick and small, "A boost now." Nan shoved against his hips. For a moment all his weight was against her and she thought he would fall. Then he dropped his stomach over the saddle and lay there a minute. When he was rested he got his legs in the stirrups and straightened. Nan caught hold of the cantle and climbed behind Merritt, feeling his body shift. She put both arms around his waist. "Can you stay on?"

"Sure," he breathed.

They went down the slope at a slow walk and reached the valley floor, plodding toward the light she had left burning. Now and then a tremor of cold gripped him from head to foot and shook him so violently that she had to shove against his weight to keep him steady. When they reached the door of the cabin she had a bad moment. His left leg was useless to him and he was weaker than before. When he rolled from the leather he nearly fell. She supported him through the doorway, over to the corner bed. He dropped on it with a long reaching groan of relief.

His eyes were coal black against the pallor of his face. Pain and chill shook him and a dull stain widened on the upper part of his left trouser leg. Water dripped from his clothes. He put the back of a hand across his eyes, shielding them against the light. She went over immediately and carried the lamp to another position; and turned to find him faintly smiling.

She was a straight shape in the room. She stood momentarily still. But she knew what had to be done and turned and pulled down the shades on the two windows and went to him. Seated on the edge of the bed she slipped her arm beneath his wet shoulders and pulled him up. "Your clothes," she said, stripping back his coat. He moved around a little to help her but the increasing slowness of his muscles made her afraid. She threw the coat on the floor and unbuttoned his shirt and undershirt, working quickly, almost urgently. She got off his boots and socks and threw a blanket over him, and stood up a moment. He had dropped full-length on the bed again and for a little while she held his glance, her lips pulled together. "Owen," she said, "it's all right," and reached beneath the blanket and stripped off the rest of his clothes. The pallor of his cheeks was constant. Water glittered through his blond hair and ran along his forehead like sweat. He held his lips straight.

"Good girl."

She was moving faster than before, her fear more and more real. She went to a trunk and pulled out a sheet, ripping it in long sections, and got a knife from the kitchen and slashed the mattress at the foot of the bed, removing a piece of batting. Pushing the blanket aside she saw the torn, chewed hole halfway between hip and knee. The bullet had struck at a shallow angle, smashing through the soft flesh and coming out near the knee. Blood soaked into the batting the moment she put it on; and this loss of blood and the shock of the cold water had deadened him. She added more batting and wrapped the strips of sheeting around it, and tucked the dry edge of the blanket beneath him. She laid all the quilts she had over him, and waited a moment. His muscles were easing a little; he was getting warm and the drawn expression around his lips began to dissolve. She said, with an almost forlorn note, "Why did you go back, Owen?"

But she didn't wait for his answer. She took the wet clothes into the kitchen, freshened the fire and filled the coffeepot. Waiting for the water to boil, she wrung out the clothes and hung them across a chair's back, as near the heat as she could put them. When the coffee was ready she took him a cup of it, black and laced with whisky from a bottle long carried in her shelf. She supported him while he drank.

"You work fast in a pinch, Nan."

She thought, with a terrible relief, "He's going to be all right." Her hand, pressed against the middle of his back, felt an increasing warmth. When he had finished the coffee she let him sink down and returned to the kitchen. All this while she had been thinking of what was to come. Now, slowly heating his clothes over the top of the stove, she made up her mind. Skull was a hard enemy and Isham would never stop now until he found Merritt. The fact that he had himself led his men to Christmas

Creek told her how much he wanted Merritt; otherwise he would have left Dutcher in charge. In the morning they would spread out and sooner or later somebody would come to this cabin. Skull's riders, or Clagg, or some other man from the Broken Buttes. All these people were quick-eyed and inquisitive and a manhunt would set them wild. She knew the Piute thoroughly.

The springs of the bed groaned. Nan went into the living room to find Owen shifting his shoulders back and forth. The coffee had warmed him and his nerves were alive again, building up the pain in his leg. She sat on the edge of the bed and slid her hand beneath his neck, as though she wished to lead some of that trouble out of him into herself. Her face showed her wish and her eyes showed it. She bent toward him, murmuring: "Is it so bad, Owen? If you can think of anything I could do — "

He murmured: "It'll go."

She said in a long, deep whisper: "I wish I could take it from you."

He looked at her with a distinct surprise. "Why?" But she didn't answer and he didn't repeat the question. Her shoulders dropped and turned round as she bent toward him and her lips were warm and faintly parted. She was a dark girl, hard to know. She didn't give herself away and she didn't talk much. But he saw something wise and grave and wondering in her eyes and he got to thinking — when the pulsing waves of pain let him alone — that it was strange he knew so little of her. Her hand was smooth and pleasant behind his neck; her nearness steadied him. There was a depth to Nan Melotte very real. It was a stillness, a fortitude. He could not get the word he wanted, he could not get close to the meaning. It was as if she held qualities strong and deep that she could not, or would not, show. When she looked at him now he caught the faint shine of it in her eyes, its steady, changeless reflection. It made him say: —

"I remember your people. That was ten years ago. They had a ranch near Corral Flats."

She nodded. "We left the country. They were both killed in a runaway at Linkville. I grew up with relatives. And came back here to teach."

Everything lay in the few slow words. She had a bluntness, sometimes, like a man's bluntness. Well, she had lived alone and asked nothing of anybody; and here she was now, silently holding him, with her lips near and soft.

"Owen," she murmured, "why did you come back to your place tonight? You knew you'd have trouble."

The whisky dissolved a little of his pain; it cushioned the steady pound in his leg. He was drowsy and his eyes were closed. He said: "A man can't run all the time, Nan. I got to thinking about that. Have to fight sooner or later."

Her voice was nearer, gentler. "You like to laugh, Owen. But I haven't seen you laugh for a long time." He thought that was all. But long later her voice, almost humble, added: "If you want me to do it, I'll find a way of getting Sally here."

He said, "I wasn't thinking of her," and opened his eyes. She drew her hand from his neck. It rested lightly on his chest and then the light in her eyes quickened into brilliance, as though coming through tears. She ran her palm across his head, pressing wetness out of it and afterwards he heard her say in the same gently uncertain way: "Sleep a little, Owen."

He was asleep soon after. She watched him a moment and rose and turned down the lamp to a vague glow. In the distance was a fugitive sound that turned and stilled her until it ran into the desert's long silence. Back in the kitchen she added wood to the stove, rearranged Merritt's clothes on the chairback and packed all the food she could find into a flour sack. She slipped from the house and took the waiting pony around to the leanto barn. The people of the district had loaned her a buggy which, so far, she had not used, preferring the saddle. Now she unsaddled the pony, harnessed it and hitched it to the buggy and returned to the house. She made three or four trips to the buggy, packing in the sack of food and a few of her own clothes. She laid out Merritt's gun and belt and her own Winchester on the room table, tore up another sheet, and returned to the kitchen. This was around ten o'clock. At midnight, with Merritt's clothes thoroughly dry, she stood over his bed, watching his face show a faint disturbance in sleep. He needed a longer rest than this; but he needed safety worse. The room was warm and sweat stood out on his forehead. His whiskers made the angles of his features more pronounced. He was a very long man and physically a powerful one, with something inside him that most people had never seen. This was what she thought as she stood there, thoroughly alive to his presence in the room. Then she said, "Owen," and drew him from the fitful nap.

He was wide-awake, immediately expecting trouble. He tried to rise, and then quit trying. He said: "Somebody coming?"

"No. But we've got to go. I put my pony to the buggy. We can get pretty far up in the Broken Buttes before daylight. You can't stay here."

He said: "Puts you in a bad position."

She turned it aside with a shrug of her shoulders. "Is it wrong, Owen?"

"Your life is yours, Nan. Don't get mixed up in mine. Give me the buggy and I'll hit out for the Fremont."

She moved around him and he caught again that hint of resoluteness which seemed to guide all her ways. She put his clothes on the bed and turned into the kitchen and stood there listening to the quick, hard labor of his breathing; and suddenly she turned back into the room and finished his dressing for him. She said: "You see?"

He sat on the edge of the bed, hard hit and half exhausted, while she stripped the blankets from the bed and put them in the buggy. She put his gunbelt around him and turned her shoulder under his arm, and so he got to the buggy. They had a few minutes' trouble but he drew himself in largely with his arms and afterwards Nan took a quilt from the house and covered him with it.

After she had extinguished the houselight and brought out the Winchester she stood a moment in the chilly blackness of the night, thinking carefully of what she might have overlooked. She made another trip to the barn for the ax — and one more trip to the house for a butcher knife. Then she got beside Merritt and turned the horse toward Stage Coach Pass. They went through the pass, into the border of East Desert, riding steadily south in the direction of Winnemucca. The moon's thin crescent hung oddly in the low sky, against which the shoulder of the Broken Butte country showed its black continuous lump. There was no talk until, long after, she said: "Owen — is it pretty bad?"

"No," he said. "No."

Following down the stage road, they came to the rocky course of a river's ancient bed and rattled over it for three or four miles. At two o'clock that morning Nan turned into the heavy shadows of the Buttes and went up a canyon, rising with it toward the sky. At three-thirty, light began to break through the east and they were lost in a world of bald ridges, rising and falling from gulch to gulch. The deeper they went the poorer became the trail. At daylight they had dropped into a deep gorge whose straight-sided walls rose a hundred feet from a shallow flowing creek. Nan Melotte found a tortuous grade down to the creek, and followed it until a rocky shoulder barred further progress with the buggy. A round tunnel led back from the creek fifteen feet or more, bored out of the sandstone in ages past by a violent eddy of the creek. Nan drove into it, threw out the blankets and made a bed on the hard floor. Owen Merritt slid from the seat, bracing his one good leg on the hub. His arms shook a little when he hung to the side of the buggy. Nan put her shoulder against him and felt his weight sag. He went to his knees, reached the blankets and rolled over once. "All right," he said in a dragging voice, "here's home."

The ride had taken all strength from him. He lay thoroughly still, with his face turned to the tunnel's ceiling and his eyes round-wide. She left him and unharnessed the horse and tied it to a boulder. Morning's light dropped into the canyon. Between these narrow walls the sound of the creek was restless and chuckling and loud. Nan watched the high-up rims a moment, then moved into the tunnel, crept beneath the quilt covering Merritt and lay listening to his disturbed breathing. She put her hand on his shoulder. She murmured: "It's all right, Owen."

XIII

"A WOMAN'S WITH HIM"

WHEN Skull splashed over Christmas Creek and opened fire on Merritt's house Hugh Clagg was swinging through the higher hills with Tempe Killeen and Pete Mariels. Meanwhile he had dispatched Ray Neale and Starr Bidwell to a lower corner of Skull's range. Later that night the five men came together and, with both Skull and Merritt beef traveling before them, fell out of the Bunchgrass Hills into East Desert, crossed the stage road, and entered the Broken Buttes country. Here and there, in one or another hidden hollow they came by, lights sparkled from isolated cabins; and sometimes they were near enough to these places to rouse a dog. But this was a well-used trail for Clagg. He knew the people along the way very well and had complete immunity. In the Broken Buttes nobody asked questions and nobody talked; and now and then when any of these inhabitants wanted beef they knew where to get it.

Far back in the wilder part of the Buttes he made camp, well pleased with himself. Three more nights of travel would see the beef sold to a cattleman over on the edge of the Black Rock Desert in Nevada, no questions asked. Next morning Clagg left Tempe Killeen in charge of the camp and drifted back toward the Piute. At the Bidwell cabin he picked up the news of the fight from

Sally's father. Near the long grade into the desert he passed one of the Cordray boys. There was, the boy said, no school and no teacher. When he reached Nan Melotte's house, Hugh Clagg knocked once and went in. He saw the ripped-up bed and the stains of blood near by, the empty kitchen shelves and, in the leanto shed, the missing horse and buggy. He knew then what had happened.

He stood in the middle of the front room, a cigarette puckered between his lips and his eyes half-closed. There was in Hugh Clagg a hatred of Owen Merritt as permanent as the color of his hair, a hatred that produced the strong desire to break or humble Merritt, to ruin him, to remove that sensation which the big man always created, which was like a sudden shadow falling on him, on Clagg. Clagg couldn't help it. And now, knowing why Nan had gone, he also realized that this girl had never at any moment thought of him in any favorable light. Careless and indifferent as Clagg seemed to be, there were in him nevertheless his moments of great desire for the good things of life, and a slowly growing knowledge that these good things would never come. He saw his own destiny pretty clearly: he hated himself for his weakness, and hated all others whose lives were better balanced. What turned him at once uncontrollable was the knowledge that Owen Merritt could, without lifting a hand, draw Nan Melotte into the hills with him while he, Hugh Clagg, roused in her nothing but fear. He wasn't a fool; he had seen fear in her eyes. And then he realized why Will Isham had at last turned Skull loose. Isham had everything except his own wife. The shadow of Merritt was on Isham too, turning Isham crazy.

He moved around the room and his leg struck the small table in the front room and knocked it over; and the sound of that crash suddenly ripped the thin covering off his restraint and he went wild. He tipped over the bed, kicking the framework to pieces with his boots. He tore the shades from the windows, knocked out the glass panes with the butt of his gun, took the little row of books standing on a corner shelf between his hands and broke them apart. He trotted into the kitchen and batted the stove-pipe down with one swing of his fist and swept all the dishes he could find to the floor, grinding them beneath his heels. He tore the shelves from the wall; he seized a stick of wood and beat in the cast-iron sides of the stove.

Ten minutes later, breathing from the bottom of his chest and drenched by the sweat of his unreasoning labors, he walked from a house as thoroughly ruined as he could make it, swung up to his horse and trotted out on the flats. He followed the tracks of Nan Melotte's buggy as far as Stage Coach Pass and there halted, bringing his knowledge of the country into play. Maybe they had gone toward Winnemucca, maybe into the east side of the Broken Buttes, or maybe straight over East Desert and out of the country. A little searching would soon enough tell, but instead of keeping on the trail he curved past Merritt's house and hit the climbing trail to Corral Flats. He passed the ranch house near enough to see what Skull had done to it, and a thoroughly unsentimental grin showed on his face. "Isham and me." Isham's frame of mind, which he so thoroughly understood right now, appealed to the latent malice in him.

Near Lankershim's meadow a Skull rider stepped out of the trees and stopped him.

"What the hell you doin' here again?"

"Isham up yonder?"

"Yeah."

Clagg brushed by the Skull man. A mile short of Corral Flats he was stopped another time. He heard men talking in the deeper timber and turned that way. Dutcher and two riders were just then coming in from some sort of scout, their ponies looking pretty tired. Isham sat on a log, small and stiff and showing Hugh Clagg no favorable regard. It made Clagg smile, for he remembered again what ate so bitterly at the Skull owner's pride.

Dutcher said brusquely, "What the hell you grinnin' at?"

"Nice day, ain't it?" suggested Clagg, and turned on Isham. "Which way you looking for friend Merritt?"

Dutcher kept breaking into this talk. "Kind of curious about the man?"

"I can look too. Maybe we can split this up and save some time. Or didn't you care about time?"

Isham stared at Clagg. "What you want with him? Why?"

Clagg's smile was a quick, thin cut across his face. "A woman," he said.

Dutcher walked nearer. Isham stood up from the log. He said, "What's that?" in a rising tone.

"A woman's with him."

"Where'd you find that out?"

Clagg looked around at the Skull crew, not sparing his insolence. "You didn't know that yet? You got a hell of a poor crew, Isham."

Dutcher said, his voice more overbearing: "He was hit and he wouldn't get far. He's around these hills somewhere."

Clagg said: "All right, you keep lookin' this way and I'll look my way." One moment he had been willing to talk, the next moment he suddenly felt affronted by the austere dislike of Isham's glance. He had come here to tell them about the wagon tracks. Now he changed his mind, impelled by that contradictory side of him which so powerfully governed his life. "You do it your way," he added, shortly. "I never waste my time on dam' fools."

"Wait," broke out Isham. "What woman?"

Everybody knew what was in Isham's mind. Hugh Clagg, watching the Skull owner's face, realized that Isham knew everybody understood what was on his mind. It was a kind of torture that could not remain altogether hidden. Clagg's unstable temper balanced on the thin edge of safety and malice — and chose the latter, risky as it was.

"Not the lady you're thinkin' about, Isham."

He thought for a moment that Isham meant to draw on him. The man's cheeks were seized by a pale killing impulse; he threw his chin quite high, he swayed forward, and for a long run of time nobody stirred. Then Isham said, scarcely opening his lips: "Go on, Clagg."

Clagg trotted away. At Pay Lankershim's meadow he slanted over the southern prow of the Bunchgrass Hills and fell into the stage road, coming upon Nan Melotte's buggy tracks. These took him well down the stage road until, in the middle of the afternoon, he saw them die in the gravelly course of a dry river-bed. Here he stopped, making his own careful conclusions. Those two, he decided, would be up in the Broken Buttes somewhere. It was a big country to cover, but there was plenty of time and the hunting would be a pleasure. He swung directly into the Butte country, aiming back to his crew. The hunting, he repeated to himself, would be a pleasure.

As soon as he had gone, Isham turned on Dutcher. "Go back to the ranch," he said, "and bring up a few more hands. Bring along some supplies."

Dutcher swung into the saddle. "He ain't far away, Mr. Isham. I just found where he camped on the crown of Bald Peak."

"We'll find out," said Isham. Then, as Dutcher turned

to go, he added, "Tell Mrs. Isham I wish her to stay on the ranch."

Dutcher went away and the other riders faded back, continuing the scout. Isham sat down on the log, crouched over with his arms across his knees, with his eyes pointed to the ground. He remembered what Clagg had said. Apparently, then, the whole country understood that he was a fool. Crouched in that cramped posture, his mind embittered beyond repair by the unforgivable fact, he was seized by the terrific desire to destroy the source of his humiliation. He would never have peace until then.

On Bourke Prine's little ranch at the base of the Bunchgrass Hills, halfway between town and Merritt's place, Prine and Pay Lankershim and Cultus Charley held a war meeting the same afternoon. Pay and Bourke had scouted the hills most of the night, out of range of the trouble which had taken place on Merritt's ranch. Going down there near daylight they had at last read the story in the wreckage. Now they were here, gloomy and disturbed. Cultus Charley had drifted in for a meal and was inclined to move along now. But Bourke stayed him.

"You're a dam' poor excuse of an Indian, Charley, but maybe I can use you."

"Well," said Pay, "if he's alive he's in these hills somewhere. He wouldn't leave the country. Not now."

"Isham will be on his trail," said Bourke. "And maybe

we just better find a spot somewhere and watch what Skull does. Charley, how good are your eyes, for trackin'?"

"My father good."

"What's your father got to do with you?"

"I almost as good."

"Then you get on that trail and find him."

"Sure. You got a drink?"

"You find where he's hidin' and I'll buy you a gallon."

Cultus Charley considered this a good while. He said, "All right," and rose and left the ranch. Bourke and Pay watched him lope into the timber, neither man harboring much hope. Pay said: "Hell, he's no good. He'll curl up and go to sleep somewhere and come back to panhandle another meal."

Bourke stamped around the room. He said, "What did Owen go back there for? Why didn't he meet us?"

Pay said: "Tom Croker told me Medary pulled out today. Went huntin'. A little scared of the fuss."

"The country's goin' to bust wide open," grumbled Bourke.

Pay stretched his long legs out from the chair and considered them with a faded, wise glance. "Let 'er bust. That gives me an idea. I don't think Mr. Isham will like it." He rose and went to the door. "I'm goin' in to town again. Maybe somethin's come up. We goin' back in the hills tonight?"

"Sure."

"Son," said Pay, reassuringly, "don't you fret about

Merritt. He's pretty tough. As for you and me — we can raise a little hell, too. I'll be back two hours after dark."

Isham left Skull's home quarters on Monday and did not return until Thursday. Those intervening three days were as bad as any Sally Isham could recall. Dutcher rode in once to take part of the crew back to the hills, but he didn't come near her and after he left she noticed that one man always made it a point to remain in the yard near the house, as though on guard. On Wednesday, hard hit by the uncertainty and the loneliness of her position, she saddled up and started for The Wells. One of the crew jumped on a horse and overtook her at the foot of the rim grade. He was blunt enough with his orders: "Mr. Isham wants you to stay by the ranch." Looking at him, she thought she saw some of Dutcher's insolent knowledge mirrored in this man's eyes. She turned back without arguing.

The silence of the house closed around her. At night she heard riders coming in and going away again, but if there was news it never reached her. Alone in the big living room, she thought of Owen Merritt, knowing that some definite break had occurred to cause all this upset on Skull; knowing that Isham would never be riding these hills so consistently unless it were because of Merritt. She remembered, at these times, Owen's long slow smile as it had been in the past, and she remembered, because she could not help it, the things he had said to her in the darkness of the hotel stairway. Those words came back; they all came back.

And then, because a need for honesty compelled her to it, she analyzed her own actions, her own thoughts. Had she been disloyal to Will Isham? Her situation here became more and more hopeless. Was it retribution for anything she had done, or had failed to do? She went back over the whole thing carefully, needing to know the answer. She had been frank with Isham in the beginning and he had known before marriage what her feelings were. She had been careful to tell him that love was not a part of the bargain. He had, she recalled, listened to that explanation very quietly, and had said: "Very well, Sally. Many marriages have started off with less honesty than this one will. I shall do my part and I know you will do yours."

She had tried to live up to her obligations. She had tried to make up, by other things, for the affection they both knew was lacking. Then, there was only one thing left — which was her visit to Owen Merritt. She knew now that this had been a mistake. And yet she had gone, not to betray Isham, but to avoid a fight.

This was what she kept remembering those long, long three days of silence and doubt. Now she understood what Owen Merritt had meant in saying that one day she would discover that her mind was one thing and her heart another. To realize it was to feel how tragic the situation had become. For now, with Isham turned against her, suspicious of her actions and

doubting her loyalty and tormented by her past friend-
ship for Merritt, she saw her hard choice turning to
nothing.

He came home Thursday night after dusk, grimed
by dust and ragged from want of sleep. When he entered the house he went past her without speaking. Always a man careful of personal appearance, he shaved
and changed his clothes, and came down to a late supper in the dining-room. She had already eaten, but she
followed him, closing both the kitchen and living-room
doors. He looked at her with an unmistakable irritation. "Can't you let a man alone when he's hungry?"

She said, gently, "All right, Will," and returned to
the living-room, waiting there. When he came out he
started for the yard again, ignoring her. This time she
knew that they had to have it out. "Wait," she said.
"There's no use putting this off. There won't be any
better time."

He was at the doorway. He stopped there, thinking
about it, and presently turned with a shrug of his
shoulders. "No," he said, "I guess not. But what can I
say, or you say, that hasn't been said?"

"I don't want this marriage to fail, Will."

He had a sharp, swift way of catching up her words.
"I suppose it is a matter of pride with you, Sally. You
don't want the Piute to know you couldn't stick on
Skull."

She repeated: "I don't want to be a failure. I made a
bargain. I want to keep it. You have been treating me

badly, Will. I have asked for nothing and I haven't expected anything. We both knew how we felt. There hasn't been any change in that. There's no reason for us to give up. I made my promise to you and I didn't come here with the idea of running away when the first quarrel came up. I won't run! I'll keep my part of the bargain. I always intended to do that. But you've got to be fair with me."

"Fair?" he said, his tone skeptical and unbelieving.

"Have I done anything wrong?"

"Not to my knowledge."

"Do you think I misled you in anything I said, before we were married?"

"No," he said. "I got just what I expected."

He had a small, humorless smile at the edge of his lips. He watched her with a consistent irony in his eyes, as though he enjoyed the scene. But she knew better. He was a man with a deep-set temper; whose pride, quick to feel affront, nourished those affronts far down in the brooding places of his memory. She could not bring them to the surface and dissolve them by reason or argument. She could not make him speak out. It caused her to say, with a growing desperateness: —

"Will, what have I done?"

He was smooth and unyielding. "Nothing. Nothing at all. Are you through, Sally? We're getting nowhere."

Then, because she knew of no other way to shatter that apparent indifference, she spoke of the one thing she knew was dangerous. "I know. You can't forget I once went with Owen."

That took the smile from his lips, instantly and completely. His eyes were gray and hot — and showed the edge of misery. "When you speak his name your voice goes soft. It gives you away, Sally."

"Will — "

He interrupted, aroused at last. "Wait a minute. You want to know what the trouble is. I think you know, but I'll just give you my side of it. I have had very little experience with women, Sally. I knew you were in love with Owen at the time I married you. You didn't say so, but it was pretty plain. I had the idea that it would pass. You see — I didn't know. But I can thank you for a good deal of education in that regard the last few days. You'll never change in a thousand years. Maybe that's the way all women are, or maybe it is just the way you are. I don't know and life is too damned short to find out, but anyhow as long as you're both alive it will be you and Owen. It won't be you and me, Sally."

"Will," she said, small and quick, "you're wrong. That's all over."

His smile came back, cheerless and bitter. "So far you haven't lied to me. Don't begin."

She went away from him, as far as the corner of the room; and turned, still desperately intent. "I wish you'd try to forget that. Whatever happened then is behind me. I came here with all that put away. I told you, the first night in this house, that I'd do what you wished to be done. That is what I want to do. If I've got to make myself over to suit you, I will. Tell me what kind of a wife you want."

It came out so headlong — this rush of eager, hard-pressed words. She stood straight, with her shoulders squared and a strong color on her cheeks; and with her hands risen and doubled, though she didn't realize it. Keyed to this emotional pitch, Sally Isham showed him a kind of iron resolution rarely seen in a woman; and showed him too, at that moment, something like actual beauty. He saw it and had his moment of awareness and was tremendously stirred. Afterwards his memory went back into its deep place and revived the smoldering animosity there.

He said in his disturbed voice: "You'd be willing to do anything to protect Owen Merritt. You'd promise anything. You're that kind of a woman and God knows the man that has your heart has a wonderful thing. You'd go to hell for him."

She flung her words at him in a low, husky intensity: "Will — Will! Don't let's quarrel! I don't want to fail! I won't let our lives be ruined like this."

He stood by the center table, one hand resting on it. His head was down and for a moment Sally thought she had reached into him and got hold of his sane impulses. When he looked up, she knew she had failed. The faint and crooked line of a smile was back on his lips. She wasn't fooled by the easy way he spoke or by the indifference covering him again.

He said: "Last night we went down to Merritt's house. He got away from us, but we'll keep on looking. I think we hit him. This morning Hugh Clagg dropped in to tell me Merritt had gone into the hills with a woman. I asked him what woman. Do you know what he said? He said: 'Not the woman you're thinking about, Isham.' It is quite a joke, isn't it? Everybody on the Piute can laugh about that, except me." He watched her with his everlastingly alert eyes. She showed him her old composure, but he thought she listened to him with a greater care. He thought he had roused her. He added: "You wouldn't know what woman did go away with him, would you?"

Her lips scarcely moved. "No."

"It will be interesting — finding out." He moved to the door. Her voice came after him, quite tired. "Will — what do you want me to do?"

He turned again, shaking his head. "It is not so hopeless, yet. There may be a change. Could you keep on loving a man, when he was dead, Sally?"

He went from the room with that last phrase hanging to the stillness, so final and so clear. She understood at last that he would never rest until he had found Owen and had killed him. His pride had that consuming, incessant reach. She walked around the room almost aimlessly, too tired at the moment to feel much, drained dry by what she had been through. From her position by the window, she saw him turn toward the hills. A Skull man walked over the yard and squatted in the late sunshine before the house. She went to the rear of the room and sat down, hands folded in her lap. There was, she realized, nothing more to say. She had said it all to him, without effect; and so her marriage, which she secretly admitted as a mistake, had come to this miserable ending — with no hope for betterment one way or the other.

She could not remain in the chair. Once more turning from wall to wall, she remembered what Isham had said about the other woman. It would be Nan Melotte, she thought, and felt an instant resentment. Well, she had surrendered many things in marriage. Most important of all, she had surrendered any claim to Owen Merritt's heart. He could do as he pleased. This she told herself, and still she could not check that feeling of anger. How could he put aside so soon — or how could he ever put aside — all that had once held them together? How could he look into another woman's eyes and touch another woman's face? If he had been hit by a bullet in the fight where was he now? Now, at this very moment, what was he saying to Nan Melotte — and what was she doing for him? This thought was hardest. This thought told her at last how great a mistake her own pride had caused her to commit. Somewhere in the hills Nan Melotte was where she, Sally, ought to be. Hard-caught in her thoughts, she built up the picture. Of Owen's long lips turned in smiling and his voice, so indolently musical, reaching out to please the girl. There was a scar near his left temple and the skin at the base of his neck had an extra ruddiness from the sun; and sometimes when he was stirred he could, by the very power of his personality, make any woman in the world come to him. Any woman. Nan Melotte.

Isham had gone and light faded out of the sky and a cold wind began to flow. The supper triangle rang; men's voices came from the mess hall adjoining. She rose and shut the door and went back to her chair. She could not run. She had made her bargain. No matter how hard the circumstances, here was her place.

That night, with full darkness covering Skull, a pale glow began to rise from the haystacks in the lower meadows, turning swiftly into great wedge-shaped masses of flame pouring crimson toward the sky. The Skull crew rushed out there; but Pay Lankersim, retreating from the fires, reached the valley's high rim and turned to laugh at what he had done; and galloped on toward Bourke Prine's ranch.

In the tunnel at the bottom of the canyon Nan Melotte slept only by shallow intervals, constantly wakened by the restless turning of the big man beside her. She could see nothing in the thorough darkness, but she heard the impact of pain on his breathing each time he tried to shift the weight of his leg. Placing her hand along his cheek she could feel its coldness. He had lost a great deal of blood. Once in the long hour before daylight he asked for a drink of water and afterwards fell into a more solid sleep. At daylight she observed that he was pale, and quite weak. Breaking up the sides of the buggy she started a fire and made a breakfast of coffee and bacon and was troubled when he only took the coffee. Even his voice was unsteady. "Where is this?"

"The east fork of Rock Creek, Owen."

"Curl up and catch a little rest."

She said: "I'm not sleepy. How do you feel?"

"All right."

She watched him drift into slumber. He had taken her hand and now she sat cross-legged beside him, patiently waiting for his grip to relax, afraid to disturb him. Long afterwards she slipped into the canyon and took her bearings.

The walls of the canyon, dark with the acute-slanted shadows of early morning, ran up a hundred feet, its course cutting generally through a rugged land she could not see but knew very well from memory. The creek was about twenty feet wide and covered the bottom of this gorge completely; it came around a sharp bend, passed the tunnel with a shallow dashing, and turned another bend. Down there, not far away, a steady, grumbling echo indicated a fall of some size. In many ways this was a good hideout, being deep in the Broken Buttes and a good distance from anybody's cabin. Water and shelter were here, but she had to find a way of getting the pony to grass.

At intervals she turned into the tunnel to watch him and to replace the blankets that his restless turning kept throwing aside. The rocky floor of the tunnel made a poor bed. His leg, she observed, never ceased troubling him. He drifted in and out of small periods of half-sleep; and at those times when he was awake she laid her hand on his chest and held it there, her lips and eyes trying to help him. He didn't talk much, but once he said: "That's a comfort."

At noon she made weak coffee and cut a piece of bread from the one loaf she had brought along. He didn't want it. She said: "Try, Owen. Try to eat." There was a weakness, a passiveness about him that troubled her and made her insist. But when she saw how poor an attempt he made at the food she gave up. His face took on color, and a fever began to heat his skin. She knew then trouble was ahead.

The wagon was all the wood they had, and of no other use to them now. She broke it apart with an ax and chopped it in small pieces, throwing the metal parts into the creek. She made a small rock dam at the creek's edge and placed the bacon and a can of condensed milk there to cool. She had a little sugar and flour, the rest of the bread, and some coffee; and that was all. Hunger made the pony restless. It kept backing into the water, it kept turning; and thinking always of discovery, she pulled it deeper into the tunnel and made a shorter tie around a rock. There wasn't anything more to do; the sense of being alone and responsible for Owen was suddenly a heavy weight on her shoulders. She sat beside him, listening to the increased labor of his breathing. His skin was hot and quite dry. She bent forward, her hands doubled up but not touching him; and she tried to throw her own strength into him by silently calling his name, by reaching out to him with her own cool resistance.

There wasn't anything else to do. That afternoon ran out its long, straining hours and the shadows of a night she actually dreaded, thickened in the canyon. Merritt was awake again.

"Owen," she murmured, "I've got to take the horse up to the rim and let him feed. I won't be gone very long."

He nodded, he showed her a smile. Leading the pony down the shallow side of the creek, she recognized the uncertainty of that smile and was increasingly troubled. The diagonal shelving of the road showed before her and she went up through the forming darkness to the surface of the Broken Butte country. The land lay around her in formless domes and ridges, barren and untimbered and gray in the thick twilight. All this cut a ragged silhouette out of the sky's empty background. The horse pulled at the rope, reaching for the scattered bunchgrass; and she followed him this way, letting him graze while the chill of a fresher breeze got through her clothes. The hunger of the pony kept him on the travel; the light died completely and the broken half-bark, half-howl of coyotes began to ride the blackness, accenting this land's loneliness. The smell of earth was in the wind, the raw pungency of it stronger than any other smell; and the feel of winter was in it, sharply imminent.

A grazing muletail, or perhaps an antelope, caught her scent and blasted the stillness with an expelled breath and went scudding away. The stars sent down their frosty glinting upon this broken land, on ridge and pocket and canyon and hidden defile; on her and on the campfires of other people camped in the hills. She had no doubt of that. Somewhere Skull and Hugh Clagg, and all those people who hated Owen Merritt for what he was, would be hunting. This was the second day and they were still distant. But they would come closer.

She led the pony into the canyon at the end of an hour or so, fearing to leave Owen longer. The small fire had died to the smallest glow on the rocky floor. Owen's breathing, when she crept beside him, was definitely heavier and the heat of his body came through his clothes. Lying there, she murmured: "Owen, how do you feel?" and got no answer. He kept turning on his shoulder blades. He threw out his arm unexpectedly and caught her across the mouth. She put her head down against him, clenching her teeth together to keep from crying, tasting blood. She could not help him and for the first time she let the fear latent in her heart have its way. What if he died? That night she passed without sleep, always beside him, always reaching out to replace the blankets he kept threshing aside.

By daylight he was deep-caught by the infection in his blood. She mixed condensed milk in a cup of water but could not get him to drink it. In the middle of the afternoon she heard the tag end of a gunshot echoing in the canyon, and crouched back in the tunnel, holding the restless pony by its rope and listening for another shot. But that was all. That dusk, with Owen lying motionless on the quilts, she did not dare take the pony up to feed, and made a double hitch around the rock for fear of losing him. She had no appetite. Her bones ached and odd thoughts, born of this lonely waiting, began to come to her. She remembered a dance long ago, herself sitting in a corner of the hall watching Sally go by with Owen Merritt — a tall girl, made beautiful by strong pride and turned gay that night because of Merritt's presence.

Lying beside Merritt again, acutely aware of the motionlessness of his body, she felt strong anger rise. All this had happened to Owen because of Sally Isham; all this. Yet Sally was still in the big man's heart, whether he knew it or not — and he was in Sally's heart. It didn't matter that Sally was married. Nothing mattered. Those two people would never change. She reached out and laid her hand on Merritt, catching the heavy beat of his heart. She had then her small moment of possession, realizing that this was all she would ever have. And she spoke through the blanketing dark — knowing Owen wouldn't hear: "I'm close to you now, my dear. As close as I'll ever get." Somewhere in the filmy grayness preceding daylight she fell asleep. When she woke it was full day. Merritt's arm lay over her and part of the blanket covered her, and for a moment she didn't move, fearing to wake him. Then she heard him say: —

"I've been watching you sleep. You've got your fist tucked up against your mouth, like a little kid."

Astonished by the clearness of his words, she lifted herself around. Whiskers blackened his jaws and his lips were cracked and the hollows of his cheeks were distinct. But his eyes were free from the cloud that had been in them and he was smiling. She knelt over him and put a hand against his neck. The fever had gone out of him.

He said: "Not much energy. But I could eat. What day is this?"

The blackness of the past hours faded and she didn't know until this moment how great the strain had been, for she felt suddenly lightheaded and irresponsible. Never thinking, she bent down and kissed him. When she drew back she watched his smile fade. For a moment they were watching each other with the deepest, completest soberness. Then she got up, trying to make her voice even. "Never mind, Owen. It was an accident — and I guess we're entitled to one accident."

XIV

AT THE CANYON'S BOTTOM

Nan built up a fire and fed Merritt a piece of bread and a cup of calico tea. He was tremendously hungry but she held him off an hour or more before letting him eat again. Meanwhile she took a piece of the torn sheet she had brought along and washed his face; and tried to re-adjust the quilts beneath him. He was extremely cheerful even though he kept shifting his shoulders on the hard flooring of the tunnel. His glance followed her as she moved about and some pleasant thought in his mind kept him smiling. After a noon meal made from the very meager supplies he fell into another sound sleep.

Relief let her down. It turned her tired and a little irritable. She had been very conscious of his eyes and for the first time in three days she was aware of her own appearance and felt ashamed. She had brought along neither soap nor comb and the ice-cold water of the creek didn't help much. Using the calm edge of the creek as a mirror she made some effort to rearrange her hair, but the blurred image she received back from it almost made her cry. In this depressed half-stormy mood he found her when he woke.

He said: "What's the matter?"

"I'm the world's ugliest woman. My face and hands are plain dirty. I didn't bring any soap. My hair — "

He was smiling again, which aroused her rebellious protest. "What's funny about it, Owen? You needn't make me feel any worse. Don't look at me so closely."

"When a woman gets to thinking about her looks I guess old times are back. What you need is some sleep. I know. It's been kind of tough on you to sit around here."

"What I need is a bath."

He said: "There's the creek. Speaking of looks, I must be a pretty poor copy of God's handiwork." His fingers scrubbed the metal edge of his whiskers. "Sounds like a coyote going through dry brush. Dam' things itch like sin. Never was able to figure how some fellows could endure wearing beards. I remember something from yesterday afternoon. A fly walked across my chin, on top of the whiskers. It felt like he was on stilts. He'd get himself on one whisker, then he'd move over to another one, all this time workin' toward my nose. Well, it was one way of keeping interested. I got to wondering if he'd break his neck when he fell off. That's a little better, Nan. I like to see you smile."

Her smile came, and soon went away. Her eyes then were very dark. "Is that all you thought about, Owen?"

"No." He read something in her glance that brought up a question. "What made you ask me if I wanted to see Sally? It was a queer idea."

"Was it? Was it such a queer idea?"

"Damned queer," he grumbled.

Something got between them, destroying the moment of ease and cheerfulness. She turned out of the tunnel.

He watched her go with a puzzled, heavy expression in his eyes. That evening she took the pony up for graze and remained away two hours. The fire was out when she returned and a coldness, damp and clinging, lay in the bottom of the canyon. She thought Merritt had fallen asleep, but his voice came through the black, unexpected enough to startle her. "You were a little long."

"He was pretty hungry."

That was all. Something had left them, so suddenly, so completely. She tied the pony and went to the creek's edge, watching the rim of the canyon pencil its charcoal line against the paler velvet of the sky. This night the roar of the falls in the lower reaches of the canyon seemed louder than before; and the loneliness and uncertainty was greater than before. What, she wondered, had so suddenly happened to her feelings? She had never been so downhearted. So she stood there, with the chill coming through her clothes, constraint holding her away from the tunnel. Quite a while later Merritt's voice came to her.

"I know. But it's too cold for you there, Nan."

She went in. Lying beside him, sharing the blankets and grateful for the added warmth of his body, she felt almost afraid to stir. It was an odd emotion, after all that had happened. It was a reaction from an intimacy that had been. Some sense of desperateness had pulled them together and his weakness had made her strong. Now that was gone and she felt almost ashamed. More than this, she remembered how irritable the mention of

Sally's name had made him and to her it was as though he had been touched in a sore spot that would not heal. This was the way it would be, always, between Merritt and Sally Isham. She thought: "It would be better if those two left everything else and went away together. Isham doesn't matter to Sally. And I don't matter to Owen. If I were Sally I'd be hunting these hills for him and I'd find him." Then she thought of the scraps of food left in the sack, and of Skull's men ranging these hills, and of Hugh Clagg, and a little tremor, both of cold and of fear, shook her body. Merritt's hand came over and dropped on her shoulder. She lay wholly still for a moment, touched by another kind of fear — of him and of herself. After a while she moved her shoulder. He pulled his hand immediately away. She didn't know when she fell asleep.

The next day she took stock of the food supply and knew they would soon be hungry. He said nothing but she noticed the way he checked himself when he ate; and she noticed, too, a restlessness growing on him. He would be thinking, she understood, of the danger hanging over them, and of his own temporary inability to help. That afternoon she slipped down the canyon a few yards and took a quick swim in the creek, and came back with her teeth chattering. But it made her much more cheerful, it restored her courage; and for a time she forgot the reserve between them. She built a small fire and sat beside him. And then, out of the long distance, came the fading roll of a gunshot. Owen stared up at the tunnel's wall, absorbing the sound and its meaning. "First one," he murmured.

"Second. I heard a gun two days ago."

He put his hands behind him and pushed to a sitting position. His revolver was at the edge of the blankets. He pulled it nearer. He said: "They'll get around this way. Sooner or later. How much have we got to eat, Nan?"

"A piece of bacon, so big." She used her hands to show him. "And some coffee. Are you getting tired of bacon?"

"Think I better try this leg tomorrow."

"For eating or for walking, Owen? If you want to eat it, all right. But you won't walk on it tomorrow."

His grin came back. "You're a help. I don't know of a better partner."

"Pretty sure of that?"

He said: "Pretty sure." He dropped on the blanket and put a hand over his eyes, not speaking. After a while she said: "What are you thinking about now, Owen?"

"You. The Piute knows you're up here with me."

She sat cross-legged near him. Light struck into the tunnel, brightening the outline of her face but leaving her features a little shadowed. He could not read her expression. Her hair was a brilliant black; it made a clean line at the edge of her temples, turning that skin whiter by contrast. Her shoulders, sitting as she was, were rounded toward him. He watched the way her thoughts kept alternately softening and firming her lips.

"I wouldn't worry about it, Owen. If you are thinking of my job at the school — don't. When we get out of this I'm going out to Linkville. I know people there. I can get another school."

He lay wholly still. He was thinking over her talk. She knew that. She couldn't have analyzed the source of her knowledge, but she knew it nevertheless. They had been as close together these few days as a man and woman could get and she knew his mannerisms and his silences — and the way his thoughts shadowed themselves on his heavy features. Presently she added: "Don't worry about it, Owen."

"If you know where you want to go, why don't you go now?"

Her shoulders lifted back from him until they were square. "Do you want me to go now?"

"No."

"Then," she said, half-angered and half-relieved, "why did you say that?"

"This is a hell of a place for you to be."

She bent nearer him, her lips touched by small sweet humor. "I never had a man to boss, Owen. I'm getting my practice on you. Here I am, and here I stay till you walk out under your own power." She let that sink in, later adding in a softer way: "Then I'll go, Owen."

He answered that by turning partially on his side. The expression in his eyes made her pull away and rise from him. He said: "Nan — " But she interrupted at once, not wanting to hear. For suddenly she was afraid to hear what he had in his head. Afraid that it might be something she wanted to hear — afraid that it might be something that would leave its hurt. From this man she wanted no sympathy and no gratitude. He was in love with Sally Isham and he had to be free. She didn't want him to be bound by anything she had done. If he felt that way and said something, out of that feeling, she knew it would cut her too hard.

"Never mind. Have you a knife?"

He grumbled, "Never mind what? How do you know what I'm going to say?" He found the knife in his pocket and handed it to her. "Never mind what?"

She turned to the horse, untying it; and took up the rifle. The pony, impatient to be out of the tunnel, dragged back on the rope.

He said: "It's a little early for that, Nan."

"I'll stay under the rim till dark. I want to look around."

But when she reached the top of the canyon trail she stopped only long enough to run a careful glance along the broken horizon of this empty country. There was a chance here she had to take and, seeing nothing to alarm her, she took it. She went into the saddle and galloped over the flat space toward a short-sided butte near by. Under its lee, with the late shadows of day crowding the sky, she let the pony graze a little while. There was a wind out of the southwest, and in that direction, on the higher slopes, a round green stain lay against the shoul-

der of a ridge, indicating water. The distance was a mile
or better and the light had started its quick dissolution
into darkness, but she saw the faint stir of antelope over
there, and put her horse into motion.

The wind was against her, which helped. Rising out
of the shelter of the butte, she made a target for any man
lying behind the roundabout crests of this tangled country. That, she knew, was a real danger, and all that kept
her going was the need of food. In a small hollow, less
than a quarter-mile from the antelope, she left the horse
to stand against its dropped reins, flattened on her stomach and began crawling in against the game. It was a
two-way race, the light fading as she got nearer. A hundred yards off, some stray sound in the dusk lifted the
antelope's head. It remained poised and beautiful
against the pale sky for a moment, and slid into a bound-
ing run.

Nan let the gun lie on the powdery ground and hit her
doubled fist against it, crying under her breath: "Damn
you, come back!" Cold came out of the earth and pene-
trated her body; cold came with the wind, striking
sharply against her face. Darkness dropped from the
sky in sudden layers until there was left only one narrow
crack of light in the west. Little flakes of soil, lifted by
the wind, hit her face. She lay still, hardening herself
against disappointment, thinking: "The wind's this
way. If he smelled something, it would send him up-
wind, toward me." She saw nothing, though.

Somewhere in the distance a shot sounded. And somewhere in the night other antelope, touched off by the echo, drummed the earth. This, she estimated, was to her left, on still higher ground. She rose and followed the slope upward. A quarter-mile of such traveling lifted her another five hundred feet above the world and from this vantage point, turning slowly to catch any sight or sound, she discovered a campfire's light burning its round orange hole through the dark. The fire lay in a gulch to the lower left. Watching it closely, she saw one man rise and step back from the light — and reappear again.

She went that way immediately. It would be Hugh Clagg, or Skull. Or it might be Bourke Prine. She had to know. Drifting down the steady slope she watched men come against the fire and settle before it, and presently discovered they were eating supper. But she was a good half-hour getting near enough — coming at last to the edge of the ridge itself — to identify Dutcher and some of Dutcher's men. She turned back at once, traveling faster. Once she had to stop and orient herself in the night's wind-raveled emptiness. A moon lay tipped on one thin-silver horn; far off, five miles away by crow-flight at least, she picked up the flash of Tom Watman's cabin light — the nearest habitation in the hills. Up in the southern heights a gun sounded again. Nan went downgrade toward her horse, guided by the angling shadow of a butte. Somewhere antelope scudded with the wind again, nearer at hand. A rock caught her shoe and sent her to her hands and knees; and not until then, openly crying from the hurt of the fall, did she realize that four days of thin diet had made her weak. She felt along the earth for her rifle and stood up, shaken enough to keep her place momentarily; and in this position, her vision blurred by tears, she saw a high-shouldered shape drift toward her.

She didn't, at the exact moment, have her gun turned that way. Not wholly sure of the substance behind this shadow, she made a slow pivot and brought the Winchester around with a painful caution. The shadow had stopped and, for Nan, the world also stopped. Gun raised, she waited to hear some sound of identity cross the fifty-foot distance. When it came, an antelope's quick blast of breath, she let go with her shot and heard its impact. She was running ahead even before she knew the result — seeing the shadow vanish. She couldn't hear anything, so noisy was the racket of her own boots against the rocky ground; and so she almost tripped on the fallen animal. It wasn't quite dead. When she touched it the antelope half-lifted itself and rammed a smooth head against her — and fell back.

She remembered the shot in the distance and she remembered the campfire below her, and was spurred to a sudden haste, reaching for the knife she had taken from Merritt. She cut straight into a hindquarter, slashing through hide and flesh and down to the tendons; and drew the knife deep through the meat, butchering it off the bone. She was happy enough to sing and only for a moment stopped to realize that the rest of the carcass might make a story for somebody else to read. This was something she could not help and so, carrying gun and meat, she hurried along the descending side of the butte. The pony had drifted toward the open flat in its grazing, giving her a moment of alarm. When she came up it caught the scent of game and fiddled around in the black. Nan said: "Stop that — stop it, or I'll brain you!" Swinging into the saddle she lined out for the canyon.

She had been gone far longer than at any other time, and knew Owen would be worried. But she had the meat to show for the delay and came up the creek with a tremendous happiness, like a child bringing back a prize. It was pitch-black at the tunnel. She dropped out of the saddle, instantly bringing Merritt's voice to her. "Good Lord, where have you been! There was a shot — then another one farther away — and then another pretty close. You've been gone two hours. Here I am down here, sweatin' blood and not able to do a damned thing not knowing. What was I to figure? Don't do that again, Nan. What held you up?"

He let it out with a cranky violence that astonished her. In his voice was an open possessiveness she had not heard before. She stepped toward the mouth of the tunnel and saw his shape vaguely placed against the lesser black. He had risen and had propped himself against the canyon wall. Nothing but the strongest kind of feeling could have caused him to make that painful effort.

She said in a small, breathless voice: "I'm sorry,

Owen. I knew I'd be late. But I shot an antelope. We had to have meat."

His wind ran out in long relief. His hand reached for her and caught her, dragging her forward. She dropped the meat, not caring at the moment what happened. For he had his arms around her, his temper thoroughly arousing him. "Nan," he said. "You gave me a hell of a wait."

Shocked and clear-headed, she realized then how deeply she had gotten into his feelings. His voice told her and the pressure of his arms told her. It wasn't, she reminded herself, love. It was something else. He was a man, lonely and discouraged, and she was a woman who happened to be near him at the moment. He had his decency and his distinct chivalry, but still he was a man — and her nearness to him these days had worn his restraint thin. It had taken him off guard.

She knew all this as she stood there, waiting for him to do whatever he meant to do. He was on the near edge of rashness; he was struggling with his impulses and any gesture on her part would sway him. So, because she knew that she would never have any more of him than she had now and that soon enough she would have nothing of him at all, she was influenced by a sweet and headlong sense of rebellion. She lifted her arms to his shoulders and tipped her face so that, dark as it was, he might see its nearness. This was the way any woman could stir a man, and it was enough for him. She knew it was a trick and yet she didn't care. Whatever doubts he had, this ended them. He pulled her against him and she took his kiss and gave it back willingly and unreservedly, and felt no regrets.

Higher in the Broken Buttes, Hugh Clagg made his supper over a fire's thin flame and rolled his blankets around him. Listening to the murmurs of the dark, placing and identifying them with a practised ear, he watched the pale black of the star-crusted sky and felt the actual rhythm of the earth beneath him. This was the fourth day, but to time's passage he paid no heed. All his grown years he had traveled these hills as a hunter, with a hunter's acuteness and patience, and a hunter's abiding satisfaction in the game itself; and this, to him, was the best kind of a hunt.

Riding the crest of the ridges all the next day, working the land with a systematic thoroughness, he saw the pattern of hoofprints, now singly and now in pairs, disturb the rock-scattered ground. Occasionally he followed these tracks until they circled into other tracks and went off on different tangents. This would be Skull; and then, remembering Isham, Hugh Clagg would grin at the empty world. Halted on butte-tops, he swept the endless rise and fall of this sundered country, infrequently viewing a handful of cattle in some two-bit rancher's isolated hollow, sometimes studying the circling wheel of distant buzzards, sometimes watching far-off dust spirals. Late in the afternoon he mounted a ridge and saw a file of men riding the yellow surface of East Desert. He kept his eye on them until they faded into a draw at the foot of the Broken Buttes.

Skull's method, he thought, with some contempt, was like a rabbit drive. This was the way Dutcher worked, it was the way Dutcher's mind ran — to just keep beating away flat-footedly until something happened. At dusk, Hugh Clagg came over a flinty ridge and found the glow of Skull's fire directly below him. Men and horses were scattered around it and in this clear desert stillness he made out the heavy pitched roll of Fay Dutcher's voice. In Hugh Clagg was a malice never far below the surface. It guided his actions always — and prompted him now to haul his rifle from its boot and take aim on the red heart of the fire. He waited until he had a clear aim, and let go, seeing the bullet break that even color into white-yellow streaks. A man down there shouted and the horses began to mill, which was warning enough for Clagg to be on his way. Hustling back over the ridge he fell into a canyon, followed it, rose from it — and struck deeper into the hills again. Diverted by the episode, hugely pleased by it, he holed up and made a dry camp.

Next afternoon, questing nearer and nearer the rim of Rock Creek's canyon, he saw buzzards wheeling and settling in a near-by pocket — thick enough to mean business. This drew him on, and so he discovered the remains of the antelope Nan had shot two days before. The coyotes and the buzzards had picked it fairly clean, but he noticed the bullet hole in the side. Skull, he knew, wouldn't have wasted so much meat; so it was somebody who had been in a hurry. Looking down the incline of the hills he noticed the road cutting into the canyon.

He had his clear hint then. It took him off the high ground and across the flat at a deliberate canter, as though nothing in the world pressed him. At the rim he observed the white water at the bottom with a good deal of care. A series of tracks showed on the trail, going both ways. As far as he could make out there wasn't much chance here for a hideout, no break being visible in the canyon. Pretty sure that he was on safe ground, he took the trail to the bottom. A feeling troubled him — the exact feeling of a man who, having followed a fruitless trail for many days, at last comes upon the trail of game. It was a faint stir of excitement, a conviction that came to him without evidence. After his pony drank he climbed back to the rim and swept the near-by pockets with a closer attention. "Around here," he said to himself, "they shot that doe, and they been down here for water. Not far away."

The feeling got stronger and he was at once keenly aware of the high rims standing around him. Merritt was a fighter and, unless badly hurt, would be watching him now. What he had to do was get back to the high ground, wherefrom he could sweep the lower pockets and hidden angles of the joining buttes with a more thorough eye. Crossing the flat he aimed for the highest single knob in the district and reached it late in the day.

He saw nothing, and moved to another knob, and repeated his search; and at dusk, having made a semicircular trip of ten miles or more, he came down from the heights again. His horse was weary and he himself felt the need of a meal. Tom Watman's cabin was six miles north; that way he turned.

He wasn't satisfied. Something in his mind nagged at him, telling him he had missed a point in the chase; and presently, drifting along the very rim of the canyon, he stopped to search his head for some fact he had picked up and forgotten, for some casual thing the day had revealed to him but which he had overlooked. He went over his trail carefully, his head ducked down, still urged by an inner voice that wouldn't let him alone. They were, he told himself, not far away.

Paused in this manner, he saw a pulse of light at the very bottom of the canyon, a reflected glow glinting on the surface of the creek and wavering on the rocks. There was no direct sight of the light's source, though, at once dismounting from the horse, he lay flat on the rim and hung his head into the canyon and tried to find that source. Somewhere below was a recess. A fire burned in the recess.

He was back on the horse at once, aiming for the canyon road. He pulled to a walk, going carefully down; he left his horse here on dropped reins, himself taking to the water. A bend in the canyon shut off the glow but wind came against him and in the wind was the smell of smoke. Excitement unsteadied Clagg. It deepened his breathing and arched his chest, it was a chill along his nerves. A sound, short and explosive and remotely like laughter, came out of him and then he was the hunter closing on his game, thoroughly alert. He went to his knees in the middle of the creek, wading its middle. A few feet onward the deepening channel forced him over to its farther wall. The water quickened and his feet slid on the stones and he fell flat, face under the surface. He came up with his mouth wide and the breath shocked out of him; and he was grinning as he turned the bend. He laid a hand against the wall, steadying himself. A fire burned on the edge of the creek, glittering yellowly against these adhesive shadows. He saw Nan behind the fire, on her knees and holding a pan. Her face, shining from the light, was sober and absorbed and her shoulders were rounded. There was a kind of recession or tunnel back of her, all black, and the shape of a horse standing there. He couldn't see Merritt, but he knew the big man was in that darkness.

For a long moment he watched every gesture Nan made and every change of expression on her face, as though he needed to know what was in her mind — what memories of these four days she was remembering now and what thoughts were hidden by the smooth composure of her features. She was a woman beyond a man's reading. She was unchangeable. In the schoolroom at the base of the Buttes, or here in this hideout, she remained the same, her character accepting either fortune. It was a calmness and a resolution; it was something better than that — it was a realism that no kind of luck could disturb. He could not name the things that shone out of her, but he felt them as a man might feel the vague edge of a glory that, sought for during all his years, at last brushed him closely and passed him by. Here was a woman.

He had, for the moment, forgotten the icy bite of the water, he had forgotten that he stood here at the end of his hunt. Then she lifted the pan from the fire and turned and said, "Owen, come and eat." Her voice had its gentleness, its little melody of possession when she spoke the big man's name; and that was the thing which roused Hugh Clagg. He lifted his gun, balancing the heavy butt in his palm; and framed the front sight against the light of the fire. A shadow materialized slowly in the tunnel and came forward. Merritt, distinctly favoring one leg, walked up to the fire.

XV

MADNESS COMES TO A MAN

THAT afternoon Merritt had risen and put weight on his leg and walked with it while Nan watched him. There was a weakness in those muscles and a puckering of formed scar tissue; and the bandage bothered him. "Otherwise," he said, "I guess we can pay our rent here and leave. Where's the landlady? I'd like to make a complaint about the bedsprings."

She had been afraid to bother the bandage. Now she said, "Let's fix that."

The padding from her mattress had soaked up a good deal of blood. It was a hard, crusted lump and had to be cut back, layer by layer. The last thickness was held to the skin and would not come off, short of pealing fresh tissue with it. She put a light bandage back on and let it go like that. "You're a hard man to kill, Owen."

She was quick to note how cheerful it made him. He was a man who needed physical action to keep his temper fresh; he needed to feel the pull of his muscles and to sweat. Confinement of any kind did something to him. He walked a circle around the tunnel, grinning now and then; and went to the edge of the creek. Standing there, building up a cigarette, he ran the overhead rim with a quick glance. He dragged the smoke into his lungs and expelled it with an audible relish. Restlessness swayed him. He kept scraping his fingers through the heavy growth of whiskers; he kept watching the sky, and his thoughts pulled his lids half together.

Nan observed this with a mixture of relief and regret. She knew now, from the sudden let-down, how insistent the strain had been. He had been helpless and her strength had been the only strength. For those few days she had possessed Owen, she had thought for him and worked for him and her will had been his will. It was a growing memory that had for her its warmth and glow. They had lived with a closeness, even their silences joining. Now he was pulling away. His mind was tracking out across the flats, alone. He had his own strength and his own will. She could look back to what had been. But, looking forward, she saw no place for her in his plans. This — all this — went through her head while she watched him. He was feeling his freedom. His pride came back and his old flash of temper, a little gay and ironic, came back. He kept pulling his shoulders into place as though the feeling pleased him. He was very tall and his fingers were long and heavy. The crop of whiskers toughened his expression.

"So," he murmured, "I guess this is about all of this." He turned then and looked at her. She didn't know she showed him any particular expression, but she noticed how quickly he quit smiling. The shadows were beginning to pile up in the canyon again. Wind strengthened and the roar of the lower falls increased.

She hadn't meant to ask him. She had meant to let

him alone. But the question slipped out. "What are you going to do, Owen?"

"Tom Watman's the nearest," he said. "I'm going down there after dark and steal his horse and saddle."

He moved around, deliberately putting the weight of his body against the leg. He was impatient with its weakness, he was forcing it to work for him. They stood face to face and she thought she saw an expression in his eyes like constraint — as though he couldn't get around his own memories of these few days, yet wanted to. As though that past had nothing to do with the future and was in the way of his thinking. He shook his shoulders together. "I've got an idea Skull's getting nearer. Ought to be."

"Or Hugh Clagg."

The name brought his attention to her. He watched her awhile, then said: "Well, the man hates me. But what would he be wanting to find me for?"

"Me," she said, gently.

As before, her talk went into him and produced its quick effect. The line of his jaw changed, his lips rolled together, stubborn and dissenting. He had a manner of weighing her words and did so now. And said: "I should have thought of that. I've made a lot of things worse for you, Nan. I know it. A man's a poor animal to say the things he ought to say. These days here — "

Fear made her break in — a fear of what he might say, of what he might not say. "Where will you go, then?"

He showed her a puzzled glance. "We'll go farther back in the buttes."

"Then what?" she insisted. "What comes after that, for you? Do you know, Owen?"

He reached for tobacco, keeping his eyes on his moving fingers as he shaped up a smoke. "That's as far as we run."

"Then you'll fight again."

"What else?"

She chose her words carefully. "It will be very hard, Owen. What's left? You can't go to your ranch. Wherever you show yourself, in the hills or on the Piute or in town — there'll be Skull, waiting. Do you think they'll give you any chance? They won't. There won't ever be a day in your life that somebody won't be waiting to kill you."

He repeated his question: "What else?"

"You could leave the country," she said. "Isham wants the Bunchgrass Hills, and he's the kind of a man who won't turn. He's small and soft and people guess wrong about him. Remember, he's got a little man's vanity. He hates anything bigger than he is. He won't rest until he's biggest of all. If you went out of the Piute you'd be through with it. There's plenty of land left, Owen. Beyond East Desert, or down in Nevada."

The shadows came down and the thwarted roar of the lower falls strengthened. She moved away from him and split the remnant of wagon wood and made a fire. She filled the coffeepot and sliced the last of the venison into the frying pan. Her face by the firelight was, he thought, serene and untouched, as though nothing had ever happened. This was the way she kept herself away from a man. She made the most of whatever came along. She didn't ask for anything.

He said: "That's the way I figured it out once. I shot up the line cabin on Corral Flats and hit the timber — and that's what I meant to do, just run and shoot and run until I got pushed out of the country or until Isham got tired. Then I changed my mind and came back to the house. Maybe it was a mistake, but I guess I'll have to stick. Trouble with running is that it gets to be a habit. Run from one thing and you'll run from another. It's a poor way to live. If a man gets to be afraid of dying, he'll die a thousand times. Life ain't that valuable to anybody. You want me to run?"

She turned from the fire, looking up to him, straight and still. "No. I want you to stay."

He didn't get it. "Sometimes, Nan, you fool a man."

She turned back, moving the frying pan over the fire. He heard her say: "I had to know what you were thinking, Owen. Come and eat."

He stepped from the tunnel and stood within the fire's round cone of light, watching the black shine of her hair and the way her white arms moved. It pulled at him, it got under his skin and he said, very rough with his talk: "What's better than this? Maybe for a minute or an hour or a week a man gets something that makes the next thirty years look flat. Nobody ever gets very much.

We take what comes — when it comes — and we make it do. There's a lot of riding and a lot of crying, but this is the thing that makes up for it."

Suddenly she dropped the frying pan and stood up, turning toward him with a swift gesture. "Owen," she said, "that's what I believe. I — "

A voice said then, level and smoothly amused, "Merritt, stay there."

Merritt threw his shoulders around hard enough to send a long sliver of pain along his bad leg and faced the mealy grayness of the canyon. A man's weight ground against gravel and disturbed the flow of the creek. Hugh Clagg, carefully stepping through the current, appeared before them, sliding into the firelight's area.

Adrip with water, he stood in the middle of the creek. Light yellowed his face and threw its brightness into the rounds of his eyes. It glittered on the dark metal of the risen gun; it hollowed out the emptiness of the muzzle. Clagg was smiling, and this smile was as fixed on them both impartially, as false and as bitter, as anything a man's lips could contrive. Merritt, who knew the man well, had no illusions concerning that expression. Clagg had his own kind of madness and this was its signal.

The smell of scorched meat came to them, whereupon the girl slowly ducked and pulled the frying pan out of the fire. She held the pan by its handle, so alive to Clagg's presence that she scarcely realized what she had done. But Clagg kept his glance carefully on her. "I'd put nothing past you, Nan," he said. "Nothing. A man never knows what's in your head. You'd like to kill me now. If you got the chance I believe you would." The water kept boiling around his feet, bothering him. He said, "Move back," and watched them give ground, himself coming on until he stepped on the dry ledge. It brought him close to the fire and it brought him against the tunnel's nearest wall, and close to the horse. There was little room. He turned sidewise, feeling the heat of the fire on his legs. Merritt and Nan were six feet back in the tunnel, almost beyond the reach of the fire's light.

Clagg said: "Where's your gun, Owen?"

Merritt lifted and lowered a hand, carrying his cigarette down from his mouth. He said, "Under the blankets."

"You get it, Nan," ordered Clagg.

She turned behind Merritt at once. She had bent, almost lost to his sight, when Clagg said, very abrupt: "Never mind. Come back." Nan straightened, standing motionless behind Merritt. "Never mind the gun. Get out of there," warned Clagg. "I know what you're thinkin'. But you'll get friend Owen shot for it. Move out."

Merritt lifted his arm, replacing the cigarette. He laid his talk against Clagg. "What the hell's eating you? Make up your mind. Don't move, Nan."

"Come on — come on," grunted Clagg. He waggled the point of the gun, up and down. Wind blew the fire's smoke into the tunnel, thickening its shadows. When Nan stepped forward, near enough Clagg to touch him, she partially blocked his view of Merritt who remained in the vague shadows, in the drifting smoke of the fire. Merritt swayed backward; and this brought its instant challenge from Clagg. "Cut that out. Get your foot off the blanket. You come this way, too."

Merritt moved forward. He came against Nan's shoulder-point. He pushed her gently around, against the tunnel wall. Clagg said, at once, "What's that for?" The stretch of Merritt's arm lay between; and he could see the shadow of doubt run across Clagg's face. This was the way they were — cramped together and silent and influenced by their changing thoughts. Clagg's eyes kept passing from Nan to Owen; his lips settled and ruddy color ran along his skin. He shook his head as though all his thoughts came to nothing more than confusion and bitterness. That was the way these three stood — the silence riding them. Hugh Clagg nodded and his resentment, so consistent and unvarying, began to shake him like an exciting drug.

"Merritt," he said, in a rising voice, "you get everything your way. You could get Sally Isham by liftin' your finger. You stumbled into Nan's cabin and she just threw away her reputation and followed. A man like you . . ." He waggled the gun in time with his incoherent speech. "What's the difference between you and me? I'd tear down the damned hills for a kind word from this girl — but I'd never get it, not in a thousand years. Listen. This girl told me she couldn't like a man that was crooked. I believed it. I used to ride the Piute, watchin' her light and thinkin' she was a thousand miles above me. I know better. Even if I was honest, she wouldn't give me a look. And if you were as crooked as hell she'd still drop everything and follow you. That's a woman. Nan, you'd lie for this man and you'd cheat and you'd do just what he wanted, if he said so."

"Pull up, Hugh," murmured Owen Merritt. "Pull up."

"No, I'm right. Both you people are fooling yourselves. I know. Well, there's a way to end it. This time I'm the honest man, Merritt, and you're the crook. I'm going to put an end to it." He was pale with what he thought and what he felt. He was a tall, narrow block against the canyon's blackness. He had set himself, he had whipped himself up to what he wanted to do. Merritt recognized that fact.

Merritt lifted his arm and pulled the cigarette from his mouth. He held the cigarette between his fingers just below his face. The smoke of it touched both of them, so close they were. The creek ran its restless, clattering way behind them, with Hugh Clagg's boot heels barely missing the edge of the creek. One backward step would drop him twelve inches into the water.

All this interval Nan had not moved. She held the frying pan, she watched Hugh Clagg's anger shake him; and now she turned her glance on Merritt and observed him pull the cigarette away from his lips and hold his arm on a level with Hugh Clagg's chest. For a long moment she considered this. There were things about Owen that gave him away to her quietly observant eyes;

other people would never see them because other people would never have the deep-lying interest in him that so habitually governed her. His lip corners showed an increase of pressure and he had stopped moving — he was thoroughly still. And so she knew what was in his head.

She turned her shoulders rather quickly and looked at the frying pan and its blackened meat. From the corner of her eyes she saw Clagg's attention swing. She made a half-swing with her body, suddenly lifted the pan and threw it into the creek. All at one motion, with her arm grazing Clagg's shoulder.

This was when Merritt's arm slid beneath the outstretched gun and knocked it upward and away from them both. He hit Clagg's chest with his shoulder, he hit Clagg's crotch with a drive of his knee. Clagg, wheeling backward, went off the foot-high ledge, and fell full-length into the water.

Merritt was on top of him, the weight of his body pressing Clagg completely under. Merritt dropped a forearm across Clagg's windpipe and moved his other arm around the dark until it struck the gun. He got the gun free and brought it down toward Clagg's head and missed; and then Clagg fought up out of the water, his wind strangling in his lungs, and capsized Merritt by a frantic roll of his body.

It was black here, beyond the fire's light, and the cold current ran completely over Merritt. He was on his bad leg and, trying to shift and rise, he lost Clagg's gun.

Clagg, still knee-deep in the creek, reached for him and then the two of them were floundering around the creek, slipping on the rocks and being swayed by the current. Clagg reached him with a wild swing and knocked him deeper into the stream. Merritt braced himself against a tall niggerhead and got up. Clagg at this moment was framed against the firelight. He had turned his back to Merritt and was wading toward the tunnel.

Merritt pushed through the water and caught the end of Clagg's coat. The man slipped and went down and Merritt jumped on him and also went down. He kicked Clagg away from him and got up and reached the ledge. From the rear of the tunnel Nan cried, "Here, Owen — here!" He couldn't turn toward her. Backed against a wall of the tunnel and momentarily sickened by the sudden fire in his bad leg, he watched Clagg rise from the water. Clagg came to his knees, shaking wetness out of his face. His mouth was open and wind sprung his chest and a scarlet film began to spread along one cheek. Merritt heard the grind of Clagg's feet on the creek's rocky bottom, he heard the man's great grunt of effort as he rose and threw himself dead in, head down and arms flung wide and forward.

Merritt hit him cleanly, bringing his fists up against the lowered face. He shook Clagg, he beat the man off his feet; he caught him on the temple with a slanting blow, and wheeled away. But his leg tricked him and his turn was too slow and Clagg, falling forward, got his

arms about Merritt's knees and brought him down on
the rock floor.

Both Merritt's elbows struck the rock. His bad leg,
twisted by Clagg's grip, took the force of the fall with all
its broken nerves as hot as pure flame. It turned his
stomach, it threw weakness through his muscles and he
lay there a moment, kicking out against Clagg's face
with his one good foot until Clagg rolled over and came
nearer. Clagg flattened on Merritt's chest and his
knuckles, sweeping the dark, cracked into Merritt's
nose; and again they were locked together in the dark,
wrestling and heaving and jamming against each other.

Merritt slid beneath Clagg, falling away on his side.
He rolled toward the creek and got on his feet and was
shocked at the effort he had to make. Clagg's shadow
reared before him and they stood, toe and toe, and
slugged it out. He reached Clagg with his punches. He
slammed into Clagg's chest, into Clagg's belly. There
was a howling in his head when Clagg knocked down his
arms and got him flush on the forehead, low between the
eyes. They were shadows in the cramped tunnel; they
fought in this blackness, the sound of their boots scraping the rock, the beat of their fists low and heavy and
flat. Merritt braced his feet against his own growing
weakness. The backs of his legs shook in steady spasms.
Feeling began to leave them and he kept leaning in as
he blocked Clagg's driving arms, knowing that if Clagg
threw him off balance he could not stand again. Clagg's

wind, like his own wind, came out in retching gasps, but he kept boring away with his silence as savage as any speech could be. Merritt's arms, slower and slower to respond, began to miss and began to drop. Clagg hit him twice, straight on the mouth. Merritt ducked his head, taking another punch there.

Nan cried, "Owen — stand aside!"

Clagg broke through Merritt's arms and slammed into him and carried him around. Merritt caught the man by the neck and pushed him into the horse. He was a dead weight that Clagg carried and tried to throw off. There was a vagueness in all this for Merritt. He could not reach deep enough, for air and a lightness got into his head, against which his will had no effect. Clagg slid behind the horse, against the tunnel wall, and Merritt kept pushing his forearm against Clagg's face, scraping the man's head and cheek along the rough surface of the wall. He let his weight hang on Clagg, at the same time beating Clagg's belly with a knee. Clagg kept swinging on toward the fire, turning to break the jolt of Merritt's knee. It threw his shoulder against Merritt who, feeling that shift, slipped his arm across Clagg's throat and made a lock with his other hand.

He was, then, riding Clagg's back and he felt the man's muscles bunch and shudder beneath the weight. Clagg carried him as far as the fire, and dropped to his knees; he swayed and, to catch his balance, plunged a hand into the fire.

His cry was a wild, shredding sound flung against the

racket of the creek and his tremendous muscular reaction carried him headlong into the stream. Merritt released his grip to save himself and rolled back on the tunnel floor, watching Clagg's head bob in and out of the water.

Nan called again, "Owen — " She came beside him, her arms pulling at his shoulders. The firelight was dim and dying and Clagg had gotten to his knees on the far edge of the light. Nan kept calling Merritt's name; it came through a kind of black hood, from a great distance. He put his good foot beneath him and hauled himself up. Clagg was fading back up the canyon. Merritt said: "Where's my gun?"

She had it for him. But she said, "No, Owen — no," when he stepped into the water. He threw a shot at the canyon and heard it echo and re-echo between the high walls. He hadn't hit anything. Clagg kept slashing along the creek toward the trail. Merritt slid uncertainly across the stony bottom, pushing at the near wall with his hand. He fired again and choked at the smoke drifting into his face; a pocket in the bed of gravel took him off his feet and the current turned him around until he lodged against a niggerhead. When he righted himself the splashing ahead of him had quit. He was at the edge of the trail, listening to Clagg's boots hit the dirt above him. He threw two shots at the sound; and sat down in the middle of the trail, so dead-beat that he could not hold his head straight. He let it drop, and was that way when Nan found him.

She dropped beside him. She pulled his shoulders forward, both her arms holding him against her breasts. "Owen — Owen!"

The wind was out of him. He had to wait for it. Every muscle in his body trembled. "I could kill that fellow."

"I know — I know."

"It's what he said. What he said about you. By God, I could kill him!"

"Owen, don't talk." She swayed a little. She was on her knees in the dust, her face very near. And then she added, silently to her honest self: "But he was right. I wouldn't care. It wouldn't matter what Owen was. Not to me." She felt the deep reach of his breathing; water dripped from his head onto her dress. Her finger tips slid across his face, touching the oily smoothness of blood. Clagg had reached the rim and had gone, the sound of his pony soon dying.

She didn't know just how long they remained like this, nor cared; but it must have been a long ten minutes later when a new sound broke through the clatter of the water, and looking up, she saw two or three shapes standing against the black sky, at the entrance of the rim road. A voice yonder began calling: "Merritt — Merritt!"

Hugh Clagg, beaten as badly as a man well could be, galloped straight east toward the Skull camp. On the ridge above it, he stopped and watched the fire a moment; and was careful this time to call down. A man stepped across the blaze and immediately challenged, whereupon Clagg descended the slope and rode into the light. There was only a part of the crew here — the rest no doubt being out on the trail. Dutcher came from the blackness; and Isham walked in. All these men stood across the fire, watching him in a way that left him no doubt as to his welcome.

Isham said: "What happened to you?"

The marks of the fight were engraved on Clagg. A long cut ran from the corner of one ear down to the edge of his jawbone, quite deep. Most of the skin on that side of his face had been scrubbed raw, which was where Merritt had shoved him against the wall of the tunnel. His lips were streaked with blood and swelling; one eye was puffed. He was soaked with creek water and his coat was torn down the back and a sleeve hung by a scant thread to the rest of the fabric.

He said: "You still looking for Merritt?"

Dutcher stepped half around the fire. "You bump into him?"

But Isham made a gesture with his hand, stopping Dutcher's talk. Isham kept watching Clagg. He said: "Where?"

"Just come with me."

"No," said Isham, "not that way. You had a little trouble. What was the trouble?"

"Then," said Clagg, "lend me a gun and I'll go back.

He's in Rock Canyon. Where the road goes down."

"You're sure?" said Isham, very quiet.

"Just lend me a gun," repeated Clagg.

Isham made one more gesture with his hand. Dutcher looked at Skull's owner for a moment, and all the other riders looked at him, not understanding. It came again and this time Dutcher stepped back from Clagg. There was a feeling around this fire hard to catch. Clagg pulled up his shoulders, not letting his eyes leave Isham. "What's that for?"

"Hugh," said Isham, very cool, "you're a free man with your tongue. As free with your tongue as with your rope. We read a few signs today. But never mind. Is Merritt alone?"

"No."

"A woman?"

"A woman," repeated Clagg and made one short step back.

Isham's little body cut its stiff shape against the yellow fire glow. There wasn't anything in his voice; there wasn't anything on his face. Yet Clagg had his growing fear and cursed himself for coming. Isham said, as smooth as before: "A woman. But maybe it's as you said to me the other time. It wouldn't be the woman I think it is, would it?" That was all. A dropping palm reached his gun and dragged it up. Clagg cried out: "I got no gun, Ish — " He threw his arms above his head; and that was the way he stood when Isham put two bullets through his chest. Clagg dropped without a sound.

Isham said, "We'll go down to the canyon. All right — all right."

XVI

PURSUIT AND BETRAYAL

AGAIN the voice came down from the rim: "Merritt —
hey, Merritt!"

Merritt pushed himself up, and stood with his shoulder against the rock wall which formed the road's inner
side. Nan put her hand on his arm, whispering: "Let's
go back!"

But Merritt at once shouted: "All right — come
down here, Bourke!"

Bourke Prine threw back a relieved and cheerful
halloo. Pay Lankershim's voice, holding an old man's
quick irritableness, dropped down: "Where in God's
name — " Horses stood momentarily silhouetted on the
rim, against the powder-black sky. Merritt counted four
of them. They filed into the canyon and came on sight-
lessly, and would have run past had not Merritt's voice
stopped them. "Wait, wait," he said.

There wasn't anything here but a blur. Voices struck
through the opaque shadows. Bourke Prine grumbled,
"Where the hell have you been?" His feet hit the rocky
trail; in a moment a match burst between his palms, the
light striking Merritt in the eyes like a fist blow. Pay
was here, and Cultus Charley. The fourth horse held nobody. Bourke Prine lifted the match nearer Nan and

even in this light his eyes showed surprise. "Why now," he said, "I didn't know — " The light burned into Bourke's fingers; he dropped it, swearing gently.

"You all right, Owen?"

"Sure — sure. How'd you get here?"

"Charley's been hangin' to Clagg's trail all day. He saw Clagg scout around here pretty steady. It looked like Clagg had stumbled into something. It was dark then, so Cultus ran back and found us — and here we are. Where's Clagg?"

"Didn't you see him?"

"Was that what we heard goin' off to the east like a bat out of hell? What was those shots for? Damnation, did we miss him that close? After roamin' around this country — "

Merritt said: "Cultus, you wade down this creek a little bit and you'll find a horse."

Cultus descended into the lower black. Pay Lanker-shim said: "Yeah — but whut made Hughie git along so fast?"

Nan broke in, "There was a fight. He ran from Owen."

"That's what the shots were," murmured Bourke. He scratched another match against his trousers and took a better look at Merritt. "It must have been a hell of a scrap. You hurt? Where you been for ten days?" The light again died. Bourke kept pumping impatient questions at Merritt, not satisfied by the silence. "Why didn't you meet us on the knob? We looked all over the country. What'd you go back to your place for? We

been all through the Bunchgrass Hills. We been eating
Broken Buttes gravel for a week."

Cultus Charley came back with Nan's horse. Merritt
said: "Let's get out of here."

They milled around the darkness until Nan spoke
with a touch of sharpness. "Bourke — give Owen a
hand."

"Well — what is it?"

"His leg."

Bourke came about Owen's horse. He put his arm
against Merritt; he rode Merritt up on his shoulder.
Merritt grunted when he hit the leather. All of them
hauled around and ascended the grade single file. Wind
strengthened from the south, pushing through Merritt's
wet clothes. His leg ached with a solid, slugging rhythm
and the taste of blood was still in his mouth. His arms
were heavy, as though the muscles had been beaten with
a club; the flesh around his knuckles began to hurt.
They paused on the rim only long enough for Merritt to
say, "We'll camp over in the northeast — up in one of
those short gulches."

Bourke rode beside him, but Merritt turned and
called "Nan — where are you?" and slowed down until
she came abreast. They put the flats behind and filed
up a canyon, crossing at its head into another cross-
canyon. An hour later, considerably higher, they stopped
in a convenient pocket and set out the ponies on picket.
Everybody rustled around to break up sagebrush for a
fire that sent its pale, clear point straight to the sky.

In this depression there was no wind, and the flame was well below the skyline. Owen crouched against the fire, soaking in its heat, facing Nan across the flame. The others were farther back, not saying anything just now. There was a continuing calmness on the girl's face and when she met his eyes he saw nothing there — nothing of that old feeling. It was as though she had put it aside, or had deliberately killed it. And so reticence hung between them. Her cheek showed a bruise.

He said at once: "How did you get that?"

She shook her head: "I don't remember, Owen. Sometime during the fight."

Pay, always a prowler and always suspecting trouble, climbed to the rim of the bowl to keep watch. Cultus came to the fire with a coffeepot and a frying pan; and a little later they had a piece of steak from some unlucky yearling, and coffee. All of them sat around the fire, with Nan drawn slightly away from the men. Bourke said: —

"Isham got most of the Skull crew in these hills. I saw his dust early this morning over east. We been cutting across his trails all week. He's covered the south half of this country with a dandruff comb."

"Clagg," said Pay Lankershim. "I wonder where that fellow is now?" He finished his meal and moved back to the rim of the bowl.

Bourke began to grin. "Pay went into Skull's home meadows and burned half their hay. Makes me feel better to think of it. Medary's left town on a vacation.

Isham, I found out, ain't been home but once since all this started. The little fellow is out to kill." An idea seemed to block the rest of his talk. He sat back from the fire, faintly rocking on his heels; and an expression, smooth and edged with scheming, showed on his cheeks. "Maybe," he murmured, "this would be just the right time for us to go down to Skull's main quarters and take it apart. Like they did to your place."

Owen only said, "No." It was a word that jumped at everybody, so instant and so round. They all looked at him with a moment's greater interest and presently Bourke's glance ran back to Nan, puzzled and very attentive. Then Bourke said, quite dry: "Why not, Owen? Anybody on the ranch you're afraid of?"

Merritt lifted his chin on Bourke and the two partners were watching each other with a long, unfriendly silence. Nan, observing this from her background position, knew they would be both thinking of Sally Isham. It was a common thought between them. She liked Bourke Prine, and yet at this moment she hated him for asking the question, for bringing out the thing she never wanted to hear. Owen said, quietly: "We'll stick around here, Bourke. No more dodging."

Pay said, from the top of the bowl, "Campfire down yonder by the canyon."

Nan rose from the group. She turned into the darkness and stopped to listen to the run of talk. It was all between these men; it held nothing for her.

Bourke said: "Then what, Owen?"

Nan waited for Merritt's answer. It came out slowly, it had a spareness and an unrelieved certainty. "We'll cross back to the Bunchgrass Hills in the morning. We'll do our fighting there."

Nan drifted on, took up the reins of her pony and stepped into the saddle. The leather squealed a little and Owen's head came about. He couldn't see her; he put his hands before him as if to rise. Nan said: "Owen — I'm going back to my place. So-long."

He called, "Wait a minute, Nan," and turned his body half-around to get his weight under his good leg. This was the way he lifted himself, breathing deeply from the effort, with his shoulders tipped over. "Nan!" he yelled. "Come back here!"

Her voice drifted in, gentle and even and softened by the distance. "So-long, Owen." Then she was over the rim of the bowl and her pony's traveling was lost to them.

Merritt said, as savage as any of these men had ever seen him: "Don't sit there, you dam' fools! Get after her! Turn her back here!"

None of them stirred. Bourke Prine's eyes were half-shut. Firelight made a frosty glint in them as he watched Merritt, sizing the big man up and suddenly understanding something that had been, until now, a puzzle to him. But he didn't move.

"What for?" he wanted to know.

Merritt started around the fire, each step jerking him sideways; each fall of his bad leg making him throw his shoulders forward. He didn't get out of the light. He quit trying and limped more slowly back to his place and dropped on his side, winded and angry and not looking at his partners. They kept entirely still.

At daybreak they broke camp and left the bowl, traveling up and down the heavy undulations of the country without hurry. The light was glass-clear and from the succeeding high points they had complete views of the formless tangle of draw and hill and butte behind them; and saw no life. To the right lay East Desert, pale silver until the first slanting blow of sunlight turned it a smoky yellow. In the north, across the low bay of Stage Coach Pass, lay the outflung prow of the Bunchgrass Hills.

Bourke had been playing a game of dodge for ten days and the slow pace bothered him now. "Push along, Owen. We're draggin'."

"Plenty of time."

"Sure," grumbled Bourke. "Plenty of time for trouble." Cultus Charley trailed behind, sitting on his saddle like a sack of meal, with his toes pointed out and his heels banging the pony. He had his head down and was indifferent to all this. Pay Lankershim ranged ahead, topping the rises and pausing to scout the land before dropping into the adjacent ravines. Pay held his rifle across the saddle. Against the clear light he was a gaunt, stringy shape. Merritt had his moment of wonder concerning the man. Here Pay had been a cattleman with considerable money — and probably still had the money. But he seemed to like this particular kind of hunt-and-run life; it supplied some renewing zest to his old frame, it put a sparkle in his black eyes; and over the night campfire he had smoked his pipe and rubbed his knees with a sly, amused expression, listening to the wind and the sounds in the wind as a man might listen to music.

They came to the last round dome of this country and traveled down toward the flats across which — a distance of three or four miles — lay the toe of the Bunchgrass Hills and its dark-rising belt of pine timber. Pay Lankersim scanned the roundabout country with a more restless turning of his head. Bourke was visibly troubled, and even Cultus Charley came out of his indifference. Bourke said: —

"We better push on faster. I don't want to get caught in the middle of the flats."

They ran for a while and pulled in again. The desert's fine dust mushroomed around the ponies' stepping feet and lifted behind them, hanging to the air as a gray-white wake.

Bourke said: "How'd Nan Melotte get into this, Owen?"

"She picked me off the yard."

"What?"

But Owen shook his head, not answering. Bourke shot him a glance wherein curiosity was brightly alive, and spoke of something else. "Helen Tague went to see

Sally at Skull day before yesterday. I saw Helen afterwards, in town."

They rode a half-mile before Owen said, "Well, what about Sally?"

Bourke grinned. "I thought maybe I could open you up. I guess Isham's left orders to keep Sally on the place. He ain't been back to the ranch but once in ten days. Accordin' to Helen, they had one hell of a talk, Sally and Isham. She started to town after Isham left, but one of the home crew stopped her. Dutcher came back once. She's afraid of Dutcher."

Owen listened to it, but didn't answer. Bourke's only clue to his partner's frame of mind was a slow reddening of skin at the back of Owen's neck. This was all. The big man had gone through something and it had changed him. Whatever he felt or whatever he had made up his mind to do lay behind a continuing silence. The old-time streak of gaiety didn't show. In its place was something very hard. As though all this trouble had brought about its permanent change.

Cultus Charley let out a short, small: "Hey!" Looking at once to the rear, Bourke and Merritt saw Skull's riders come off the Broken Buttes in a cloudy swirl of dust. The distance was around two miles.

Merritt said, "I thought they'd be that close," and swept on at a full gallop.

Bourke yelled: "I told you we should have done this faster."

They raced over the flat, keeping the Skull outfit at

its distance. A coyote rose out of a dry wash and loped away. At the base of the Bunchgrass Hills, they pulled in to thread their way through an area of scab rock. When they were past it Skull had closed up to a mile or less; someone back there began an aimless firing. Merritt hit the climbing grade. At the edge of the pines, five hundred feet from the desert floor, he turned to let the horses blow. Dismounted, he pulled the Winchester from its boot and watched Skull come slowly through the rocks. At this distance he could distinguish both Dutcher and Isham; and it was on Dutcher he lined his sights and let go. A streak of dust showed the bullet strike short of its mark. Meanwhile Bourke and Pay and Cultus Charley opened up, and all this put Skull into a mill at the foot of the grade. A horse went down, throwing the rider back into the rocks.

Bourke said: "Now what's that?"

The party had split. Dutcher waved his arm and took part of the men back through the rocks toward Stage Coach Pass. Isham led the rest of the outfit eastward, curving around the point of the hills.

"Figure to squeeze in from both sides," said Bourke. "Isham will come up through Corral Flats. Dutcher's cutting around by your house."

Pay said, "Ahee — that was a dam' good shot." He pulled down his gun, watching one of the horses in Isham's outfit drop to its knees and turn end for end. The rider rolled free, jumped up, and ran full-tilt after the other Skull men. But nobody lagged back to give him a lift, and after a short chase the stranded man retreated to his horse — Pay again pumping bullets at him — and dropped on the lee side of it. Pay's chance firing lifted dimples of dust around the horse.

Merritt said, "Come on," and returned to his saddle. He led them upgrade until they came to the dome on which he had camped ten days before.

Bourke said: "I don't like this spot. Now what?"

"I'm back on my own land," said Merritt.

"Better hustle," counseled Bourke. "Dutcher won't be another thirty minutes gettin' up this way."

"They're split. Dutcher's got three men with him. Isham's got four. We'll go after Isham first."

"Then," said Bourke impatiently, "let's be on the move."

Merritt held his place a little longer. "You fellows don't have to get into it. I don't want to rap you into anything."

They didn't at the moment say anything. They watched him. They showed him a tough indifference. Bourke's face had a steady grin. Pay Lankershim folded both arms over the gun on his saddle horn, his weathered cheeks seamed and smart. Cultus Charley never stirred, and there was no sentiment at all in his muddy-black eyes. Bourke suddenly spoke out his unfavorable judgment. "You got a soft streak in you, Owen. It won't do."

"No," answered Owen, "not now. I've made up my mind."

"Then we're wastin' time. A fight's a fight and we're in it, kill or cure. You just said a fool thing. If we didn't want to get in it we wouldn't be here." Another thought struck him. "You pretty sure your mind's made up? Suppose you run into Isham? Suppose it comes to you and him? What would you do, Owen?"

Merritt said, "Time to go," and drifted downslope into the heavy pines. They came behind him with Bourke Prine repeating his question in a sharper voice: "What would you do? You got to get that clear in your head. If it ain't clear when you bump into him you're a dead man. If you're still thinkin' of Sally when you find Isham . . ."

Merritt didn't answer. They ran through the still shadows of the red-bodied pines, the ponies' feet sinking into the soft carpeting and making almost no sound. Sunlight now and then pierced the green mat of overhead branches and burned round golden patches on the earth. Bourke caught Pay Lankershim's eyes. He moved his head from side to side, thus conveying his uncertain sentiments.

Hugh Clagg lay dead within the circle of Skull's campfire and Will Isham's voice kept rising against his crew. "All right — all right!" For a moment these men looked on, not moving. They were a rough and unsentimental bunch, and they had few illusions and no nerves; but the pure deliberateness of this killing set them back; it gave them something to think about. The dead Clagg meant nothing to them. It was Isham they studied with the speculative interest of men who had long ago learned to put their own survival above every other thing. They took Isham's pay and they took his orders, and if they paused now it was to realize they were following a boss who had changed his skin; who was wilder than they had believed him to be. Dutcher was a hulking outline in the light, thoroughly absorbed by the almost frozen expression on his chief's features. Isham, feeling no response, whipped himself around and caught that stare. He put his little frame against Dutcher, speaking again: "Dutcher, did you hear me? God damn you, move!"

The crew retreated toward the horses. Dutcher held his place a little longer. He was too black a man to show the flush of his temper and yet his temper made its appearance in the sudden gesture of his shoulders and in the way his lips rolled together. He had used this kind of talk habitually on his crew; he had never allowed another man to use it on him. His dark, overbearing pride slammed around him and left him resentful and ready to talk back. He was on the edge of speaking when one of the men called to him from the darkness. "Come on, Fay." He turned away.

They ran away from this camp, up the ravine and through the broken hills and down to the flats. Isham found the road into the canyon and led the crew to its bottom. He called at them: "Get down there. Wade both ways."

Dutcher remained beside him. Dutcher said: "I wouldn't put no trust in Hugh Clagg's talk — "

"Shut up, Dutcher."

Dutcher laid his big hands around the saddle horn, squeezing into it with all the fury he felt. He murmured, "Mr. Isham, you been drivin' this crew pretty hard. It's a good crew and you got no reason — "

Men splashed back from the creek. One of them spoke through the solid black. "They been below. There was a fire on the gravel. It's still warm."

"Look farther down."

"They couldn't go no farther. There's a fifty foot drop in the creek."

Dutcher said: "They had this fight with Clagg — and skipped out."

"They?"

Dutcher added: "A woman's with him." When it was out he knew he had said the wrong thing, and so did the crew. Everybody remained still, waiting for Isham to speak or move. The creek beat up its clacking rumors and wind scoured between the canyon walls and whirled around them. Isham led the way back to the rim. He said: "We camp here."

Dutcher murmured: "Here? It's a little bit risky."

Isham said: "Never mind."

They made a fire of sagebrush, rolling up in their blankets well away from it. Dutcher crouched on one edge of the light, smoking his cigarette slowly, still looking at Isham, who stood on the very edge of the night.

The glow of the cigarette flickered against the foreman's eyes; and now and then, looking around the circle, he saw the pale shape of men's faces. The crew was watching him. This was the end of ten days and Isham had ridden everybody to a wire edge. His words had scraped the skin off the men, leaving them sullen, leaving them jumpy. Dutcher sat cross-legged, his huge shoulders lumped forward. He could make this crew mind him, he could whip any man in it. But he could not stop the things in their minds — and he knew the tongue-lashings given him by Isham had made them lose respect for him. He had his own fear of Isham. Against this fear his pride pushed with a greater and greater insistence.

At daybreak they took the trail made by Merritt, and reached the black scar of Merritt's campfire in the hills. The ashes were still warm.

Isham said: "He saw our blaze last night, from here. He was looking down at us. We've been followin' this man for ten days, without a sign till now. Dutcher, if you or any of this crew you picked had the sense God gave geese you'd have found his trail a week ago. I thought you knew how to follow a track."

Dutcher fired back: "You been leadin' this outfit, not me. You been givin' the orders and disregardin' my advice. When an owner starts monkeyin' with his foreman's job it's dam' high time he got a new foreman. Maybe that's what you better do now. You ain't asked my advice lately."

Isham's answer, so cool and so calculated in its ironic courtesy, was like a drop of acid on Dutcher's nerves. "We're getting close now, Dutcher. Maybe that's why you want to leave. Maybe you figure Merritt will make a sucker out of you again — as in Winnemucca."

Dutcher drew a deep, deep breath. The crew sat around in a half-circle, listening to this quarrel with an expressionless attention, listening to an owner rake over his foreman — a thing not seemly and not to be let pass. Yet Dutcher, bulked hugely against the day's growing light, held his hands on the saddle horn, and spoke with a labored evenness. "You get yourself another man, when this hunt is over, Mister Isham." They turned to follow the tracks again, going upgrade toward the succeeding summits. Dutcher dropped behind, riding in the dust with his head tipped down, knowing his soft answer had lost him his control forever over Skull's crew. Knowing it, and growing more and more bitter.

At the last rise, they saw dust roll up in the flats. Isham said in the same dead level voice: "Now we'll close in" — and led them down the sharp pitch at a full run. Merritt's party, somewhat scattered, pulled together at once and raced on, keeping the distance until the rock rubble at the foot of the Bunchgrass Hills slowed them. Isham turned to Jake Strange and said: "Try a shot," and Strange began to peg his Winchester's bullets through the distance, without effect. When they reached the foot of the hill, Isham waved at his crew to follow him up the slope, but at that moment Merritt's crowd began firing from the timber line above. Skull broke back. Isham swung in the leather and cursed them with a terrible softness, even while the lead rutted up the dust around them. He kept cursing them, looking straight at one man and another, grinding his contempt into them, one by one. Then, seeing them drift a little, he said: "We'll go around the base," and started that way.

Dutcher shouted: "I'll try the other side," and motioned to some of the men to follow. Isham howled at him, but three of the crew wheeled with Dutcher, recklessly running the scab rock. A bullet knocked down Hale Everett's pony and Everett shouted, "Wait a minute, boys!" Nobody stopped, whereupon Everett cursed Isham by name, and all of them by name, and dropped behind the shelter of the dead horse. Dutcher kept going.

He hit the hills at Merritt's abandoned house and took the climbing trail toward Corral Flats. At Lankershim's little meadow he stopped, and said: "We'll wait a minute." The three men with him slackened in their saddles and scanned the surrounding timber with a close, lively interest. There was no sound at all in the dreaming stillness of the hills.

Dutcher rolled a cigarette, his eyes hanging to it while he remembered all the talk Isham had thrown at him and all the contempt in Isham's manner. The man was crazy; turned so by a woman. It was a weak spot in

Isham, a kind of disease that was eating out his insides. In ten days he had ruined the crew and destroyed a foreman. Dutcher lighted the cigarette and dragged in the smoke; he took up the reins, moving on. This time he avoided the trail, ducking in and around the pines, climbing the grade at a deliberate gait. Somewhere in the southeast, firing began to roll back, irregular and faded. It was, perhaps, a mile away, or more.

He stopped and faced the three men who were so closely watching him now. He said: "You in a hurry?"

They didn't answer but they knew what he meant, for they were men born to trickery and sudden change. Skull's pay check had held them a little while, but the time was gone now. After ten days of this they didn't give a damn about Isham.

The firing rolled up, closer-spaced. Dutcher listened to the oncoming reports, visualizing the kind of a fight it was — duck and dodge through the timber, with Skull's five men against Merritt's four. And as he listened to it his own deep and sly and sultry temper governed him completely. He had his own rules of conduct and he had his own ambitions; and now he knew the time had come to play the game his own way. Isham and Merritt. One of them would go under.

Jack McGinnis spoke up, summer-soft with his talk: "Maybe, Fay, maybe. But if Isham drops, there's still the woman to run the ranch. And there's still friend Merritt."

Dutcher pinched out the cigarette and said: "The woman won't stay on Skull. As for Merritt, I'd ride through hot-pitch after him. We'll drift that way. No hurry."

XVII

FATAL MEETING

HALFWAY between the high knob of the hills and Corral Flats, Merritt saw the flicker of motion at the end of a long vista in the pines. The trees rose, thick-bodied and closely ranked, out of the dark earth-mold. Pay Lankershim threw up his hand at once. "They're crossin' toward the flats."

"We'll cut in front of them," Merritt said.

They turned from west to northwest, swinging around the pines, up and down with the potholes of the uneven earth. There was no shock from this urgent running, so deep was the cushioning layer of humus; there was only a soft "tunk-a-tunk" of sound. Sun brightened the overhead green and day's heat began to cut the long-held chill of night. Merritt rode with his bad leg free of the stirrup, in a degree easing the pain which slugged its way from toe to hip. Sweat collected under his hat-band; the raw bruises around his mouth began to throb and burn. Bourke stayed beside him, Cultus ran behind, and Pay Lankershim was stretching farther and farther to the front. He rode like an Indian, his shoulders going high at each jump of the horse, his feet pushed straight and his arms carrying the gun up against his chest. He said, like a long sigh, "Ahee," and hauled his body back, throwing the horse on its haunches. The others overran him and heard his sudden swearing. "Dammit — get out of my tracks — back — back!"

Skull's riders came up through the deeper timber, riding very fast. One man shouted and the compact group scattered; and at once both outfits were wheeling around the gray and golden light. Pay Lankershim flung his rifle forward and was immediately firing. Cultus Charley and Bourke moved against those turning and vanishing and reappearing shapes. Merritt sighted Isham just as the latter threw his horse behind the partial shelter of a pine, fifty yards away. Bringing up his gun, Merritt rushed at the tree. The sound of this quick racket was compressed beneath the pine boughs, rolling through the corridors of the hills, slamming and echoing, and breaking into smaller whorls of sound in the deep distance. A bullet chipped the edge of a tree, shedding bark particles on Merritt's hat as he rushed ahead. Isham fired and faded. Merritt's bullets went wide as his pony bucked back.

Isham kept sliding to the rear, toward his own men. Lead whipped by Merritt and slugs spatted into the adjacent pines, closely seeking him. Pay Lankershim yelled, "Owen — don't git so far over there!"

The alternate patches of sunlight and shadow blurred a man's eyes and the crisscrossing motion of the rider made them hard to place. He swung wider, racing on to catch a better sight of the elusive Isham. The pony hit a hollow, throwing Merritt flat against the saddle horn. When he straightened Isham wasn't to be seen.

Prine streaked past. A Skull man galloped into the open, his body twisted half-around to snap a shot at Pay Lankershim. Bourke, still on the dead run, swept his long arm around, fired and rushed on. The Skull rider, still twisted in the saddle, raised one elbow, as if to protect himself against an unseen blow. His head snapped far back and his hat fell off and Merritt saw the wide-stretched expression of shock on his face. All this came to him as a succession of brief, flittering glimpses as he threw himself into the lower slopes of the forest. Looking back, later, he saw the Skull rider lying in the smoky dust. The horse had stopped.

Both these groups kept shifting ground; they kept wheeling and swinging, with the area shattered by the close-held detonations and dust thickening and the smell of powder rank in the air. Merritt saw the rump of Isham's gray horse on the far right, away from the center of the fight. Skull's owner had made a deep, fast cut through the timber to catch Merritt off guard.

Merritt rushed at him, upgrade. Bourke Prine's voice was behind. "Owen — hey!" Behind him, too, a ricocheting bullet howled dismally. Isham came into plain view, head on. His gun steadied itself against Merritt and Merritt saw it kick back against Isham's fist. Wind vaguely breathed on his cheek. Then Isham had faded behind the close-ranked trees once more and Merritt saw the rump of the gray horse appear and disappear.

The distance was something better than a hundred

yards, which Merritt sought to close up. The way was downgrade for a short distance, thereafter rolling up toward a high knob. The firing behind him was increasingly softened by the intervening trees, and, as from a great distance, Bourke Prine called: "Merritt — hey, Merritt!" A quickening crackle of gunfire stopped the yell.

He saw the gray horse cross a small alley in the timber and fade behind the endless pines; and then, remembering that it was Isham who forced this fight, and would never run from it, Merritt pulled in behind a tree and waited. Around him the ground lay rougher, the root systems of occasional deadfalls lying fan-shaped in the shadows. Dust clung to the air and where sunlight slid through the overhead branches this dust boiled in the stained-gold brilliance.

Other than the far-off burst of shots — which seemed to be at less frequent intervals — there was no sound in the forest, and the lagging minutes went on and the tension piled up until Merritt felt as though, somewhere, a rifle's round snout lay steadily against him. Strain was that definite, and he caught himself bracing his muscles against an awaited explosion.

He was troubled by the occasional streaks of sunlight. Back of those yellow-gold bars was a kind of diffused grayness his eyes could not quite penetrate; and he was thinking, carefully and quickly, of the way he would circle, drop to the ground, and use the adjacent deadfalls for shelter — if he were Isham. The man had a mind hard to read and Merritt wasn't sure of his ways. Never ceasing to sweep the broken earth, its little pockets and fallen timber and its close-ranked pines stretching away without end, he saw nothing to give him a cue.

On his right, suddenly, a crow high in the trees shattered the silence with a squawking racket that filled all the corners of the hills. Merritt had been looking elsewhere; not turning, he saw Isham's gray horse pull out from a little roll of land and rush straight forward.

Merritt dropped from the saddle, ran around his pony, and lifted his gun for a steadier aim than he had used all day. Isham's was three hundred feet away, lying low on the horse as he raced in. Now and then he had to turn around the standing trees; and once he dipped into a hollow until only his shoulders were visible. Merritt slid his free hand forward to cushion the gun. His front sight struck a straight black mark against the gray horse's nearing breast.

At fifty yards Isham drove the dust around Merritt's legs with two quick shots, checked the gray horse and made a long, free jump from the saddle. The horse ran away, ruining Merritt's shot. Isham rolled head-over-heels for a good fifteen feet, jumped up and raced for the shelter of a deadfall. He went over the deadfall in a low, flat dive, Merritt's following shot never catching him. Bourke Prine's distant calling ran insistently through the oncoming silence.

Merritt stepped behind the nearest tree, keeping his glance pinned to the log while he pushed fresh shells into his gun. A little streak of dust rose from the far side of the log, showing Isham in motion. Merritt had a moment here, a risky moment; and ran out from the tree toward the log. He covered the last ten feet on his hands and knees, came against the log and so crouched, with a weather eye lifted toward the log's top line. When he put his ear against the wood he very plainly heard the continuing scrape of Isham's body on the other side.

The log was high enough to cover him when he crouched on his knees. It ran slightly downgrade toward its up-ended roots, thirty feet away. In falling, the pine had pulled up a great cake of earth with the roots, and this was a solid bulwark toward which Isham seemed to be moving. Beyond, though Merritt couldn't see it from his location, was a hole fifteen feet broad, where the tree had formerly stood.

Bourke Prine's voice was a steady halloo in the lower forest; it swelled through the morning air. "Merritt — hey! Hey!" The fight there had quit. Merritt listened to the steady scrape of Isham's body beyond the log, holding his place until he was certain the man meant to reach the lower end. Then, paralleling Isham, he moved forward.

He heard Isham grunt. He heard Isham jump into the depression beyond the roots. Reared back, half-upright, Merritt waited again while sweat rolled along the back of his neck and pain pounded its steady rhythm through his leg. Dirt rattled directly beyond

the root fan. Isham grunted again, seeming to fight
his way up from the depression. Merritt rose and
backed away and at this moment Isham appeared
around the edge of the root fan, flung one shot at
Merritt, and ducked out of sight.

Merritt went over the log in one jump and ran
away from it a few yards and turned. He cut a short,
quick circle around the roots, sighting Isham at the
same time Isham saw him. Isham was in the depression,
his shoulders level with its rim. He had been moving
forward. Now he held himself steady. There was no
more ducking for either of them, and no more waiting. Twenty feet separated them. The little man's gun
pointed toward the earth. And it was his, Merritt's,
shot if he wanted it.

What kept him from taking his shot was a thought
he believed he had killed during the long wait at the
bottom of the canyon. This man was Sally's husband.
It was something he couldn't forget, though he had
tried to forget. It weakened him, it shamed him, it
made him discount all these hard days of hiding. Looking now at the narrow-white face below him he saw
the eyes of a man turned mad. There was that chill in
them, that rage which takes a man and grinds all
human feeling out of him, which turns him cold instead
of hot. Isham was like that.

Isham had thrown his head slightly to one side, with
his little shoulders pulled together and with his face
smooth and thin. He had lost his hat and his black

hair lay down on his forehead and his white shirt showed the streaking of dust. Not even the exertion of the chase seemed to have greatly disturbed his breathing.

"Will," said Merritt, "come up here. Let's talk, like a couple of white men. There's a couple maggots in your brain. One of them makes you grab land you don't need and the other makes you doubt a girl that never did a crooked thing in her life. It is time . . ."

Isham was paler and paler, and a twist of his lip corners put an expression of irony there, that same expression which had held people away from him so long. He raised his gun with a gesture as deliberate as a man could make, and fired.

Half-turned, Merritt missed the bullet. His own shot shook Isham's shoulders and drove him backward to the earth. Isham was dead when he fell and it was only an accident that one arm rolled up and rested on his face in a gesture that seemed to express a weary annoyance at the light shining against his eyes.

Merritt stepped away. He crossed the log, lifting his bad leg with a distinct effort. He returned to his horse and put his shoulder against the adjacent tree for a support he needed. At this moment it wasn't Isham he remembered at all; it was Sally whose face was before him, and it was her voice, low and soft and sad, he heard.

Coming through the timber, drawn by the last shots

fired, Bourke and Pay and Cultus found him still leaning against the tree. He had rolled a cigarette. The smoke of it covered his face, and Bourke, looking sharply at him, saw little of his eyes. Merritt nodded toward the base of the fallen tree, whereupon the other three went over that way. Bourke soon came back.

"Owen," he said, "did you give him a break?"

"He had his chance. I tried to talk it out with him."

"That," said Bourke, "is what I was afraid of. You had something in your head. Sally kept gettin' in front of you. I knew you'd try to talk to Isham. I knew you'd rather lose a leg than put a bullet in him. By God, you're a fool for softness. It might of been you down there behind that tree."

Merritt moved his shoulders. The cigarette trailed in the corner of his mouth; smoke kept rising in front of his face. There was an indifference around this big man as solid as a wall, and Bourke's sharp eyes couldn't read much. But he thought he knew what lay in Owen Merritt's head, heavy and constant.

"She's still in your system," he said. "And you'll never get her out of it."

Merritt seized the cigarette from his lips and crushed it between his fingers. He stared at Bourke, glowing. He said, soft enough to be dangerous: "Shut up, Bourke. Shut up."

Cultus Charley and Pay came back. Pay moved his skinny shoulders around to show his dissatisfaction.

His eyes sought remote points in the forest. "Whut's keepin' Dutcher? I'd like to know where that jug-headed such an' so is right now."

Cultus Charley murmured: "Not far, not far."

They stood in a half-circle, watching Merritt. Silence lay long and thick and warm under the trees. The scent of dust held on. Merritt rubbed a hand across his cheeks. He pushed himself from the tree, limping over to his horse. He made two tries before reaching the saddle. A little stain of blood showed through his trousers. "Well," he said, "let's go down to the house."

"Dutcher's still in this country," pointed out Lankershim.

"Let him do the hunting," grumbled Merritt.

They rode around the knob, keeping well off the occasional little trails streaking through the timber, and came upon Lankershim's meadow. This they avoided, descending the steady slope leading toward Merritt's house. Christmas Creek curved out of the shadows and fell with them. They watered their horses, afterwards going deeper into the timber. Presently Pay halted.

"No," he said, "I ain't goin' down there yet. Dutcher's around, damned if he ain't. I'll be along later. Charley, you come with me. I'm goin' to camp by the main trail and see what I see. We'll be close by."

There was the sound of quick-running horses on the trail, whereupon Dutcher motioned to the men with

him. They pulled off the trail, and from this conceal-
ment saw Tuck Ring rushing up. Ring had followed
Isham but was alone now. When he was near enough,
Dutcher called to him and came out of the timber.
Dutcher's challenge had turned Ring into the trees;
he took his time moving out to Dutcher.

He said: "Where you been? Where you been all this
time? Porky's dead and I dunno what happened to
Tip. Karl Grash is gone. They all just faded. So I faded.
Isham's dead, that's plain certain. His horse drifted
up from the timber. I heard shootin' somewhere. Then
his horse drifted up. He's dead. Where the hell have
you been, Dutcher? My God, we sure got caught.
What'd you split the bunch for?"

Dutcher looked at the other men. Jack McGinnis
gave him a wry, hard grin. "It is too bad," he commented. Then he added: "But there's still Merritt.
And the woman. You got your wish, didn't you? Well,
you're a cool one with other people's skins. Only, it
ain't over yet."

Dutcher said: "You boys cut back to Skull. I'll be
along."

When they were gone Dutcher crossed the trail,
circled Lankershim's meadow and left his horse a
good distance from the house. He dropped into Merritt's yard by the back road, went over the yard and
stopped in the kitchen. He kicked away the broken
rubbish around his feet, saw a tin dipper, and remembered then that he was thirsty. He took up the

dipper and walked back to the well on the porch.
There was a little stale water in the well bucket. He
dumped it on the porch floor and drew a fresh bucket
and took his drink. He sloshed the rest of it around
his face, and entered the house. All the doors were
broken from the hinges and all the windows smashed;
and though he tried one room and another, none of
them seemed to suit him. There was a door inside the
house that hadn't been bothered, one that closed off
the attic stairs. He pulled this open and sat on the
stairs, bringing the door against him until it was almost shut. Through the narrow crack thus made he
had a view of the back doorway and the kitchen.
Seated there while the moments went by, he rolled
himself a cigarette.

After leaving Dutcher, the five Skull riders turned
through the hills, heading for home quarters in complete silence. Somewhere near the main trail along the
ridge of the hills, Jack McGinnis suddenly slapped a
hand across his thigh and reined in. He looked at the
rest of the crowd — a smart, sly man who never let
his eyes or ears miss anything. He had been on the
dodge all his mature life, and his own skin was his chief
concern. He said now: —

"I guess not, brethren. The old man's dead and I
ain't so sure about this business. I'm going into The
Wells and get me a meal and a drink. Then I just guess
I'll keep goin'."

They remained in a solemn circle, studying it out. There wasn't a man in this party who didn't have something to run from. There wasn't a one of them who could ride a trail without needing to look back. So they studied it, silently and taciturnly under the fresh morning sunlight. Mike Strange said: "Maybe," and turned his horse. Presently, saying nothing more at all, Strange and Jack McGinnis trotted down the slope toward the Piute and toward town. The other two headed for the ranch.

XVIII

"YOUR HUSBAND IS DEAD"

EACH of these ten long days had brought its increasing suspense and its added weight and its deeper loneliness to Sally. Isham made but one trip to the place, leaving immediately after their painful interview. Helen Tague came up from Wagon Rim two days later, stayed a short while and went away. Afterwards silence closed in and there was nothing to do but wait and go over the old thoughts again in search of some answer she could not find. She kept telling herself, "There's got to be a way. I won't give up." But there was, though she sought it hour after hour, no way. The stillness of the house oppressed her and the speechless distance of the home crew angered her and through all this was the everlasting question that would not leave: Where was Owen — how was Owen?

On the tenth morning she rose from a sleepless night, crossed the yard to the horse barn and saddled her own personal pony. She had ridden only as far as the Skull bridge when the ever-present guard galloped forward and rounded her in. He was cool about it, staring at her with a faint boldness — as though she might be easy with a man. It was an attitude she had noticed before, though never so openly.

He said: "Sorry, Miz Isham. If it was somethin' you wanted from town I'll go get it."

"Ben," she said, "I'm tired of this foolishness. Pull aside."

His eyelids stretched rounder, showing some surprise. "Why, I can't do that. Mr. Isham —"

"Pull aside, Ben. I mean it."

He shook his head, and displayed a small gesture of irritation. This, she realized, was Skull. It had always been a man's ranch; and none of this crew had ever accepted her. She was the intruder. This Ben, now, let her see the edge of his own intolerance. He didn't trust her and he wouldn't listen. She was a woman.

She wore a coat against the morning's crispness. Reaching into one of its deep pockets she drew out the .38 she always carried when riding alone. "Ben," she said, as stubbornly even about it as he was, "get out of my way."

He revealed the instant anger of a man physically challenged by a woman. Instead of giving ground he urged his horse toward her, leaning out and extending his arm. He said, "Give me that damned thing —"

She put a shot within a foot of his head, making him haul away. His horse pitched aside, half-unseating Ben. He righted himself, punishing the horse with his spurs, and kicked it back toward her. But he kept a little distance between them, cautiously judging her temper. She could see quite distinctly what he wanted to do; she could see that he was on the edge of rushing her again. It made her say: —

"You're a fool, Ben. I've carried this gun for years and I could tear your collarbone to pieces before you moved. It might be a good idea. You're a brush-jumper and you run for shelter every time a stranger drops off the rim. Just like a dog tucking his tail down. Go on back."

Ben said, between his lips: "We'll see about this, ma'm. We'll sure see when Mr. Isham—" He had made up his mind she'd use her gun again and so he started away, to be stopped by her sharper voice.

"Come back here and take your hat off."

He said, at once outraged: "I'll be damned—"

She put a second shot at him, the bullet's nearness making him flinch. Three or four of the home crew collected back by the house to watch this. Ben rode toward her and removed his hat, a killing blackness in his glance. He said, "Yes ma'm," and wheeled and galloped away. She started on, but he had reached the group and he was openly cursing her — and suddenly she turned about and charged him. The other hands gave ground. Ben, swinging his horse around, showed her an odd, half-shocked glance. She was a tall girl, almost as tall as this ordinary-sized Ben; and she sat straight on the saddle, willful and composed and thoroughly unafraid. The man was a tough one, as were the rest of Skull's crew, and he hated her and showed it. But her own temper had been ten days in the making. She meant to break this Ben, she meant to break the crew to a woman's presence.

"Get down, Ben."

He dropped from the saddle, with a slowness intended to show her his independence.

"Walk in front of me — and run when I tell you to run."

He had long, thin lips. They closed, and his eyes were very black again as he shook his head. He said: "Not from you, ma'm — "

"Ben," she said, "don't make a mistake. I'm not a lady. I'm the Bidwell girl and I was raised among harder men than I think you are. I am going to live on Skull, and if I have got to whip some of you boys to make you mind me, now is the time. Get in front of me, Ben. If you stop before I say so I'll shoot you." Then her voice hit him twice as hard: "Damn you, I mean that!"

Ben went around her horse. His knees bent and dust squirmed up around his boots. She pulled her horse into a slow trot and watched him run before her with the angular, shambling gait of a rider who had never walked more than fifty feet at a time. Across the bridge she began to hear his breath deepen. At the foot of the long grade up the rim, he turned his face back toward her, showing a strained anxiety. She pointed the gun at him, whereupon he hit the grade, his boots scuffing the rock. Sweat rolled off his face.

He sawed his arms back and forth and his head jerked up and down; and when he sucked in air it was like a gusty cry. He looked back once more, halfway up the grade, caught his foot on a rock and fell flat.

She said: "Keep running."

He struggled to his knees and to his feet. His head kept dropping on him and she saw his legs shake. His mouth was round and wide, faintly purpling at the edges. But he flung himself into a run and went another hundred yards, each pace dragging him lower and lower until his whole body was in a crouch. When he fell, utterly exhausted, he rolled over and was half-unconscious.

Sally watched him a moment, without pity; and turned to see the distant men in Skull's yard observing this. It was a lesson for them. Afterwards she reached the rim and fell into a steady canter across the high flats, going toward The Wells. Cruelty was all Skull's crew understood; and she had been cruel. She was thinking, with a singular coolness, that this was the way she would be with them — until they acknowledged her. Her will was up; and so she rode, swinging to the horse with a born sureness, with more confidence than she had known for a long while. Color turned her cheeks rose-red and the pleasantness of the day restored some of her old spirit.

In town she went directly to Sam Nankervell's

blacksmith shop. Sam was her friend and a notorious gossip.

"Any news come into town yet, Sam?"

He said no, there wasn't, and rested his broad back against the door of the shop and took time to fire up his corncob. Medary, he told her, had gone off on a hunting trip, which was probably smart. Bourke Prine had ridden into town a couple times, looking for Merritt. Nobody knew where Merritt was. His house had been busted up and he had, apparently, been cornered and shot. Story seemed to be he had gotten down to Nan Melotte's place. She had patched him up — her front room showed bloodstains. Then she had hit into the hills with him. And that was everything.

"Well," he added, "almost everything."

Sally said instantly: "What else, Sam?"

He took the corncob from his mouth, reversing the stem and pointing at Shannon's store across the street. "Nan came in, this mornin'. She's over there."

Sally caught her breath. "Well, hasn't anyone asked her — "

"No," answered the blacksmith, looking at her directly. "Nobody ain't."

Excitement rushed through her, strong and hard; and fear turned her faintly cold. She murmured, "I will," and went immediately over the street. Nan's horse stood at Shannon's rack. The sun was half up in the sky, shining fully on The Wells's almost empty street, and a brown dog lay before the saloon, and a small wind boosted a scrap of paper along the dust. These things she noted with the idle edges of her vision, even while her mind went its own way.

When she stepped into the store Nan Melotte turned from a corner counter and looked at her very casually, for a moment not identifying Sally because of the light shining against her eyes. Then Sally saw the girl's face change a little — change and darken and turn away expression. Shannon was waiting on her; and Shannon's wife was at the back end.

Sally said, "Did you just come in?"

"Yes," answered Nan.

They were watching each other carefully as the silence lengthened, with feeling lying between them that wouldn't change as long as they lived. Sally Isham was the taller girl, the more dominating. She had a self-assurance in the way she held her head. There was a poise to her shoulders, a firm line to her long lips and a driving directness in her manner. Against her Nan Melotte maintained a sober reserve, her dark eyes interested and very attentive to the other girl's least expression. This was the difference between them — a self-certain woman with copper-colored hair facing a dark girl caught in a strange quiet.

Shannon's wife suddenly called: "Shannon — come here."

Shannon was quite embarrassed, and glad to go. He went immediately toward his wife. Both of them left the store, closing the rear door.

Nan spoke up. "Owen's all right. That's what you want to know, isn't it?"

"Yes."

"He's up in the hills, with Bourke and Pay Lankershim and Cultus Charley." Nan paused, adding another phrase afterwards, more slowly. "I think your husband is up there, too."

Sally said: "Was he hurt?" For a moment she let the question lie. But something in Nan's expression made Sally add with an impatient quickness: "I'm talking about Owen."

"Your husband, and his crew, trailed Owen to his house and shot him in the leg."

Sally said: "Why do you keep speaking of my husband?"

Nan shrugged her shoulders, not bothering to answer. Sally said: "If you were with him so long, why did you leave him now?"

"He doesn't need me any more."

Sally's chin tilted a little higher. Her tone strengthened. "Are you so sure he needed you at all?"

"Yes," said Nan. "I'm sure." Her lips came gently, softly together, and her voice made a little melody.

"I see," breathed Sally.

"It hurts you," murmured Nan, cool and direct. "It hurts you to think of it. And you'd give anything to know what those days were like. What he said to me and what I did or didn't do."

"Of course," admitted Sally. And again they were watching each other, so carefully and with so much speculation. "I knew it would be like that," went on Sally. "He's the kind of a man to attract any woman."

"Then," said Nan, with the first appearance of resentment in her voice, "why didn't you keep him? Why did you make the terrible mistake you have made? If he really wanted me, I'd still be in the hills. But he doesn't. You're still in his blood. You always will be. Maybe you're glad to know that. I do not admire you, but I do not blame you for being what you are, or doing what you have done. Only, you have caused him more trouble than you dream. How could you leave Owen, no matter what the reason or the reward, for a man like Isham? Well, here you are. You have no right to him now, but you don't want to let him go. You will want to have your way with him. What excuse can you have? You made your bargain. It didn't include Owen — so why don't you leave him alone? Or go to him outright? One thing or the other. You can't have everything."

"I know," murmured Sally. "But I'm not going to him. I just wanted to know how he was. I won't be seeing him. Maybe — maybe I could wish you luck."

Nan said, "It wouldn't do any good. I'm like Owen. Half of something isn't enough. I'm leaving the country in the morning."

"Then — " said Sally, and stopped. Riders came into the town at a fast pace. Shannon raced up from the back of the store. By common impulse both women turned toward the street, reaching it in time to see Jack McGinnis and Mike Strange haul up before the saloon. People were coming out of all the buildings, crossing toward the Skull men; and Jack McGinnis saw Sally and strode toward her. There was a thinness to his expression, as though deep in him a gray joke had its way. He removed his hat, polite and drawling and ironic.

"Your husband shot and killed Hugh Clagg last night. This mornin' your husband was killed. By Merritt."

He wheeled away, his spurs jingling on the walk. Voices rose around Sally as she stood there. Shannon kept calling, "Where's Merritt? Where's Dutcher?" Nan Melotte touched Sally's shoulder and Sally looked up and saw the look in the girl's face, so dark, so distantly curious. "You see?" murmured Nan, and went to her pony and rode down the street. Sally walked straight to the hotel and up to the room always kept for Isham. Hoyle Daugherty, who ran the place, called to her, across the lobby: "Sally, I'm — " She didn't look at him; she went up the stairs rapidly and turned into the room. Nan's "You see?" kept ringing through her head. It meant so much. It meant so terribly much.

XIX

THIS MAN AND THIS WOMAN

Bourke Prine said: "I don't like this so much, Owen. Dutcher ain't a man to run. He's got too much gall in him, and he hates you like a wolf."

"No," said Merritt. "He wouldn't run."

"Then," said Bourke, "why didn't he come up and help Isham?"

They quartered the hill, dropping gently with the grade. Light began to swell through the thinning timber, marking the approach of Merritt's ranch yard. Merritt said, idly and not much interested, "He sold Isham out. Which is what I figured some time ago. But he won't leave the Piute. I made him run once. He wouldn't forget it in a million years. The man wants to run Skull."

"Then," murmured Bourke, more and more dissatisfied, "there's Clagg. We ain't in such good shape yet." He quit talking and, as was his habit, watched his partner with his consistent, close curiosity. The big man showed a taciturn expression. Everything was inside, churning its way around and producing a hard, aloof silence. Bourke recognized it, and spoke again. "Kid, I'm sorry you had to be the one to drop Isham. I wish it had been me."

"Doesn't matter, does it?"

"It makes a difference," observed Bourke. "For you, it makes a difference."

Merritt only shrugged his shoulders, but Bourke knew his partner was thinking, as he too was thinking, of Sally. Sally was in the big man's blood and wouldn't ever get out. Her marriage to Isham had been a mistake and Bourke, who was no fool when it came to the ways of people, knew that both Sally and Owen knew it to be a mistake. It had been something that grew out of a quarrel, something that grew out of pride. Both of them were strong-willed, both of them were individualists. Their courtship, as Bourke well knew, had been a stormy time — reaching the heights and the depths; and then, because they were what they were, she had married Isham. But they were still in love and now Sally was free again to repair the hard mistake made. Only — and this was the fact that kept sticking to Bourke's mind, troubling him — it was Merritt who had faced Isham and had sent him down to the dust. It put something between those two people, between Sally and Owen: a barrier, a memory, a stain. The more Bourke considered it, the worse he saw the picture. And though the big man was always hard to read, he knew Owen had this on his mind as he rode silently along. Nan, Bourke figured, was just an incident to Owen. She had been in his life for ten days, a pretty woman and a desirable woman who had stuck by him when he needed somebody. There would be, he guessed, a warm memory there for a man with feelings as strong as Owen's were. But it would pass. Sally was the one.

Bourke pulled himself out of this analytical frame of mind as they came nearer the break in the timber. Through a between-tree alley they saw the clearing below and the house. The falls began to send back its flat, dashing echoes and light brightened considerably. Bourke said: —

"I don't like it very much, Owen. Too damned many loose ends around here to trip a fellow. Dutcher wouldn't let go this easy. Don't ride so blind."

Owen looked at his partner. "It's in the book, one way or another, Bourke. So why worry?"

"It don't hurt to keep an eye peeled," grumbled Bourke. "That's the first lesson in my book — and should be in yours. Just wait a minute."

They were at the edge of timber, traveling the back trail which led them into the yard by way of the barn. Bourke repeated, "Just wait a minute," and rode along the margin of the trees, cutting toward the main hill trail. All this land was fairly open and he spent a good ten minutes angling around the pine trunks. He was only partly satisfied when he returned. "Nothin'," he admitted. "Nothin' at all. But I don't like it."

They came into the yard. Bourke, keyed up by his suspicions, hooked around the barn, entered it from the front and trotted through it, coming out the back door. Merritt circled the house, Bourke immediately joining him. All the windows were smashed; both doors were wrecked. They had their quick views of the interior and its littered emptiness. Paused by the front porch, Bourke saw the big man show his first real expression of temper. "They did a damned complete job," Merritt said, "on the house. It'll take a lot of work to put it right. Wonder why Isham didn't burn it while he was in the business?"

"Maybe," said Bourke, "he was thinkin' it would make a good spot for Skull's headquarters on the south end of the hills. He was a hell of a man to figure ahead. Nobody ever did know just what went on in that little head."

Merritt, he observed, now considered the Piute with a freshening expression. He was watching Nan's cabin out in the flats, he was sweeping all the far country with a kind of confident, pleased anticipation. As though he returned to old times and was happy over it. Sun lifted in the sky, building up the tawny coloring of the Broken Butte's slopes, building up the long transverse shadows of the gullies yonder; and turning the floor of the Piute a silver-yellow. Yet even though the sun fell out of a pure, cloudless sky there was distinctly in the air the gray shimmer of coming winter. Wind, small and slow, turned the day really crisp.

"Snow any time now," murmured Merritt. "It's a fine country, Bourke. A man couldn't spend his life better anywhere in the world. I'd like to get over into the Fremont before the weather breaks. Just to watch the antelope busting the breeze." He reached for his tobacco, rolling up a smoke with his glance still running the horizon. The sight of all this lightened him. "You know why I didn't meet you up on the knob that day? I had it figured out — to bushwhack and then run. But I got to thinkin'. Why run? This is my country. Wouldn't make any difference where I went, I'd be thinking about this spot. I'd be a man on the drift, wishin' I was back. Better be buried here than alive somewhere else. Sounds damned foolish. Anyhow, I got down here — and got shot. If there's anything in this business of living at all, it must be to stand fast when the pinch comes. Somewhere, along the years, every living creature has to make that answer for himself: Stick or run. We're dead soon enough and maybe we miss a lot of fun in going too soon. Still, there's nothing in the world like the pleasure of knowin' you toughed it out and got through. Puts salt in a man's food, puts wind in his lungs. Makes him feel the blood running through him." He threw a quick side glance at Bourke, and grinned a trace sheepishly. "Now you can take up the collection, brother."

Bourke had his mind still on the hills. He turned his pony half around the house, watching the timber line closely. After a while he said: "I'm going up there and get Pay and Cultus. I don't like this. Not any. You stay here. Right here, understand?"

"Sure," said Merritt, and watched his partner cross the creek and take the hill trail.

Merritt circled the house again, reviewing the damage done; and came to the rear and got down, going to the kitchen door. Everything lay on the floor. Every dish had been broken. They had knocked the stove off its legs and pulled the pipe down, and thus the wreckage was mixed with a foundation of soot and ashes and glass and crockery fragments. He reached down to rescue a cup that had survived all this, putting it on the table. Turning back to the porch he took the tin dipper and scooped a drink from the well bucket.

It was then, exactly then, with the water running down his throat and his head tipped up, that certain stray things, idly observed, came home to him with a tremendous jolt. The water he drank was cold and fresh, the dipper handle wet from prior usage; and the scent of smoke came out of the kitchen. It was the pungency of the smoke which told him the man still was in the house.

He had then one of the hard moments of his life, which was to hold himself still and finish the drink and lower the dipper to the bucket without sign of haste. He was cold at once — deeply, chillingly cold. His nerves jerked at him, almost compelling him to swing around. But he stood fast, with his back to the kitchen door, while his thoughts raced around the house, exploring it until at last he remembered something his eyes had seen and his mind had failed to understand. The door leading up to the attic, he recalled, stood ajar.

He grew colder and colder, as if a hard strong current poured from the door, and his heart slugged against his chest and he could feel the reverberation of it in the artery in his neck. The impulse to swing was greater and greater. He swashed the dipper around the bucket, keeping his eyes down — and took a slow step sidewise until he cleared the well box and stood behind it. That move put him out of the direct area of the doorway, it turned him so that he looked into a corner of the kitchen. From this position he could not, without bending forward, sight the attic door.

He reached forward, lifted the bucket, and softly stepped from the porch. He put the bucket down and banged the dipper against it to create a little incidental noise, and cat-walked around the house. Coming along the edge of the front porch, he sighted the kitchen again through the front door. The attic door was still ajar — its opening facing the other way; and he studied it until he was certain it stood too nearly shut to leave a crack on the hinge edge. The fellow in there had only a one-way view — a view of the rear yard.

Merritt put a foot on the porch step, eased his weight into it and rose to the porch. When he changed his weight to the bad leg, pain started along it, fresh and keen. He had to wait a moment; he had to shift his weight away. Afterwards he moved to the front door. A faint spiral of smoke trailed from the attic doorway — betraying the man there. Merritt thought of that carelessness with a gray amusement, knowing it had saved him from sudden ambush. Clagg or Dutcher — he wasn't sure. But he thought it was Dutcher. Clagg was too much of a schemer to overlook little things like cigarette smoke and fresh water in well buckets. Well, it was Dutcher. Skull's foreman was heavy and direct in everything. It would be like him to come here and wait his chance, to satisfy a hurt that rankled in his sullen head.

The door moved an inch outward, stopped, and moved another inch; and these moments were longer and longer. Merritt let his right hand drop to the top of his gun and remain there. He was on the right side of the doorway and this, it suddenly occurred to him, blanked his draw unless he threw the gun over to his left hand. He started to move across to the left side of the door, but checked himself when he saw the attic door swing again. A board on those stairs let out a thin, crisp explosion, whereupon the door came wide and Dutcher stepped into the kitchen.

He faced the other way, his big shoulders dropping and his knees bending a little as he looked into the rear yard. This was the way he stood, huge and solid, tensed against the silence and the uncertainty. He was a man with a slow mind, a dogged mind; and his suspicions so strongly flowed toward the back yard that it was a full thirty seconds before some warning crossed the house and reached him. In that time Merritt stepped away from the casing of the front door and came broadside with the opening. Dutcher threw himself wholly around — and saw Merritt.

The most apparent expression on Dutcher's face then was not surprise and not fear; it was a definite chagrin, as though this mistake of judgment hurt his pride. He pulled his wide shoulders fully up and his hands made a pushing gesture against the floor. Light struck up a swift glinting in his round eyes. His lips rolled together and so he stood, granite-sure of himself and controlled by the sullen self-confidence which left no place for any kind of doubt. He never spoke. He had his look and he made up his mind and when he drove his hand toward the gun on his hip his chin dropped a little to give Merritt a fractional warning.

There were two shots, explosion running into explosion. Dutcher's bullet ripped the casing beside Merritt — level with Merritt's belly, and within an inch of his hip. Merritt's slug hit Dutcher with a brief, muffled, tearing sound. It knocked the wind from Dutcher and doubled him over. He bowed his head until Merritt couldn't see the changing expression on the man's face, it made him seize the casing of the kitchen inner door with his free hand. The gun fell out of his fist and his shoulders, so massive and solid, dropped. That capsizing weight sent him down, face forward into the ashes and soot and broken dishes.

Smoke sluggishly drifted in the house. A horse

pounded the hill trail, with Bourke Prine's hard howl coming before: "Hey — Owen!" Merritt watched Dutcher's head turn, and go still, and he knew the man was dead. He put back his gun and stepped away from the door. Prine appeared on the slope with Cultus and Pay behind. Prine hit the shallow creek hard enough to throw water completely over him; he jumped from the saddle and raced over the porch, his ruddy cheeks stained to crimson from his run. He saw Dutcher lying inside and wind sighed out of him and he murmured, "Good God," and put his arm against the house wall. Pay and Cultus trotted forward to have a look.

Merritt backed away. He limped around the house. He scooped another drink of water from the bucket and stood there, drinking with his legs wide apart. Somewhere during these crowded moments he had thrown undue strain on his bad leg; its ache was steady and powerful. He went to his horse, riding over the yard and waiting for the rest of them. Bourke said: "Where to?"

"Town."

They swung up and quartered along the slope. Pay Lankershim said: "The rest of that outfit has gone back to Skull. Or they have just scattered."

Cultus murmured: "What they do? Kitchen all bad. Stove busted. Dishes no good. Dam' fellas."

Out on the Piute a solitary rider bound toward the Broken Buttes lifted a streak of trail dust. Merritt held his glance over there until the rider turned at Nan

Melotte's cabin. Bourke, keeping his covert attention on Merritt, saw the big man start to pull in on the reins; and Bourke pulled in at once. But Merritt looked back at his partner, revealing a faint irritation. "No," he said. "No."

There was a question in Bourke's mind and it grew larger and more insistent as they rode along, though he could not bring himself to the point of openly asking it. The sun climbed up. Distant in the west, toward the homestead settlements, a cloudy horizon showed other riders coming in. Merritt said: "What day's this?"

"Saturday."

They entered town directly after noon and went into the saloon. Tom Croker stared at Merritt. He came over and seized Merritt's hand. "You sure you want to be around here? My God, man, I'm glad to see you. We just heard about Isham."

Merritt put down his whisky. "How's that?"

"Jack McGinnis and Mike Strange came through here two hours ago. They said he was dead. They said Isham killed Clagg last night. You boys know anything about that?"

The four men stood around, thinking of this, solemnly. Merritt said, "Clagg? He could have been a pretty smart man. But something went wrong in his head. Well." He looked at Bourke, at Pay and Cultus. The four of them drank together, not saying anything then. Bourke ranged the place restlessly. He stopped at the doorway of the small rear room, staring at the picture of the two riders holding a bear by their ropes. He said: "That fellow didn't know anything about drawin' a horse's hind legs." He came back, leaning on the bar. There was a long silence in the room. Merritt placed both hands on the bar and his head tipped, and he kept watching his fingers. Croker said: "On the house, boys. Have another cheer."

"No," murmured Merritt, "not now, Tom. Thanks." Nankervell and Shannon came into the saloon. Nankervell seized Merritt's fist and shook it vigorously. "That's all right, Owen. That's all right. You seen Dutcher any place?"

Bourke Prine, standing a little behind Merritt, signaled at Nankervell with his hand. He shook his head slowly; he pointed his finger at Merritt, and made a dismissing gesture with his palm. Nankervell cleared his throat and changed the question at once. "Goin' any place, Owen?"

The liquor thawed Merritt. It caused him to look up to Nankervell, faintly smiling. "You talkin' about this world or the next one, Sam?"

"You got enough whiskers for a major prophet," said Nankervell.

"I'm going to eat," said Owen. "Then I'm going to run down to Skull."

Other men came into the saloon, making a small crowd here. Nobody said anything for a moment. The silence seemed to mean something. Nankervell removed his corncob and reversed the stem. He pointed the stem through the saloon's back mirror. "That," he remarked, "might not be necessary. If it was Sally you figured to find, she's in the hotel. Been there for a couple hours."

Merritt said, dry and distant, "Thanks," and left the saloon at once. The street was empty and his boots knocked small and quick echoes around the stillness, reminding him of the dismal night not so long back when he had brought George Vird into town. He passed Shannon's store with his head lowered. He walked with his weight unevenly falling, with a limp that turned him to one side each time he used his bad leg, and from her window in the hotel Sally saw this and felt pain each time he swayed. He didn't see her. He kept thinking of George Vird, all across the front of Shannon's and as far as the hotel. Then excitement raveled through him and memory of Vird went away. He took the stairs one at a time, slowly and with difficulty, and was winded when he reached the upper landing. He turned toward her room and stood before its door to remember that slightly less than three weeks ago he had come up the outer stairs to this hall. She had met him in the shadows of this place and had waited for him to take her away. He knew that now; he hadn't known it then. For a moment he lived it all over, feeling even the freshness, the heat of her kiss. Then he drew a long, long breath and said, "Sally," in a level voice.

She opened the door to him at once, as though she had been paused on the other side, ready and waiting. She stepped back and let him come in, her eyes widening when she saw how thin his face was. She never took her glance from him; she watched him with a care and an indrawn interest, with almost an anxiety. Merritt closed the door and rested his shoulders against it.

"Sally," he said, "Will's dead."

"I know — I know."

He said: "We came together in the timber between Corral Flats and my place. After that it was just a question — Will or me."

She listened to him so carefully, she observed the way his face changed as he spoke, the way his wide chest lifted and fell. Heavy whiskers darkened him and toughened him. She didn't have to question him about the fight. She saw it and she heard it, in his attitude and in his few words.

She said: "Owen — have you seen Nan?"

"Not this morning." He looked at her with a faint curiosity, wondering at the question.

She had brought Nan's name between them so that she might see how the sound of that name affected him; and now, noticing the faint reaction of his features, she had her own private thoughts and very quickly changed the subject. "Are you through now, Owen? What happened to the crew — and Dutcher?"

He said: "The crew, I guess, is scattered. Some of them will be on Skull by now. Dutcher's dead."

"I hated that man," she murmured.

The silence came on again, even while a thousand things pressed against them and waited to be said. She stood in the center of the room, tall and composed, with her lips held resolutely together, as though to restrain any impulsive word that might betray her. About this girl was a certain beauty, born of pride and will. She showed it now, her copper hair making its dull shine in the shadows of the room and her expression holding back so much. She said in a small, husky voice: —

"I know, Owen. I know."

"Then," he said, "I'll do no more explaining."

"It's Will," she murmured. "When I heard that you had shot him I knew nothing would ever be right. Between you and me. If there was ever any chance for us, it died with Will. He stands between us, more now than when he was alive."

He said: "What are you going to do, Sally? What — "

But she broke in. "You know it's true, don't you?"

"Yes," he said. "Yes."

She came nearer, looking into his eyes with a straining soberness; and her voice then was humble and level. "Owen, I've got all my life to live down a mistake. You were right when you stood here that night and told me I'd someday know what I had done. In these three weeks I guess I've lived a hundred years. You don't know how hard it was. I tried to convince

Will I was loyal to him. I was — and I meant to be, always. But he shut himself up and I couldn't reach his mind. I couldn't make him see." She drew a long breath, so serious, so drawn. "Well, I made the bargain, Owen. And there never was a minute in all that time when I ever thought of going back on it. I can be proud of that. I just want you to know I can take my punishment and not cry. I am taking it now."

She had always owned the power to stir him, and had it still. It was a quality in her he could feel — a kind of sternness toward herself, an honesty she clung to when everything went wrong. He said: "I know, Sally."

She looked at him with a show of eagerness. Her lips were soft and she spoke his name in a way that brought back for a moment a memory of older times to him. "Owen — how different it might have been! That's what I keep thinking, through all this. I'm going back to the Broken Buttes — back to where I started. That doesn't leave me very much, does it? I wish I could know one thing. It would help a little. It would give me at least one pleasant memory to go on. Suppose I had come to you a week ago, wherever you were — would you have taken me then, Owen? You were in love with me once. Do you still remember? Does any of those old days ever come back to you?"

He laid his shoulder point against the door casing, easing the solid beating in his leg. He lowered his head, thinking back in some surprise. This girl had been his life. She had put color into his world, she had been in his mind, wherever he rode, like music; he had walked the earth with a swing and with a secret laughter, because of her. He remembered, in this room's absolute silence, the fire and the tumult she had wakened in him and could recall the way her lips answered his own heavy impulses. Where was that now? Here he stood, so quiet and so solemn, trying to bring it back — and as he tried to bring it back Nan Melotte's shape came before him, outlined by the light of the campfire in the tunnel, and then a strong feeling brushed through him, impatient and eager, and he knew suddenly what had happened to him.

He said nothing but it was all there for Sally to read. She spoke in a sighing, resigned voice. "Of course." Then she came quite near to him, looking up at him, crying out: "How could you forget me so soon? Or forget everything we used to be! How — Owen?"

He shook his head. "I don't know," he answered, very gentle. "But that's the same question I asked about you when I stood in the stairway here, three weeks ago. Things happen and then everything changes and nothing brings the old times back again."

She said, "I hate your Nan. I can't help it — and never will be able to help it. But I wish you happiness. I could never wish you anything else, my dear." She put her arm to his shoulder and at once bent against him. Her head turned a little and lay on his chest, and then this girl, so willfully strong, was silently crying.

He put his arms around her, hard-hit. He waited, holding her this way while the long moments passed. Then he said: "Go on back to Skull, Sally. It's yours. You kept your bargain."

She pulled away and turned definitely from him. She said, with half the room between them, "So-long, Owen."

He went out, limping painfully down the stairs and into the street. Bourke and Pay and Cultus were coming up from the saloon, all of them a little mellow from their drinking. Bourke said: "We're going to eat. Come on." But Merritt passed them and got to his horse. He had trouble swinging up; and a small crowd stood on the walk and watched him with a closeness that unaccountably irritated him. Bourke and Pay and Cultus came back to their horses. Merritt said bluntly: —

"Dammit, quit trailing me."

But when he turned out of town, heading south, they were behind him. Pay said: "Great Judas, I'm hungry!"

"You'll be a hell of a lot hungrier before you eat," grumbled Bourke.

Merritt ran down the long road, never speaking to them. There was a greater shimmer of winter fog in the day and the wind had risen and had turned colder. He paced on, seeing Nan Melotte's house rise up from the distance. When he reached it he looked back to find that his three partners had stopped in the distance. He struggled out of the saddle and went into the cabin without knocking.

Nan Melotte was in the center of her wrecked room, waiting. She had seen him coming, and this was the way she met him — color on her cheeks and a reserve in her eyes. He said, not knowing what else to say just then: "A man gets pretty hungry riding this country."

"Was there no other place to go?"

"A lot of places," he said. "But none of them seemed to suit."

She was almost severe with him. "You've been to town?"

"Yes. I went to town."

"Owen — did you see her? Did you kiss her?"

"Don't ask me about that, Nan. I'm here now."

She said: "Owen, you don't owe me anything, if it's gratitude or if it's pity — "

"No, Nan."

She watched him, with her dark face changing, with its severity breaking before softness, before a smile that made her cry. She let out a long breath and came suddenly against him, seizing his arms. "Then," she said, "if you are sure — if you are really sure — "

This was the end of it. She put up her face, her smile unsteady and brilliant and the light in her eyes stronger than before. He bowed his head to kiss her. Afterwards, long afterwards when they had forgotten the run of time, they heard Bourke Prine outside the cabin, howling like a wolf.

Nan stepped back, excitement glowing through her. She said: "Owen — everything I am is yours. Everything you are, is mine."

THE END